WORKS BY J. W. JUDGE

Fiction

Watch Party

Casual Business with Fairies

Vulcan Rising (The Zauberi Chronicles, Book 1)

Seeking Sanctuary (The Zauberi Chronicles, Book 2)

Forging Bonds (The Zauberi Chronicles, Book 3)

The Murder Tree (A Short Story)

Non-Fiction

Write Your Novel One Day at a Time: How to Write a Novel While Having a Career, a Family, and a Life

WATCH PARTY

J. W. JUDGE

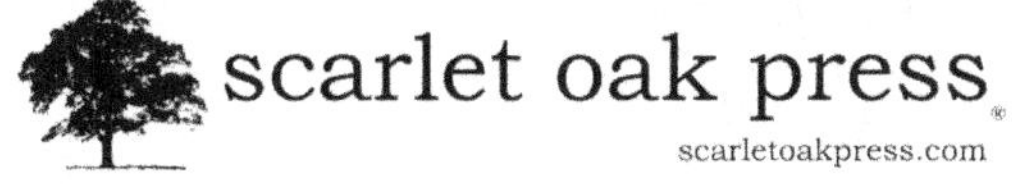

scarlet oak press
scarletoakpress.com

For permissions and information about special discounts for bulk purchases, contact Scarlet Oak Press at contact@scarletoakpress.com.

ISBN: 978-1-954974-20-3 (Paperback)

ISBN: 978-1-954974-19-7 (eBook)

ISBN: 978-1-954974-21-0 (Hard Cover)

Library of Congress Control Number: 2023923766

Published by Scarlet Oak Press (scarletoakpress.com)

CONTENTS

WATCH PARTY

But humans are born for trouble
as surely as sparks fly upward.
Job 5:7

CHAPTER 1
THROUGH THE OPENING

I TUGGED at Daryl's shoulder, but buckled in like I was, I couldn't get any leverage. Tom sloshed past, pulling me off my tiny island of narrowly focused attention. He stumbled into something that was submerged, swore, and splashed down. I held my phone as high as I could, trying both to see Tom and give him light to see by. He pushed himself up and continued toward the front of the plane. The water deepened as he went.

I unlatched my belt, slid off the seat, and fell forward harder than expected. Kneeling in the murky water in front of Daryl, I pushed him up by the shoulders and shined my phone's flashlight in his face. The temperature of the light gave everything a blue hue, so I couldn't tell by his coloring whether he was still breathing.

When I sensed movement behind Daryl's seat, I stood up and looked over the headrests. Jac was wiggling around.

"You okay?"

She didn't acknowledge me.

Someone splashed down the aisle from the front of the plane. I pivoted to find the flight attendant, flashlight in hand.

There was blood on her blouse, and she held her left arm tight against her chest.

She paused after she saw our state of affairs, turned around, and took one step before stopping. I called her name. "Denisha. I need some help." She looked down and waded back into deeper water.

As she moved away from us, I recognized two related things that I should have already realized. The water was much deeper at the front of the plane than at the back, and the reason I'd nearly fallen out of my chair was that the front was downhill.

I squinted toward the galley to see what Tom and Denisha were doing. They were at the door trying to unlatch it. Denisha gave him instructions, even though it seemed straightforward. Tom unclasped the latch and pushed outward, but the door didn't unfold. He looked back at Denisha, who shrugged.

"Push harder," she said.

Tom really leaned into it and pushed with this back and shoulders. Everything happened all at once.

Two arms of water reached into the plane from the crevice created by the opening door. The water pried the door the rest of the way open and poured into the cabin at an alarming rate. By the time I looked back down at still-unconscious Daryl, the ocean was already in his lap.

I half-turned back to the front to call for help from Denisha and Tom, but they were gone. Instead, Norman stood in front of the seat where he'd been sitting. He was looking down at Henry.

"Norm," I called.

He looked up slowly, nearly chest deep in water now.

"Norm, is Henry okay?"

Norman shook his head.

"Can you help Jac? I think she's in shock."

He shook his head again, then swam to the door and pushed into the blackness.

I yelled something at him that I immediately hoped he wouldn't remember later. If there was a later for any of us to worry about.

What's even out there? I didn't have the luxury of worrying about the answer to that question. At least two people needed help getting off this plane, and that wasn't even counting the cockpit. I hadn't seen or heard anything from the pilots.

I grabbed the front of Daryl's shirt, shaking him violently. Nothing. I plunged my hands into the seawater, groping for his seatbelt. This would be another bad time for him to wake up. I could already hear him telling the story to some buddies, everybody several beers deep into the night. "There I was, knocked out, and the girl from HR was trying to give me a h—" I couldn't even finish the thought. It was just too gruesome.

The latch wouldn't release. I fiddled with it every way I could think of. The thing opened, but it didn't let go. I grabbed him under the armpits and tugged, but there was no way that was going to work.

I pushed Daryl backward against the seat. Time to change plans. I'd have to come back to him. Jac still sat there, almost helplessly. I left Daryl and went back to her.

"Jac, come on now. We've got to get out of here."

Jacqueline didn't so much as redirect her eyes toward me, no matter how much I leered down at her.

Every second was precious. The water was rising up my thighs. At least it wasn't cold.

I raised my hand to my shoulder, took a deep breath, and slapped Jac as hard as I could. There were plenty of days I would have reveled in being able to do that. This wasn't one of them.

Jacqueline's eyes blazed to life, and she gulped air like she hadn't breathed in a couple of minutes.

"Let's go," I said.

Jacqueline brought a hand to her cheek.

"Sorry. Now, come on."

She finally realized that water had crept up to her rib cage. When she couldn't immediately release her seatbelt, she wriggled out over the top of it. I grabbed her by the hand and started dragging her toward the doorway that was an inch or two shy of being fully submerged.

My toes lost contact with the ground, and I treaded water the rest of the way while still tugging at Jac. I looked for Henry as I passed the front row of seats, but only the back of his head was still visible under the waterline.

"You have to go under to get out," I said to Jac when we'd reached the door.

"And go where?"

"I don't know, but the others are out there … somewhere."

The plane groaned and shifted. Waves thumped at the hull in a rhythmic barrage.

"You go first," Jac said.

I shook her head. "I've got to check on the pilots."

Jac grabbed me by the wrist. "If they're still in there, they're already dead. I need you," she pleaded.

I ignored the fear and the lump in my throat. "I have to see. Go."

Jacqueline hugged me quickly, then dunked her head under the inky water and disappeared through the doorway. I turned the light toward the back of the plane.

Doing a quick head count, I realized I hadn't seen Walt. "Walt. Walt!" No one answered the call. It would have been a greater surprise if they had.

Daryl still hadn't budged, and the water was up to his neck. I almost became frantic knowing that I was leaving him there to drown, but I was out of time. There was nothing I could do for him.

My head bobbed against the ceiling of the plane as I turned the light to maximum on my phone.

The thought of diving into that black water was almost intolerable. My brain chose that moment to remind me of a line from an Ernest Hemingway novel: "It is awfully easy to be hard-boiled about everything in the daytime, but at night it is another thing." Never mind that I was half fish as a child, spending as much time as I could in the water. This was not like that. This was voluntarily burying myself alive in an already occupied coffin.

I took a deep breath and pushed myself under, swimming toward the cockpit. I resisted the urge to look behind me for Henry's body.

As soon as I used the door frame to pull myself into the cockpit, I saw the windshield was mostly gone, which explained why the plane had taken on water so quickly. That question had preoccupied a small part of my brain. I remembered from the Miracle on the Hudson that the airliner had been watertight, and ours was leaking like a mobile home. I knew something wasn't adding up.

More importantly, though, the pilots' seats were empty. Both of them. Hopefully, they had escaped through the broken windshield and hadn't been ejected into the glass.

It was time for me to get out. My plan had been to go back the way I had come, but at the rate the cabin was taking on water, I didn't know where or whether I could come up again.

Concerns about bumping into my boss' dead body made up my mind for me. I pushed off from the pilot seat and torpedoed through the opening in the windshield.

CHAPTER 2
A SLIVER OF ISLAND

ONCE I WAS certain that I was clear of the windshield's broken glass, I swam upward. Not knowing how far up I had to go brought with it the third adrenaline kick of the night. When I'd swum further than I thought necessary, I blew bubbles out of my mouth and watched them go up to make sure I hadn't gotten disoriented.

Breaking the surface came as a shock. It almost felt like running into something. My aching lungs coveted the air I took in.

I twirled frantically, looking for anything that wasn't water. The only distinction between the blackness of the water and the blanket of the sky were the stars that had started poking holes in the clouds.

Sounds of screaming reached my ears as a swell lifted me. I thought maybe something worse than drowning in a plane had happened to those who escaped. At the crest of the wave, I saw not-water. Maybe land. The screams were my name.

I turned myself toward the noise and swam with all the energy I had left. The voices didn't sound that far away, and the tide seemed to help.

The yelling grew stronger as I paddled. A line of lightness

grew out of the water and expanded outward. A wave caught me as though I were body-surfing on a beach trip with my family. It smashed me into the lightness. Sand.

Hands grabbed me and pulled me out of the water. They dragged me up the beach, out of the tide's grasp. I lay on my back and sputtered a couple of times while I got my bearings. A small congregation gathered at my feet.

A woman asked, "Are you okay?"

I pushed myself upright and did a quick assessment. My second or third of the night. I was losing count. "I think so. Maybe."

Tom said, "Is there anybody else?"

I shook my head. When there was no response, I realized it was still too dark for anyone to easily see the gesture. "No." My voice cracked. I cleared my throat. "How did you know to yell for me?"

Norman said, "We've been yelling for everyone."

Jacqueline added, "I washed up a couple minutes ahead of you and told them to look for you."

Tom pointed at my hand. "The flashlight helped."

I looked down, surprised to find my phone still in my hand, the light now shoved into the wet sand of the beach.

"What now?" Norman asked. "Wait for search and rescue?"

The band of survivors turned to the pilots. I couldn't remember either of their names.

"Bad news on that front," the co-pilot said.

"Ryan," the pilot pleaded softly.

"What? Everybody deserves to know what we're in for." He waited, but there was no further protest. "There's almost no tracking on international private flights, especially coming from South America. I mean, we filed a flight plan, and folks will eventually figure out we didn't arrive in Birmingham, but they won't know where or when we went down."

"Besides," the pilot chimed in, "Henry had me block

third-party tracking. He didn't want Drummond or Warrior Met to follow where we were going."

Panic and acid rose in my throat.

Tom spoke in a voice chock full of emotion. "You're telling us we crash landed on a deserted island with no chance of rescue?"

It was weird having this conversation in the dark of night with everyone's disembodied voices. But maybe it would have been a strange conversation regardless of the lighting.

"It's not as straightforward as that," Ryan said. "There's shipping lanes and flight paths and … I don't know, bruh. I'm still processing."

Norman said, "We don't know that the island's deserted. There could be other people here."

"Like the ones you left for dead," a voice said in the darkness.

Jacqueline screamed in surprise.

The group instinctively huddled.

I found myself on the outside of the huddle and shined my light toward the voice. Daryl stood dripping wet a dozen feet from us with his arms crossed.

Jac hurried toward him to give him a hug. He put out an arm that barred her from closing the gap between them. "A hug? You left me to drown," he accused.

"Alexis tried, Daryl." She looked back toward me. "She really tried. You were stuck."

"And the rest of you?"

The collective silence answered the question.

In the coming days, a lot of folks would reckon with how they'd responded in the face of any emergency. Usually, you'd say they would have to take a hard look in the mirror, but it appeared there wouldn't be any mirrors for the foreseeable future. Any self-reflection would have to take a more figurative route.

"What do we do now?" Denisha asked.

The pilot said, "Wait until morning and …"

Tom finished the sentence when she refused to. "See how bad it is."

"It's going to be a long night," Norm said.

I wished somebody would say the pilot's name so I knew what to call her. It felt like we were already over that threshold where I could ask without being embarrassed about it. Something about being stranded on an island with seven other people lent an instant intimacy to things that kept me from introducing myself like we were at a conference.

Clouds blew away to the east enough that a three-quarter moon came out, giving us enough light to see each other and a sliver of the island. A couple dozen yards away, the sand gave way to foliage that ranged in shades from gray to black under the moonlight.

I shivered to think about what might be lurking there, looking back out at us, itself unseen. Then I recognized that I'd been shivering for a while, probably since I got pulled out of the water. The air would have been warm enough to be comfortable if I was dry, but my wet clothes drew away all my body heat.

Tom asked, "Who all has their phones?"

All the men and I spoke up. For all the gaps that were being closed in gender inequality in recent decades, the lack of useful pockets in women's business attire was still an egregious oversight.

"Anybody have service?"

I checked but had only dashes where I'd hoped to have escalating steps. The others' expressions indicated the same result.

Ryan suggested, "Probably be best if we turn them off so we don't waste the battery. Then we can check again in the morning."

"What about the sat phone?" Tom asked.

Norman shook his head. "Henry was on it when every-thing went sideways."

"So it's still on the plane?"

"Hell if I know."

"What happened up there?" Denisha asked. "I thought the plane could take a lightning strike."

"We were," Ryan said. "I don't know. It just kind of killed everything. Rhonda almost had the engine back for a minute, but …"

We all knew what had followed. There was no reason to say it. One dead. One missing. One abandoned, who had escaped anyway. Eight survivors stranded on an island waiting on the light of morning to figure out how bad our situation was.

CHAPTER 3
THE CENTER OF ATTENTION
ONE HOUR EARLIER

DARYL NUDGED me with his elbow. "What's the stewardess' name again?"

"Flight attendant," I said, rolling my eyes. He knew that. It's not like he was a boomer who'd been calling them stewardesses his whole life. "Denisha."

Denisha made her way along each of the sets of seats, taking requests for snacks and drinks. On these private planes, the alcohol flowed like jet fuel. I would just as soon they didn't serve alcohol on company trips. It was an HR nightmare. Everyone reverted to their teenage selves despite all of them being at least thirty years beyond that stage of life. Some of them had to be creeping up on forty-year high school reunions. Despite being the baby of the group, since I was the only one who was totally sober, I was basically the only adult.

When Denisha stopped at our row, she rested a hand on the top of Daryl's seat and flashed a professional smile. "Is there anything I can get you?"

Daryl slid his arm along Denisha's waist, settling his hand on her far hip. She stiffened immediately, and her smile disappeared. With his free hand, Daryl rattled his tumbler, "Another rum and Coke, if you don't mind, honey."

"Get your hand off her," I said, more loudly than I'd intended.

The noise drew Norman's attention, who sat two rows in front of us, next to Henry. He envisioned himself as the CEO's right hand, but I wasn't convinced the perspective was mutual. "Hey, man. You can't do that."

"Y'all mind your own business." Daryl barked in response to being chastised. "She doesn't mind. Do you, babydoll?"

Denisha found herself in the unenviable position of being the center of attention for seven people who were now talking about her and her body in third person.

Daryl doubled down and squeezed her toward himself. "I'm sorry if this bothers you. You can tell me to stop if you want."

From the row behind us, Tom said, "That's not how consent works, dude."

Denisha finally found her voice. "I don't think my husband would appreciate this very much." She waggled the fingers of her left hand, letting the still-new wedding band and matching engagement ring sparkle at them.

Without letting go, Daryl said, "Well, that's not the same thing as *you* not appreciating it, so how about we just don't tell him?"

Daryl yelped in pain when Tom reached forward, grabbing Daryl's thumb and wrenching it backward. With his arm suddenly bent at an awkward angle, Daryl came up out of the chair, trying to relieve the pressure.

Tom growled, "She was being polite. I'm not. Don't touch anyone else on this flight." He released the offending hand.

Daryl slid back into his seat. "Geez, man. I was just messing around. It's no big deal."

Tom said, "All you had to do was tell me to stop if you didn't like it — isn't that how unwanted touching works?"

The alcohol-induced redness in Daryl's face deepened with anger. He stood up and side-stepped into the aisle. Tom remained casually in his seat, a smirk on his face. "This is such a bad idea."

Everyone knew it was a bad idea, even Daryl. If Tom wasn't talking about the chemical makeup of the coal deposits the company was mining in Central and South America, then he was carrying on about mixed martial arts. Cross-fitters had nothing on him when it came to gabbing about his fitness method of choice. He was a constant stream of information about either his own training or the matches he had watched the weekend before.

Daryl, however, had the physique of someone whose physical peak was too far distant in the rearview mirror to be discernible.

Much to her credit, Denisha said, "Mr. Roberts." After several seconds, during which Daryl and Tom eyed each other like rival chimps, she repeated his name. Finally, Daryl turned around to face her. "If you'll take your seat, I'll go get that drink you asked for."

Daryl nodded his head and sat back down, muttering slurs about Tom's wife and mother, quiet enough for only me to make out.

I would have to talk to Henry about whether this was something he wanted me to write up. Denisha wasn't a company employee, and the jet wasn't company property, but this was definitely company time. He could make that call. That's why he got paid the big bucks. Really, *really* big bucks. The corner office in the C-suite came with a bunch of money and some nice perks, but it was also fraught with problems.

When Henry and I were the last two left in the conference room at the end of meetings, he liked to mimic taking off the crown that had been weighing him down. His posture always improved dramatically as soon as the invisible crown touched the table.

I sat up and looked over Walt's headrest toward the front of the plane. Henry had the satellite phone plastered to his ear. His muffled voice trickled back our way. He usually made a point of being unreachable while in the air, so whatever this was, it must have been important.

When the flight attendant returned with his drink, Daryl accepted it and said thanks without even looking up. He fidgeted with the glass and said with quiet earnestness, "Alexis, Gabriela will literally murder me if she finds out about this."

I shrugged. "That was pretty gross."

Daryl shot a hard look at me. "Not helpful."

"What? I'm just saying. I'm not married, but murder sounds reasonable to me." I was uncertain how far I wanted to go with this conversation, but my curiosity got the best of me. "Does that happen a lot?"

"I like to flirt sometimes, that's all." He added defensively, "But I have never cheated on my wife."

Daryl was notoriously flirty in the office. It had never led to complaints, so I'd never had to deal with it. But my HR yellow flags went up every time I saw it. To my knowledge, he hadn't touched anyone inappropriately. Of course, it was super unlikely this was a one-time occurrence.

"Umm, no. Flirting uses words. Getting handsy is … something else. You might not think it's cheating, but I bet y'all wouldn't agree on that definition."

Worry was written all over his face. "Do you think someone will tell her?"

I scanned the plane, considering its occupants. Walt couldn't even be bothered enough to pay attention to it. Besides, he was an old guy, and I had a strong suspicion that he lived by the code that people's office improprieties stayed within the confines of the building. I'd heard a theory (which I had no trouble believing) about why Boomers were so keen to get back into the office after COVID: they wanted to resume their indiscretions.

Norman had interjected briefly, but he too was mostly indifferent about people's personal stuff.

If some young upstart encroaching on the attention that Daryl usually directed at Jacqueline spurned her enough, she might stir up some drama. Even so, I didn't think it was likely that she'd involve his wife. More likely, she would redouble her efforts to attract Daryl's attention.

That left Tom, Henry, and me. "Nah. That seems pretty unlikely to me."

"I'm a little drunk," he offered as an excuse.

I frowned. "That's only your third drink, and you haven't even touched it yet."

"Whatever," he said sullenly.

The pilot's voice came over the cabin intercom. "Denisha, return to your jump seat. Passengers, buckle your seatbelts." Tension laced her voice.

I lifted the shade that I'd drawn down over the window earlier in the flight. I hoped for an amazing view of the sunset, but quickly discovered that dark clouds eclipsed my view of the Caribbean Sea. Lightning jumped from one cloud to the next in the distance. My heart stumbled a bit, and I pulled the shade back down. Flying isn't my strong suit, and I would rather not know what we were flying into. I considered digging around in my bag for my Zoloft. Present-me regretted that past-me hadn't taken it before we boarded.

Daryl set his tumbler in the cup holder and unbuckled his seatbelt.

"Where are you going?"

"To apologize."

"Now? I don't think that's a good idea."

CHAPTER 4
RUMBLING OVER SPEED BUMPS

IGNORING MY SUGGESTION, Daryl slid back into the aisle and made his way to the front of the jet. I shook my head. There were just some people who refused to be told anything.

I reached into my bag under the seat in front of me and dug out my tablet and earbuds. Maybe if I immersed myself in a movie, I wouldn't notice the turbulence as much, assuming that's what the message had been about. Why else would they tell the flight attendant to go to her seat?

I wished I had my big over-the-ear noise canceling headphones, the ones capable of transporting me to another world. The ones I put on when I wanted everyone to know I'm not to be disturbed. I was technically complying with Henry's mandate that the executive team and HR have an open-door policy. The human resource functions I managed generated a ton of paperwork, and I couldn't get my work done while having people pop in all day to gripe about how their cubicle mate's lunch smells like cat pee.

The plane dropped.

And kept dropping.

For a full three or four seconds, my stomach wedged itself

between my ears. My tablet went from laying in my lap to hugging the ceiling.

Someone cried out. It sounded like Jac.

There was a loud thud at the front of the plane. My seatbelt strained against my hips as my body struggled to keep pace with our descent.

When the plane quit falling out of the sky, several things happened all at once. Everything that had been experiencing weightlessness for the last few seconds crashed to the ground or into its owners.

A second thud pierced the clattering noise.

One of the guys in front of me blew chunks. I hoped he'd had time to grab a barf bag, assuming private jets came equipped with those. I hadn't had cause to check before.

"Help!" Tom yelled. He was somehow at the front of the plane, not immediately behind my row like he had been earlier. I didn't even see him go forward when I zoned out. "We need help!"

I unbuckled and pushed into the aisle. Between the galley where Denisha had latched in and the door to the restroom, Daryl lay in the aisle. Tom and I hovered over him. Blood streamed from a gash in his forehead.

Daryl wasn't moving or responding to Tom saying his name.

"First aid kit?" I asked.

When Denisha didn't respond, I put a hand on her shoulder and repeated the question, which snapped the flight attendant out of her daze. She nodded and stood up.

The plane shimmied.

Tom and I caught each other's eyes, each of us wondering if we were about to add to the number of casualties.

"Do you know first aid?" Tom asked.

"'Know first aid'? I mean, it's not like knowing CPR. But yes, I had brothers. I can wrap something in gauze, at least good enough to keep him from slinging blood all over the cabin."

"That'll work. You think it's okay to move him?"

I shrugged and took a second to look up the aisle. Several heads peered our way, but no one else wanted to risk being turned into a pinball. "How should I know?"

Denisha returned with a glorified white lunch box with a red cross on it. When she handed it to me, I flung the lid open and pulled out a roll of gauze. I started unspooling the roll and got ready to wrap Daryl's head.

"Use the gloves," Denisha said. "You never know."

I snapped a latex glove on each hand, then hesitated. My college roommate had a latex allergy and wore a dog-tag, so first responders would know in case she ever needed medical attention and was unconscious. "Check to see if he's got an allergy necklace."

Tom popped open the top of Daryl's shirt. He shook his head.

"Wait. One more thing," Denisha said.

Tom and I looked up.

"Can I kick him in the dick while he's out?"

I grinned. "I'll turn a blind eye."

Tom was more diplomatic. Sort of. "Better wait 'til he comes around. Otherwise, he'll just wake up with sore junk and won't know what to attribute it to."

Denisha crossed her arms. "Fine."

I wrapped Daryl's head four times, but even before I was done, the wound started bleeding through the gauze. "Geez Louise." I muttered.

"Do you kiss your mother with that mouth?" Tom teased as he rummaged through the first aid kit. There were no bandages big enough to help.

I had an idea. "Have any maxi pads?"

Denisha's cheeks immediately flushed. "No. I use—What? Why?"

"Not you. On the plane."

"Oh, right." She pushed into the bathroom and rattled around in the cabinets before popping out and handing me a couple of puffy rectangular packages.

"Perfect." I ripped the packaging open on one, then lifted the wrapped gauze with one hand, and shoved in the pad with the other.

Tom handed me an antiseptic napkin. "Wipe his face, and I'll carry him back there and buckle him in."

Denisha said, "Then we all need to get buckled up before we go on another roller coaster ride."

"Yeah, what was that?" I asked, as I cleaned the blood off Daryl's face. Even as I asked, I wasn't sure I wanted to know the answer.

"Air pocket," she said. "Happens sometimes, but not usually that bad. It always feels like the plane's about to fall out of the sky, but sometimes there are sudden air pressure changes with these storms. Honestly, it probably won't be the last."

"Great."

As if to emphasize Denisha's words, the jet bounced several times like it was rumbling over speed bumps.

"We've got to hurry," Tom said. He stood up and pulled Daryl by the hands to a sitting position. He leaned down, scooped Daryl under the armpits, then stood him upright. It looked a lot like trying to get jelly to stand. "Hold him there for a sec."

I got behind Daryl and wrapped my arms around his chest. When Tom briefly let go, it felt like I was bear-hugging a bag of concrete. A bag that Tom then threw over his shoulder and waddled to his chair, hanging onto seat backs as he went. He then dumped the unconscious man and buckled him.

"Hey," Denisha said, "we've got to get rid of those gloves and wash your hands."

I turned around and followed her the several steps to the galley. Denisha pressed a latch, and a trash receptacle popped out of the back wall. I used one blood-smeared glove to remove the other, wadded them into an inside-out ball, and dropped them in.

The plane shuddered. Both of us braced ourselves against the galley walls, like Samson preparing to pull down the Philistine temple.

"Wash your hands," Denisha prompted.

"If I'm dead, it won't matter," I said with a smirk.

"If you live, it will. Wash 'em."

CHAPTER 5
LIGHTNING STRIKE

I SCRAMBLED TO MY SEAT. Tom gestured to catch my attention before I turned around to sit. "Good work up there."

"You, too."

I climbed over Daryl to get to my window seat. *Hopefully, he won't come to while I'm straddling him. Then we'll have a real situation on our hands. Or maybe I'd be the situation in his hands. Eww.*

From beside Tom, Jacqueline asked, "Is he going to be okay?"

I didn't hear his answer, but it was probably kinder than what I had in mind. *If you were so worried about it, you could have come up there and helped.* But realistically, there wasn't room for anyone else, so their self-preservation instincts were just as well.

After dropping into my seat with no stirring from Daryl, I latched my belt as quickly as possible. I had visions of myself as one of those super bouncy balls pinging all over every surface of the cabin before landing in Henry's lap, which would require several rounds of counseling to work through. *So many coworker-related lap thoughts. Maybe I need counseling regardless.*

Daryl's head rolled downward until his chin rested on his chest. If it weren't for the gauze headband, he'd look like he was sleeping off a drunken binge. He'd been unconscious for a solid ten minutes. *Is that long enough to worry?* I scoffed. Any amount of unconsciousness was worrisome. The only other two times I'd been around someone who got knocked out, it had lasted seconds, not minutes. Did that mean it was more likely he was concussed? And if so, did I need to rouse him?

A tingle crawled across my skin. My arm hairs — I hated them so much; thanks to Mom's Greek heritage, they're a couple of shades too dark, and I have long considered laser removal for them — stood on end. The hair on my head (appropriately dark) took its cue and began wandering away from my body.

A flash of blue light invaded the cabin. The plane jolted violently to the left.

All went black.

Thunder displaced every other sound. When it dissipated, it left devastation in its wake. The jet and all of us occupying it were quiet as a coffin. The only noise was the wind buffeting the plane as it ripped through the sky, but even that lessened noticeably as everyone listened to the obvious absence of engine noise.

The jet listed to the right, and its nose dipped.

We began losing altitude rapidly. My body pushed upward against the seat back, and the seatbelt strained against my hips. Things that had broken loose during the tumult skittered toward the cockpit or tore away from the floor's grip, evolving into projectiles. Among the clambering, I heard several grunts from those closer to the front. Cries and shouts emerged as the situation became clear.

Shortly after takeoff, the pilot had announced we would cruise at 41,000 feet. Assuming that was still our altitude, how long would it take us to fall? Depended on our terminal velocity. A memory from high school science made a flitting appearance, telling me terminal velocity for a human who wasn't diving was about 120 mph, but panic and terror tag-teamed to take over my brain before I could even attempt any math.

Surrounded by darkness, there was no way to know how soon we would hit the water, though it seemed inevitable that would be the outcome.

Mom was right. I never should have taken the job with a company that was coal mining in the jungles of South America and killing the planet. The boring gig at the Honda plant in east Alabama would never have had me in a private jet hurrying toward my death. It would be a small mercy if the impact killed me, rather than drowning.

The overhead lights in the cabin flickered on momentarily, revealing chaos around me. The wings made mechanical noises. Their trajectory flattened somewhat. The turbine at the back of the fuselage whined and groaned.

Hope crowded the cabin but did not last.

The engine went quiet as darkness descended over us again.

Someone was crying.

Despite most of my consciousness telling me not to, I pushed up the blind on my window. I couldn't not know when and what we were going to hit. Moments later, we broke through the bottom layer of clouds. Rain continued to pelt the plane as it descended toward a turbulent ocean.

I pressed my forehead to the window to see what was ahead of us. It wouldn't be long until we struck that particular patch of water, not that it would look different from any other water.

But I didn't see water in front of us. Correction. I didn't see only water. A strip of sand peaked out from under the fuselage. It was too dark outside to make out much more than the distinct color contrast between sand and water. I couldn't see enough to know whether it was a sandbar or an island. My depth perception was a mess.

I wondered whether it was better to crash into land or water. Either way, the most likely result seemed like it would be our messy deaths. Bits of plane and people littering the Caribbean.

The cockpit door slammed open. The male co-pilot yelled, "Brace!"

The crying person renewed their sobs.

I tore my eyes away from the window and strained forward to grab my pillow from under my chair. Daryl moved beside me. His eyes fluttered, and he groaned. *A helluva time to wake up, buddy. Just in time to be dead.* I tugged at the sleeve of his shirt. "Lay your head down." He resisted.

With my head turned, I saw Jac from between the seats. She sat stoic and upright. I thought Jac was the one crying earlier. Apparently not. *Nice work, HR, assuming it was the woman crying.* It had to be Walt or Norman, then.

I didn't have time to fuss with Daryl anymore. I squeezed my eyes shut and buried my head in my pillow. My heart raced raggedly in my chest. My throat hurt in the same way it did when I tried to not cry.

Impulsively, I decided not to die without seeing it.

Beside me, Daryl's body lurched forward before my nervous system registered the impact. Stuff from the back of the plane launched past us. The next bit of eternity was too chaotic to be coherent.

The plane tried to buck me out of my seat.

Something inside of my abdomen felt like it tore.

The earth ground against the bottom of the fancy private jet, shredding it to bits.

So loud. It was all so loud.

Another crash. The grinding went away. A new noise. The nose of the plane dipped again.

Momentum stopped.

Stillness.

When I realized my feet were wet, I sat upright. *I'm not dead.* But I wondered how bad my injuries must be that blood was pooling in my socks so quickly. I looked down but could see nothing. The blackness was almost tangible.

Tenuously, I felt for injuries with my hands, starting at the tops of my thighs and worked my way down. After I got to my calves, my hands found water.

My relief that my pants weren't wet with blood was immediately replaced with renewed terror as I realized water was filling the plane. I reached under my seat. By some miracle, my purse was still lodged under there. I pulled out my phone and tapped it to make my flashlight come on. *Thank God for waterproof phones.*

I shined the light over myself. All my visible bits looked like they were intact. Another miracle. I turned the light to Daryl and grimaced. He was folded forward and motionless.

"Daryl."

No response.

CHAPTER 6
I CONTAIN MULTITUDES

IT WOULD BE nice if there was a word for exhaustion combined with dread and a little bit of excitement. *The Germans probably have a word for it.* That's how I found myself approaching our new day when the eastern sky began turning gray. I couldn't tell how much of my soreness I should attribute to whiplash and taking a beating on the plane versus trying to sleep sitting upright cuddled against my new friend, Denisha.

Before we settled in for the night, I helped her search for the cut that left the blood on her shirt. Not finding one, we concluded it was Daryl's blood. After that, we converted her flight attendant's jacket into a sling for her injured left arm.

Slowly and reluctantly, I got up. "Going to check on Daryl."

Denisha said, "Can you deliver a message for me?"

"Sure."

She stuck her good arm up in the air and raised her middle finger in salute.

I scrunched up my face. "If it's all the same, I might try playing the role of peacemaker, especially since, you know, we might be the only people any of us ever see again."

Denisha's eyes welled with tears. "Please don't say that."

My hands went to my mouth, and I dropped to my knees in the sand beside her. "I'm so sorry. I have an inappropriate sense of humor when things go bad. Coping mechanism. Not a good one either. My mother almost murdered me at my grandfather's funeral a couple of years ago when she overheard me tell my cousin, 'You can't spell funeral without f-u-n.' Then at my brother's funeral, I told a story about the time I almost killed us when I was learning to drive a stick shift."

Snickers replaced Denisha's sniffles. "You're kind of a hot mess, aren't you?"

"A bit, yeah."

"And aren't you the HR person?"

I grinned and held my arms out. "What can I say? I contain multitudes." I stood up with a grunt. "You okay?"

"I guess?"

"We'll be alright" was the best I could offer. It wasn't very compelling. There was no evidence to support it, and both of us knew there was a pretty low likelihood of us being alright. I shuffled through the sand as the sky added more color and the sun breached the horizon.

Daryl didn't acknowledge me when I plopped down beside him.

"How's your head?"

"Hurts," he grumbled.

"And your feelings?" I asked lightly.

"Don't make fun. This isn't some light offense, Alexis. Y'all literally left me for dead. To drown. Do you know how much drowning sucks?"

"No, but neither do you, fortunately." Still trying to keep it light.

He scowled.

I opted for sincerity instead. "I did everything I could. Really. Your seatbelt was stuck. I had to help Jac and check on the pilots, then I couldn't get back."

"And the others?"

"Everybody was doing their best … except Norm. He sucks and didn't help anyone."

"Yeah, well, that drunk, old curmudgeon wouldn't have been strong enough to keep me from sinking anyway."

I nudged him with my forearm. "That a way to look at the bright side. You were way better off strapped to your death chair."

I could tell he wasn't going to let go of this easily, and could I blame him?

"Daryl, how much do you remember of the flight?"

"Takeoff? Not much after that. It's all fuzzy."

"What about your interactions with Denisha?"

He shook his head. "Who?"

I nodded at the figure sitting with her knees curled up to her chest. "The flight attendant." This was the worst part of my job — confronting grown-ups about their inappropriate behavior. I always had to swallow my apprehensions and inhibitions and pretend to be the adult who knew what I was doing, like my age said I was.

I'd always thought that at a certain age, everything would finally make sense and get easier, the same way that algebra just clicked one day. But I was beginning to suspect that my parents never actually knew what they were doing and were mostly flying by the seat of their pants. It would explain a lot about the upbringing my brothers and I had.

Myself, I was still waiting for that day. In the meantime, I would continue to fake it. "You kind of — no, not kind of — you groped her. Grabbed her butt and put your arm around her waist."

"Oh, no." He hung his head before looking at me with widened eyes. "Who knows?"

"Pretty much everybody. You weren't real shy about it."

He went from shame to indignation pretty quickly, clenching his jaw. "And that justifies them letting me die?"

"What? No. That's not why I'm telling you this. I mean, you have that bandage on your head because Tom and Denisha helped me put you back together like Humpty Dumpty after you got rocked the first time we hit turbulence."

He felt the bandage wrapped around his head, as if noticing it for the first time. "How bad is it?"

"Not terrible on the outside. You have a cut that probably could have used a couple of butterflies if we'd had them. But based on you getting knocked out twice and having a headache and memory loss, I'd venture to guess you earned yourself a concussion."

He sat with that for a couple of minutes. I didn't interrupt him as he ruminated, then I couldn't help myself. "You know, with any luck, you'll live long en—"

"Hold on." He stuck out a hand, interrupting me. "Are you about to be super irreverent about me dying?"

"I am."

"You think that's appropriate?"

I shrugged. "If I can't say irreverent things to you, then who?"

"Fair. Carry on."

"Maybe you'll live long enough to die of CTE."

He shook his head at me. "That was grim."

"Well, the delivery would have been better if you wouldn't have interrupted me."

Up the beach from us, there was activity among the group as the sunlight grew bright enough to make any kind of exploration meaningful.

"Was I drunk?"

"No, just being a perv."

Daryl gave me side-eye. When he saw my smirk, he nodded.

"An apology would go a long way. As would, you know, not doing it again."

"You realize this is like my kid sister telling me what to do, right?"

"That isn't lost on me. You know the solution?"

"Don't be a perv?"

I tapped the end of my nose, then stood up. "I'm going to see what I can do to help." I reached my hand down to him. "You coming?"

"Not yet."

"Well, don't wait so long that it gets awkward."

"More awkward," he corrected.

I made my way back to Denisha, whose dark blue hose were lying beside her. With her good arm, she was trying to shake the sand and salt out of the blouse she'd taken off now that it was mostly dry.

I looked past Denisha to see that she was drawing indiscreet glances from the rest of the group. It reminded me of the "They're real, and they're spectacular" episode of Seinfeld. But if we were going to be here any length of time, this kind of thing was unavoidable. Might as well break the ice early.

"Let me help you."

Denisha handed me the blouse. I turned around and gave it several violent shakes. Sand flew in all directions. "Need help putting it back on?"

Denisha held her left arm close to her body, trying to keep it still. "That'd be nice."

We methodically got both arms into the shirt and draped it over her shoulders.

"Do you need help buttoning it?"

"I'll manage. I think you dressing me may be too much for the men among us to handle."

I laughed, uncomfortably. She'd noticed too, then.

"Is he sorry?" She gestured her chin toward Daryl.

"Doesn't remember it."

"So he says."

"What do you mean?"

"That's the story I'd go with if I were him."

"Maybe," I said noncommittally. "He seemed embarrassed when I told him what had happened."

"Whatever. Can I ask one more favor?"

I nodded.

"I haven't figured out everybody's names yet and can't keep them straight."

"You seemed to know everybody on the flight?"

"Trick of the trade. Pet names and surface-level friendliness make it seem that way."

"Ah, okay. So, Norm and Tom go together. Tom is the head of engineering, and Norm is the COO."

"Which one is Norm?"

"He's … ummm …" I gestured at the skin on my arm.

"The Black guy?"

"Yeah."

Denisha rolled her eyes. "We can use physical descriptions to identify people. Just don't be weird about it. How else are you going to do it? Tell me how he smells?"

"Oh, he does smell nice."

She raised an eyebrow at me. "You're not like Uncle Joe going around sniffing people's hair, are you?"

I laughed nervously and protested. "No!"

She looked at me sideways before dropping a bomb on the conversation. "Also, and unrelated, you know ole Norm's going to die first, right?"

My jaw dropped. "Nobody's going to die. What are you talking about?"

"Well, look who got sensitive all of a sudden. What happened to that gallows humor you were bragging about? Besides, people have already died."

"One has died. One." I held up a finger to emphasize my point. "Walt is … just … missing."

"Uh-huh. Missing in the ocean, but not dead. But since you're technically right, Norm will be the *next* to die."

"Okay, I'll bite. Why's that?"

"He's Black."

I stopped mid-stride, mildly stunned. "So are you!"

Denisha whirled around playfully, though the blazer-turned-sling holding her left arm nullified the effect somewhat, and gestured at her figure. "Yeah, but I'm hot. And mixed. So I'm only like a third as likely to die."

"Hot and humble."

"Don't be mad at the facts."

"Noted," I said, not really knowing else what to say. So I moved on to the next person. "Anyway. Moving on. Walt, Daryl, and Jac are a trio. Walt's the CFO." I nearly auto-corrected to past tense, but wasn't ready for that concession yet. "Jac is accounts payable. Receivables is Daryl."

"Yeah, I know Daryl," she said sourly.

"That leaves me and you three from the plane."

Denisha put a hand to her chest and, in her best sorority voice, said, "Well, I'm Denisha."

"Yep. Got that."

"Rhonda's the pilot. She's pretty vanilla, both in skin tone and personality. Ryan is kind of an enigma. I haven't flown with him before. He did his own thing while we were in Colombia. I hardly saw him at all."

"Thanks," I nodded with a wry smile. "Wanna go see what the others have in mind to do?"

CHAPTER 7
FIRST THINGS FIRST

DENISHA and I approached to the sound of Tom doling out instructions. "First things first. We need to locate a source of fresh water and make a shelter nearby. We should split up and go in different directions. If everyone gets a buddy, we can look in four directions, okay?"

No one dissented.

Daryl wandered around nearby but lingered slightly away from the group. The pilots stayed together. Norman immediately approached Tom, who nodded, but not without casting a disappointed glance toward Denisha.

Jac motioned Daryl forward to join her. He did as beckoned.

Denisha crooked her arm through mine and said, "Hang on a sec." She leaned toward Daryl and whispered something in his ear. He nodded solemnly. As soon as she finished, he took a side-step away from her.

"Great," Tom said, looking over the four pairs. "Now look, everybody stay with your partner no matter what. I don't want to scare anyone, but we do not know what's here. One pair should head up the beach to the north. One to the south. A group should go inland to the northwest. And one to the southwest."

"It's not like we have compasses," Ryan said.

"Sure, sure. We'll have to do our best. Just pay attention to where the sunlight is coming from. We are on the eastern side of the island. Keep an eye out for landmarks that can help you find your way back here."

"Are you some kind of survivalist?" Jac asked.

"Not really," Tom said, growing shy. "I watch a lot of survival shows."

"Great. We're taking instructions from a reality TV junkie."

Tom raised his hands in mock surrender. "I'm not trying to be in charge or anything. Just helping us get started. I'm open to other suggestions."

No one offered any.

Jac didn't have any better ideas. She was scared and lashing out.

Denisha said, "We'll go this way," and pointed down the beach to the south.

Jac said she and Daryl would go the opposite direction. The pilots, Tom, and Norm discussed among themselves what directions they'd take.

Once we were sufficiently far from the group on our beach trek, I asked, "What was it you said to Daryl?"

"Told him if he ever touched me again, I'd kill him slowly and drape his entrails over him like a shawl."

My disgust at the visual showed on my face. "Gnarly. I wouldn't have guessed you had that in you."

Denisha shrugged. "I wanted to leave a lasting impression."

"High marks for sticking the landing then."

She smiled and bent down to pick up a long, slender piece of driftwood. "Now, I can play whack-a-mole with any creatures that jump out at us."

I glanced into the line of brush and trees, hoping against hope a jaguar or something wasn't hiding in there, trying to decide which of us would make the easiest meal. To change the subject, I asked, "So, what should we be looking for?"

"No idea. This may be the longest consecutive amount of time I've spent outside in my life. I got cousins and uncles down in lower Mississippi who'll hunt anything that moves, but my people are city folk. I guess *city* is relative, but not-country anyway."

The rising sun warmed both the air and the sand. I was already chafing in all the worst places from my still-damp clothes. I paused to roll up my pants legs, but Denisha kept walking. "Hang on."

"There's something up there," Denisha called over her shoulder while pointing ahead.

I stood up and once I saw it — whatever it was — I was surprised we hadn't seen it before. I hurried to catch up to Denisha.

Our pace picked up as we closed on what revealed itself to be wreckage from the plane. What Denisha had initially spotted was a piece of the landing gear. It wasn't alone, though. A debris field of aluminum and steel surrounded the tire and its accompanying bits.

"We need to salvage this stuff," Denisha said.

We picked up metal shards and parts of all sizes and moved them to the fluffy part of the sand, where it was clearly above the high tide mark.

I said, "We must have hit here and bounced over to where we skidded into the water."

Denisha squatted in front of the tire and began flipping it end-over-end up the beach.

"You don't think it would be easier to ... you know ... roll it? That's like the whole advantage of the wheel is that it rolls."

"Force of habit. They have us flip tractor-trailer tires at the gym, so this little guy is nothing."

I resolved to join a gym if I didn't die first from starvation or exposure to the elements. She was doing one-armed what I wouldn't have tried with both.

After we'd gathered everything we could find, we surveyed our collection of carnage.

"Well?" Denisha said.

"Well, I'm not sure what use any of it's going to be, but here it is."

Denisha pointed at the tire. "That right there can be made into sandals for those of us unfortunate enough to have been wearing heels."

I looked at her like she had two faces. "What are you talking about?"

"There's this tribe in Mexico that make sandals out of tire tread and leather. I read about it in a book about ultra-marathoners. As long as somebody's got a knife."

"Oh, I guarantee you at least two of those guys have pocket knives. Never mind that, until now, they've mostly been used as letter openers. How else can the office-dwelling male expect to stay attached to his hunter-gatherer roots and assert his dominance?"

"You … seem to have thought about this a lot."

"In the wintertime, the place is full of duck boots and knife clips on pockets like there's about to be a bird hunting company retreat. It's absurd."

"Anything else?" Denisha said with a smirk.

"Probably. If you give me a minute. HR rarely gets to release all our pent-up mockery since we're the workplace neutrals. But maybe I should pace myself."

"That works. We can always come back to this. I'm eager to hear your specific gripes about people as long as they're entertaining. In the meantime, we should probably look for some fresh water because we're all going to die without it."

"I guess. Since you seem to think it's so urgent, I should probably mention that I think I saw a stream up ahead coming out of the jungle. Is that a jungle? We need to figure out what we're calling it."

CHAPTER 8
WHAT HAPPENS IN THE BUSH

BY THE TIME Denisha and I got back to the place we'd set out from, each of us carrying several scraps of aluminum as proof of our find, two of the other three pairs had already returned. The pilots stood at the water's edge, letting the low-tide waves lap at their feet. They faced the tail of the plane, which was the only part that wasn't submerged. Denisha excused herself and joined them.

I wandered over to Jac and Daryl, dropping my haul in front of them. "Parts of the plane."

Daryl said, "Well, I didn't figure you'd found a smelting plant."

"Don't be snarky at her," Jac said. "She's the only one who even tried to save your raggedy old self."

"Y'all have any luck?" I asked.

Daryl pointed his thumb over his shoulder at a collection of coconuts. "There's no shortage of those if we can figure a way to get into them."

"Is that going to be a problem?"

"Haven't you ever been to a resort?" Jac said. "They use machetes to open them up. And unless one of these guys is hiding one in their pants—"

Daryl opened his mouth, but Jac gave him the stink-eye, so he closed it.

"Anyway, we don't have a machete, so we'll have to figure out something else."

I hadn't been to a resort, or anywhere else remotely exotic. My experience with coconut ended at Mounds bars (nasty) and cream pies (not nasty).

"What about them?" I nodded toward the pilots. "They find anything?"

"Mentioned seeing some papayas, but no water."

"Oh, we found water," I said excitedly. "Not sure if it's fresh or anything. But it was coming out of the jungle and going down to the ocean. Denisha wouldn't go in there and check out the source. She was scared of snakes and big cats."

"You're damn right I was," Denisha hollered, having heard her name. She scanned the tree line, putting an exaggerated hand above her eyes to shield the sun, even though it was at her back. "What am I going to do, flog an attacker like a goose?" She flapped her injured arm like a wing and winced. She was adjusting the makeshift sling when her head popped up and she pointed. "See, you never know what's going to come out of there."

We all turned in unison. Tom and Norman walked toward the group. Tom appeared to be holding something in his hand and was being careful to keep it well away from his body. Everyone converged on them.

Daryl asked, "What you got there, Tom?"

Norman shook his head with mild embarrassment.

Tom smiled with one side of his mouth, held his closed hand palm up, and let his fingers open. He held several brown pellets that could have been a seed or bean or almost anything. But it wasn't any of those things.

"What's that supposed to be?" Rhonda asked.

"Not 'supposed to be,' Captain. *Is.* That's poop."

"Gross," Denisha said.

Norman shook his head again. "No, gross was him tasting it to see what it was. Just disgusting."

The group let out a collective groan, and Tom looked betrayed. "Norm, my man, what ever happened to 'what happens in the bush, stays in the bush.'"

"I can assure you, we are still very much in the bush."

Tom pitched the handful of pellets over his shoulder. "Anyway, somewhere on this island is a herd of goats or deer or sheep, which also means there's fresh water. So that means this place is habitable … for as long as we need it to be."

Our little band of survivors didn't receive the news in the positive way Tom had intended. The prospect of having to think about being here for long enough to worry about its long-term habitability was both daunting and devastating.

Tom saw the deflation as it was occurring and tried to patch the hole. "Guys, this is great news. We have everything we need."

"What we need," Jacqueline said defiantly, "is to be rescued, not to be the Swiss Family Robinson."

I looked at the pilots. "When they figure out we're missing, won't they retrace our steps and find us?"

Ryan said, "Do you know how many islands there are in the Caribbean?"

Rhonda nudged him with her elbow. "Don't be a jerk."

"Go ahead. Guess."

"A few hundred?" I said. "I don't know."

Norman offered, "Seven hundred."

"Seven *thousand*," Ryan said. "Want to know how many of those are occupied? About a hundred."

"Please pardon my partner's lack of tact." Rhonda sighed. "The problem with all that real estate is that there's no way for anyone to know that we went way out of our way to the east to get around the storm that hit us. It was just too big and caught up with us. Then when we got hit by lightning, we glided further to the east, riding the wind. At this point, I have no idea how far off the flight plan we are. Did you all see *Cast Away*?"

Only Denisha and I didn't nod.

"Alright, in the movie, Tom Hanks' character figures out they flew off course about an hour, roughly four hundred miles. He did some math and figured out that rescuers would have to search about 500,000 square miles to find him. I remember he said that's twice the size of the State of Texas. Well, assume that we were only 200 miles off course. That's still about … help me with the math, Ryan."

"That's 125,600 square miles."

"Right. So, half the State of Texas."

Several minutes of grim silence descended over us as we mulled over our newfound reality.

Tom tried to lighten the atmosphere again. "At least we have goats, right?"

It didn't elicit any of the smiles he'd been shooting for.

As the group started to break apart, I said, "Wait."

Everyone paused and faced me.

"If we're going to be here for the rest of our natural lives, I want to be called 'Alex.' That's what I was my whole life until some career counselor told me it wasn't professional. So I've been Alexis ever since college, and I hate it so much. And I won't die here with you people while being called a name I hate."

That drew smiles. Only a couple. But still, it was more than Tom got. And the amount of relief I felt more than compensated for any lack of response from my fellow marooned compatriots.

CHAPTER 9
IN ORDER OF IMPORTANCE

AS THE SUN continued its upward arc, we sought shelter from the heat under the trees. I joined Denisha and Norman, who sat with their backs against a palm.

"Been an eventful …" Denisha looked down at her smart watch, "… fourteen hours."

Norman only grunted.

My first thought was that if her watch was made by Apple, she probably only had another twenty-four hours or so until it was just an expensive decoration, while my fancy-pants Citizen would go on for years. Not that it mattered. Watches had about as much meaning to us now as teats on a boar hog.

I said, "Is there a customer service desk somewhere? I'd like to tell a rep this isn't the trip I signed up for."

"Maybe you—"

"Y'all may be giving up on being rescued! But not me!"

Startled, I looked across Denisha to check out the commotion. Jac stood in front of Tom, pointing her finger at him.

"No one's giving up. I don't even really know what that means in this context. But whether we're here for three days or three months, there are things we need to do to survive. That's all I'm saying."

Jac crossed her arms and stalked off, apparently unconvinced. Or in denial. Or both.

I sat forward, about to push myself up and go intervene. Then, acting against my usual proclivities, I leaned back against the tree. The Enneagram test I'd taken said I was a Peacemaker with some Challenger tendencies, which served as a good explanation for my career choice. I was keen on making other people's problems my own problems and trying to fix them. It took a lot of restraint not to go try to set things straight. But hunger and a lack of sleep made compelling arguments for doing nothing.

"Good girl," Denisha said. "They can get their own selves sorted out. Or not. It's not your job anymore."

I let my head rest against the palm tree. "It kind of feels like it is, though."

"If you want," Norman said, "I could fire you."

"Heck, no!" I said. "Do you know how fat my bank account is going to get, collecting all those paychecks without paying any bills?"

"And think of all the overtime we're accruing," Denisha said.

"Not us." Norman shook his head. "We're exempt employees."

"Sucks to be you."

A minute later, I got up anyway, incapable of not doing anything for an extended stretch. I'd always found that relaxing and doing nothing are kind of stressful. "I'm going to talk to Tom. See what we need to do next. There's got to be something he needs help with."

"He's probably already etched a to-do list into a stone," Norman said. "Man likes a to-do list."

I strode over to Tom, who was collecting small sticks and piling them up. When he saw me, he said, "Kindling. And also, I didn't pick that fight with her."

I smiled and raised my hands to show I didn't have any

weapons. "I come in peace." He seemed to turn his defenses down a bit with that. "I was wondering what you think we need to be doing."

"That's easy. In order of importance — water, shelter, and food. We can get by for a few days without a shelter and without food, but we won't make it long without water. To have drinkable water, we need fire so we can boil it, though we can probably collect rainwater from the storm and be okay drinking that while it lasts. We also need to decide on a campsite and make a latrine well away from camp."

I looked around and took a mental inventory of our belongings. "I don't think we have anything that can hold water."

Tom seemed surprised, like he hadn't considered our lack of any resources. Maybe he was in camping mode, where he made sure to bring everything with him and had a list he went through days in advance, checking and rechecking to make sure he left nothing behind that he might need. "Of course." He considered for a minute. "What about any of the metal you found?"

"Most of it's pretty small. There are some bigger pieces, but they're all wrinkled up."

"Okay, okay. That might work still, if we can figure out a way to flatten them out, then make them into a kind of bowl."

Some of the others had loosely congregated around us, doing anything productive being preferable to sitting around being miserable.

Rhonda said, "Denisha, what's in the galley?"

Denisha nodded and started listing things as they came to her. "Glasses, but they're probably broken. A couple of small pots and pans, but nothing bigger than would go on a hot plate. Oh, there's an air fryer. It has the pullout part that's metal."

"And then there's the baggage compartment," Ryan said as he settled next to Denisha.

"What do you mean?" Norman asked.

"It's accessible from the lavatory. So unless the door won't open or something's blocking it, we can get to the luggage."

"Anybody have anything useful back there?"

"I've got a couple extra packs of cigarettes," Jac said from where she stood just outside the circle. "And I would literally murder any one of you bastards for a smoke right now."

That helped explain the earlier outburst.

Excitement shined on Tom's face. "Does that mean you have a lighter?"

The joy was fleeting.

Jac shook her head. "In my purse. Forgot to grab it."

"So it's still on the plane?"

"Maybe. How should I know? Could have floated all the way to Antigua by now."

Several people cast sidelong glances at the plane. The prospect of going back into the tube-shaped prison that had landed us on the island wasn't particularly inviting.

Tom stood and ran his hands through his hair, then gestured wildly with both hands. A hundred years earlier, people would have thought he was having some kind of fit. "Holy smokes! The suitcases. We can use the suitcases to store water, and even food. Who all has the clam shell ones?"

Most of us raised our hands like school children. Thanks to the baggage fees on commercial flights that had coerced passengers to get new bags to fit in overhead bins, we mostly had hard-cased bags that should be watertight up to the zipper line ... if they hadn't been cracked or broken during the crash.

Jac griped at him. "You're more excited about figuring out how to survive here than you would be about being rescued."

"That's ..." Tom floundered before landing on "preposterous."

It wasn't preposterous, though. Tom was always in search of an adventure. Increasing salaries and bonus structures fueled his ambition to climb the corporate ladder so that he could afford bolder and more exclusive adventures. The downside was that becoming a nearly indispensable executive limited his opportunities to disconnect entirely and fall off the grid in the Chilean mountains or the Sonoran Desert.

Of course, the company was about to find out whether the majority of the executives were indispensable after all.

"After we get the lighter, should we start a signal fire or something?" Daryl had finally slunk to the outer edge of the gathering.

"*If* we find the lighter," Tom corrected. "I'm not sure that really works, anyway. Maybe we should use rocks and drift-wood to spell out S.O.S."

That seemed suspect and lent credence to Jac's suggestion that he'd be content to stay out here. It seemed to me that spelling something out in the sand wasn't all that likely to be seen.

Rhonda spoke those same thoughts aloud. "I can tell you that I'm a whole lot more likely to see a pillar of smoke rising into the sky than some rocks on a tiny island." She looked to Ryan for support.

"Agreed. When there were all those wildfires in Texas a few years ago, you could see the smoke for … I don't know … a long way."

"Well, yeah, a wildfire. Sure. But that's acres of forest. It's not like we can set the entire island on fire and hope for the best."

It was weird that he was so defensive about his anti-fire position. If he was going to be the leader like it appeared he wanted to be, he'd have to be more pliable and willing to concede things.

Denisha asked, "So what now?"

"Now, we ask for volunteers to go climb back into the plane when the tide goes out in a little while."

CHAPTER 10
THE LAST OF THE LASHINGS

THANK God for men and their pocket knives, and that we were on a private jet where they could carry them. Although we probably wouldn't be here at all if we'd flown commercial. 'One thing at a time, baby girl,' as Daddy always said. I wish I could turn off my internal monologue sometimes. What about people who say they don't have it? Is it just quiet inside their head? That must be nice.

Ryan tied off the last of the lashings in our bamboo and driftwood raft. It wasn't the sturdiest thing any of us had seen, but all it had to do was hold together long enough to get things from the plane to shore.

Tom mopped the sweat off his face with his forearm. "Those knots good?"

"We had a sailboat when I was a kid," Ryan said. "My dad used to make me tie knots as punishment whenever I got in trouble. He didn't much care for spanking us. He'd had a rough go of things, I guess. He thought time out was a stupid waste of time, but if he could make us do something mind-numbingly repetitive while simultaneously learning a useful skill, that seemed about right to him. So, yeah, the knots are good."

Norman clapped Daryl on the back. "The raft was a good idea."

"I know."

Jac quipped, "Not that either one of you did anything to build it."

Norman said, "I'm old and fragile."

"Not so old that you've retired and given up that fat salary and bonus."

He shrugged. "Old and wise."

He wasn't that old. I knew their personnel files by heart. Not necessarily because I needed to, but mostly because I'm a nosy snoop. It wasn't a *required* skill for people in my position, but it was useful. Unlike being a gossip, which is a terrible characteristic for someone in HR. How gossiping hadn't made the deadly sins list, I'd never understand. Gossip had harmed far more people than slothfulness. Wars had started because of gossip.

I stepped a few paces away from the group and motioned for Denisha to join me.

"Yeah?"

"I don't want my clothes to get wet again."

It took Denisha a second, but she caught on. "There's only one way to do this, then. Quick and bold. Just slip out of them, jump into the water, and start swimming. Remember, underwear is basically a bikini."

"If the girls on Survivor can do it, I can too, right?"

"Yup."

Tom called. "Y'all ready?"

Ryan affirmed.

I nodded.

"Okay. Ryan and I will pull the raft. Alexi—sorry. Alex, you make for the side door."

Having already ditched my shoes, I ripped off my top and pants, throwing them to Denisha and running to the water.

Behind her, Norman yelled, "I need to complain about a violation of company policy."

"You know you're not complaining," Jac said.

Thankfully, the waves and my splashing drowned out the rest of it. As I got deep enough that swimming became the better option to running, I realized the plane was further out than I'd thought it to be. *How did any of us, much less all — nope, not all — Walt got lost in all the commotion — make it to shore.* I hoped for his sake that whatever happened to him had happened quickly.

With the low tide, much of the top of the hull was visible, and I could see a gap between the water and the top of the side door. That was good. Once I was inside, I wouldn't have to worry about breathing. There was no reason to go into the cockpit, which was still fully submerged. By the time I got through the galley into the passenger compartment, I should be able to stand relatively easily.

After a few final kicks, I bobbed down the back side of a swell and ducked my head as I slipped into the jet. My breaths came in great heaves. I wasn't in swimming shape any more. I forced my eyes wider, trying to make them acclimate more quickly to the relative darkness.

The plane bucked gently as waves rolled into it. I made an effort to plant my feet and had to crane my neck back to keep my mouth and nose above water. *Being short sucks sometimes. Most of the time.*

With my eyes adjusted, I moved from the entryway across the galley to where I remembered seeing the air fryer when we boarded. Most jets would have had a microwave, but not this one. Air fryers made Henry's chicken nuggets crispier, and Henry had mandated that he have nuggets when he flew. Crispy ones. It was a small wonder it wasn't the dinosaur-shaped nuggets my niece and nephew love.

Henry, who was still strapped into his seat just a few feet from me. Henry, who'd probably already been nibbled on by things that had smelled him and made their way in. Things that were probably still here and could smell me.

I covered my mouth, thinking I might be sick. Behind me, something bumped against the outside of the fuselage. I shrieked and whirled around.

Tom's face appeared through the slit between the water and the top of the door frame. The bumping noise was the raft. "You okay in there?"

"Uh-huh." I took deep breaths, trying to slow my heart rate.

"Coming in," he said, a moment before going under and resurfacing inside the plane. "Found anything yet?"

"No. Just … uhh … getting my bearings."

"You scared of seeing the boss-man with half his face missing from crabs and sharks?" He laughed as he said it.

"Stop it."

"Wait here." Tom waded through the galley into the passenger compartment. He splashed and made a racket as he rustled around, but I couldn't make myself look. Half an eternity later, Tom said, "Okay, come on back."

My feet found the ground with more certainty as I pushed through the galley. I slunk down to keep my torso below water, knowing even as I did so that I was going to have to get over my self-consciousness (and regret) about shirking my clothes, or we'd never get all the things we came for.

"Oh, Tom!" I covered my mouth in surprise. A brown leather messenger bag sat upside-down over Henry's head, which was only partially above water. "Don't you think that's kind of disrespectful?"

Tom waved me off. "I asked him about it. He said he's freakin' dead, so he doesn't care."

I glared at him. "That's messed up."

"Any sign of Walter?"

I shook my head.

"He's probably washed up on the beach somewhere. Either that, or he got carried out to sea."

Goose eggs crawled over my skin, and I shivered.

"Cold?"

"No. The thought of that happening is horrifying."

"All of this is kind of horrifying."

"True. You got your phone?"

Tom pulled the phone out of his pocket and read aloud through the list of things we were supposed to look for. When he'd finished, he shoved the phone back into his pocket and sloshed back to the galley for the air fryer. I pushed past bag-headed Henry toward the seat Jac had been sitting in, hoping that the strap of her purse had gotten tangled in something and kept it in the vicinity.

CHAPTER 11
TAKING INVENTORY

TOM AND RYAN beached the raft with the aid of Rhonda and Daryl, who waded into the surf to help. We had no more made landfall than a rogue wave snuck in behind us and upended the overloaded raft. Luggage, appliances, and personal possessions went every which direction, sending all eight of us into a mad scramble to recover our things.

After several minutes, we sat amid a collection of items, huffing and puffing and burning under the Caribbean sun. I slipped Jac's purse over my head and handed it across to her. "Glad you had a crossbody and not a shoulder bag."

Jac all but ripped the purse open and yanked out a pack of cigarettes. There has never been a more dejected expression than the one she wore when water dripped from the pack. She nearly cried when she opened it and peaked inside.

When she stood up and turned to walk away, Tom asked, "Jac? The lighter? Is it in there?"

She glared at him but reached into her purse again, pulling something out. She threw it at Tom. He ducked to the left. Ryan jabbed a hand out just in time to catch the lighter before it drove into the sand.

"Hey!" Tom yelled.

"Hey yourself. Me smoking is about to save our lives, but I don't get to have one last cigarette when I didn't even want to quit."

Daryl said, "Didn't you say you brought some extra packs in your bag?"

Her eyes lit up. She pulled her bag toward her and unzipped it with all the eagerness of a child at Christmas expecting a puppy. Jac reached beneath the damp layers of pants suits and pulled out a cellophane-wrapped carton. She cradled it close to her chest as she demanded the lighter back. Tom leaned forward and handed it across to her.

Jac unwrapped the carton and pulled out a pack, inspecting it to make sure it was dry. She flipped the lid back and looked greedily at the contents. She took a cigarette out and placed it gently between her lips.

I felt like a voyeur and wanted to turn away, but didn't.

Jac unclasped the lid of the lighter and pressed the button. There was no fire, but the cigarette began glowing anyway.

"What kind of lighter is that?"

Jac inhaled deeply, held it, and moaned softly as she blew out. "Better than any sex I've ever had. I'm going to answer your question then walk over there so none of y'all ruin this for me. It's a plasma lighter." Tom opened his mouth, but Jac continued talking before he could get any words out. "And yes, it makes fire." She waggled the cigarette between her fingers, then tossed the lighter back to Tom. More gently this time. "Obviously. Now, I'm going to have a threesome. Y'all do whatever you need to." She pulled a second cigarette from the box, turned, and walked away. As she walked, she lit the second cigarette with the first and put them both between her lips.

Norm said, "Shouldn't you ration those?"

She raised a middle finger without looking back and meandered over to some shade.

Rhonda said, "We need to take an inventory of everything useful. Anyone have food or drinks?"

The sounds of zippers winding around luggage could heard around the huddle. Rhonda took a towel out of her bag and unfolded it to lie flat across the sand between us all. Norman flung a bag of corn flour and a couple of bags of coffee onto the towel. "The missus won't be happy about me coming back without that masa, assuming … you know."

We all knew, and no one wanted him to finish that sentence.

More flour and coffee were added to the pile. Bags of dried plantains, along with candies and several bottles of a Colombian liquor called aguardiente. The last addition was a small package wrapped in duct tape. Heads snapped toward Ryan.

"Bruh, we were in Colombia. You think nobody's going to pick up some of the local produce?"

Jac, who had made her way back to the group, squatted down by her luggage, pulled out a similar package and tossed it next to Ryan's. "Things are shaping up for quite a party."

That drew some uncomfortable giggles.

Tom looked around. "Anyone else have anything useful … or recreational to contribute?"

Ryan reached back into his bag.

Rhonda covered her eyes. "God help us. I can't even imagine what you're about to drag out."

He smirked and pulled out a machete that he threw onto the pile.

"Oh, you're a lifesaver," Tom said. "A couple of pocketknives weren't going to make things very easy."

While Ryan's machete looked somewhat like a cutlass, the one Norman pulled out of his suitcase and pitched into the middle of the ring appeared to be designed to fell small trees.

"Norm, my man!" I said.

He wore a self-satisfied grin, knowing no one expected this

from him. "I've got a kudzu problem in the woods behind the house."

"And no matter how well you sling that thing," Tom said, "you'll still have a kudzu problem. That stuff is like a hydra. You can only kill it with an herbicide. Problem is, anything strong enough to kudzu will kill everything else in those woods, too."

Daryl seemed bewildered. "Y'all know you can go down to your local Ace Hardware pick up any manner of brush-clearing tools, right?"

"But these," Norm said, "are the genuine article. Right out of the rainforest."

Jac picked one up and inspected it. "Genuinely made in Vietnam. I guess it's fortunate for us that you two haven't gotten the memo about toxic masculinity yet." She turned her head and whispered to Rhonda, still loud enough for everyone to hear. "Or maybe they're overcompensating?"

"For what?" I asked with a wink.

"Look at you being a saucy little instigator now that you've shed that human resources mantle. Well, you see, when men have small peni—"

"Alright," Tom said, standing up, "I think I'm about done with this conversation. But if anybody wants to help me gather wood for a fire, that would be a lot more helpful than discussing the relative sizes of dudes' parts."

Because Ryan and Norman were the ones being discussed, they were only too eager to have a reason to do anything else, and Daryl wasn't about to be the only man left sitting around.

I figured I needed to learn how to make fire, so I too joined the firebrand brigade, a name I came up with right there on the spot. I was proud of it but knew I wouldn't tell any of them. It was too hokey and sounded like the name of a 1980s movie made for kids, right alongside The ButterCream Gang. Before long, all eight of us were scrounging around for wood, from kindling to fallen logs.

"Keep an eye out for pine trees," Tom said. "We can use the sap to start the fire. It's super flammable. And if you see any old dry coconuts lying around, bring those too."

"Everybody stay within eyesight of at least one other person," Rhonda said. "We still don't know what's in this jungle."

Tom said, "There aren't any big cats, if that's what you're worried about."

"And just how do you know that?" Jac asked.

"Not a big enough habitat."

She rolled her eyes. "First of all, you don't have any idea how big of an island we're on. Second, if you really did find pig crap—"

"Sheep, probably."

"Whatever. Where there's prey, there is likely a predator."

CHAPTER 12
A PILGRIMAGE

TOM GRUNTED IN FRUSTRATION. "Look, there's no reason for us to stay here, where we washed up. But there's about a half-dozen reasons to move closer to the stream Alex and Denisha found."

"What about the plane?" Jac asked.

I couldn't prove that these two were going out of their way to butt heads at every turn, but it sure as heck seemed like that was the case.

"What about it? It's not like it's going anywhere, and we've scavenged everything we can from it."

"Shouldn't we stay close to it?" Norman asked.

"No. Don't you think if someone comes along and finds the plane that (a) we'll be acutely aware of their approach, and (b) they'll go to the trouble of looking around a little to see if anybody's home? I'm not proposing we move to the other side of the island, just a few hundred yards closer to fresh water. In fact, I'm not proposing anything. I'm telling you what I'm going to do and recommending that you join me."

Ryan added, "Besides, we can't make decisions based on being rescued. We haven't seen a ship, or a plane, or even so much as a contrail. We have to decide based on what gives us the best chance to survive."

If someone chimed in with *not just survive, but thrive* like some kind of misbegotten motivational speaker, I might puke. Or drown them. Maybe both. Drown them in my puke. That's disgusting. I was ashamed of myself for taking it that far. Fortunately, both of our lecturers relished playing the role of bad cop, so we were spared any frivolous niceties.

Tom gave his final word on the subject. "It's going to be dark in two hours. We need to move camp and start a fire while we can still see." He and Ryan didn't wait for further questions or commentary. They loaded their arms with stuff and walked down the beach in the direction that Denisha and I had explored.

Explored may have been overstating it since all we'd done was follow the beach south a ways. Because we hadn't encountered any evidence of prior human inhabitants, I guess that qualifies us as explorers. Of course, my European ancestors would have counted themselves as explorers regardless of its prior or current status of human habitation, but that's a topic for another time.

Denisha grabbed the handle of her suitcase and started pulling. She waggled her sling-strapped left arm and said, "There are some advantages to having a broken wing."

I grunted, wedged three coconuts in a pyramid that crooked between my left arm and chin, and towed my suitcase in Denisha's wake. While I hoped the bags that had gone before me would have packed the sand a bit and made my traverse a little easier, it turns out that tiny luggage wheels aren't ideal for long walks on the beach. By the time we got to the stream, which had included several pauses to let my heart rate come down from redlining, I was sweating like a racehorse.

Everyone else had fallen in line as well. We were a procession of pilgrims making our ragged way to a new home, except that it took several processions to get everything relocated. After the first trek, we had no more conversation, just huffing and puffing. And sweating. So much sweating. You could have cut through the humidity with a knife.

For a group of people who'd been in a fatal plane crash on a deserted island just under forty-eight hours earlier, we sure had a lot of stuff. The sun was nearly setting on the other side of the island by the time we finished.

"I was thinking about something," Denisha said.

"I'm game."

"The whole world is made up of islands, from tiny islands like this one to the continents. Because even they are islands if you think about it — land surrounded on all sides by water. So how big does a land mass have to be before we don't call it an island any more?"

"You know, that's an interesting question — not to me, but probably to someone. And since I'm not a cartographer or a geographer, I have no clue. Maybe you can pose that to the group over family dinner."

Tom gathered both a collection of materials to burn and a crowd around himself. He balled up dozens of dried fibers from coconut husks and built a tiny teepee around it. A stack of dead palm fronds lay close at hand.

"Okay," he said to himself, reaching into his pants pocket for the lighter and coming up empty.

When he hadn't used it right away earlier, he'd given it back to Jacqueline, who'd smoked another couple of cigarettes in the interim. Tom whistled sharply at her and gestured for her to give him the lighter.

He flipped open the lid and mashed the button on the side. Two purple plasma arcs crisscrossed with a small sizzling sound. I couldn't help remembering Egon telling the other Ghostbusters not to cross the streams.

Tom held the plasma arcs down to the coconut fibers. An orange glow crawled out from the contact point like a spider, but no flames emerged. Everyone's anxiety dial turned up several degrees.

Once the ball of fibers was mostly glowing, Tom inhaled deeply, then blew a slow, steady stream of air at its base. Flames danced outward, lapping at the kindling. "Give me the stick with the pine tar on it." Ryan picked it up and handed it over. When Tom shoved it into the infantile fire, it caught immediately, and the fire grew more substantial. It no longer looked to be on the verge of going out. A cheer went up.

"Not so fast," Tom said. "We've got a long row to hoe here. More kindling."

Ryan and Norman helped assemble a second teepee over the top of the first. I got the idea that this would be like Russian nesting dolls, but only if they got consumed from the inside out.

I remembered from the few camping trips I'd gone on with my dad and brothers that we needed to establish a good base of hot coals before the fire would be truly stable. At least we were well on our way to that. Maybe we could get the fire big enough that it would put off gobs of smoke and get us noticed.

It was only then that I looked up and realized how dark it had gotten, and much more quickly than I'd expected. We had all been so focused on the task at hand that the sky had gone from sunset to darkness without our noticing.

After Tom helped the fire evolve from a couple of flames into a blaze, he stepped back a few paces, tore off his shirt, and did his best Tom Hanks impression. "I have made fire!"

The line, accompanied by gesticulating arms, got a good deal more laughter than it would have warranted in any other circumstance. But with the prospect of a warm night's sleep and knowing that we could boil water for drinking, everyone's spirits soared.

Off to the west, thunder rolled toward us as a warning. Our soaring spirits plummeted. Tom let go of the most creative string of curse words I'd ever heard, then leapt back toward the fire.

With a large stick, he knocked over the upright pile of burning driftwood.

"What are you doing?" Denisha asked.

"We've got to smother this thing and cover it in layers of green fronds so maybe the rain will roll off them and away from the fire pit. That way, we'll still have a bed of coals and won't have to start from scratch tomorrow."

Jac said, "But what if the storm goes around us?"

Lightning sprinted from cloud to cloud, and a concussion followed in its wake.

"Oh, it's coming for us," Rhonda said. "That's just the luck we have."

She was right.

CHAPTER 13
A LATRINE AND A LEAN-TO

BY THE TIME the rain let up several hours later, everything was soaked. We rode out the storm in a huddle under the tree line. Not that either of those things — the huddle of bodies or the trees — gave us any warmth or relief from the deluge, but it was still better than sitting alone in the open. Shared misery creates a strong bond.

While it was still dark, Tom wandered over to where the campfire had been. We went with him, not having anything better to do and being too cold to sleep. He peeled the palm fronds back one at a time, hoping that when he removed the last one, he'd find an orange glow waiting for him. Instead, he found a puddle.

If we were going to have another fire (and we were), we would have to start all over. Discouraging, but not disheartening. If we hadn't had the lighter, it would have been a more aggravating task, for sure.

No one had spoken in a long time; maybe not since Tom's stream-of-consciousness cursing fit. Fatigue and stress were wearing on everyone. Fortunately, so far, we had all become quiet and morose rather than hostile. We'd had a few dust-ups, but nothing to send home a message in a bottle about. You could rest assured it was coming, though. There's no way to corral this many strong personalities and not have a major clash or two.

I sat down by Tom, who was looking forlornly into the puddle that had been a fire. "You alright?"

"Missing the fam a bit."

"Yeah, I can't imagine. I mean, all I have are siblings and parents, and I'm missing them. I wouldn't even have talked to them in the last couple of days. Except my mom. I talk to her almost every day. She's probably beside herself with worry."

"Every day? What do y'all talk about?"

I thought about it, trying to remember, then shrugged. "I don't know. Stuff."

"There's nobody in my life who I talk to every single day unless I see them."

"So your wife and kids, then."

"Right, and to be honest, now that Meg is a teenager, I'm not entirely sure she talks to me every day. Until now, I was kind of okay with it. There's not a single topic that isn't a minefield. Her tween sister seems to be taking notes and getting a head start. It's going to be a rough few years."

"Decade. Rough decade."

He laughed. It was good to hear.

Daryl walked up. "What are you two hens clucking about?"

"Teenagers."

"Good Lord Almighty," Daryl said, shaking his head. He sat on the wet sand beside Tom. "Ours nearly caused our divorce — I know you're not supposed to say that, but it's true. Then we figured out that neither one of us would survive them alone. We teamed up, and they didn't know what happened. You could see the fear in their eyes. It was glorious."

His tone said the story didn't end there. "But?" I asked.

"You remember how in the first *Jurassic Park* movie, the

velociraptors started figuring out how to open doors and trap the humans? It was a lot like that."

Tom and I both laughed.

Our laughter was a magnet, drawing the rest of the group. All eight of us sat in the damp sand around our thoroughly drowned campfire. To keep things from lulling back into a depressed quiet, I asked, "So what's the plan come sunup?"

Ryan answered first. "We need a latrine and a lean-to that we can sleep under. A hut would be even better, but I think we're better off starting simple. Something to get us up off the ground with a roof over our heads, then we can go from there."

The silence that followed was unmistakably the group awaiting Tom's endorsement. Ryan's alpha ego couldn't have loved that, assuming he had enough emotional intelligence to pick up on it.

Tom announced his agreement. "Yep. We need to collect some of this rainwater too, if we can. Anybody willing to give up their suitcase for the greater good?"

Daryl surprised everyone by volunteering. "So long as someone will rent me some space for my stuff."

"Glad to," Tom said. "My clamshell has separate compartments for the top and bottom. I can get all my gear into one side, and you can have the other. We may need another bag later. We'll see how far this gets us. Probably ought to make a platform for the firewood to help keep it drier, which should be pretty easy."

Denisha said, "What about the raft we made for the luggage?"

Tom hit his forehead with the heel of his hand. "Of course. That's perfect. We can mark that off the list. Collecting firewood is going to be like a full-time job. Scratch that. Part-time. No one is accruing any PTO or health insurance."

"Speaking of PTO," I said, "none of you have turned in

your paperwork yet for your beach vacation." The waves of the beach were all the louder for the silence that followed what I thought was a decent joke. "Wow. Tough crowd."

"Bring better jokes," Jac said.

Someone made a sizzling sound.

I'd readily take the loss if it would help to keep morale up.

By the time the sun arrived, the team was eager to get the day's work under way. We divided up the labor, and everyone knew their respective jobs. I'd stuck with Tom, whose priorities were to gather wood and get the fire going.

Carrying things seemed to fit my lack of skills better than either of the other two tasks. I was incompetent at building and couldn't fancy myself taking orders from Ryan for the next several hours, though Denisha seemed unexpectedly keen on the idea. On top of that, wielding a machete to chop down bamboo was a recipe for me to lose a digit or two.

Daryl and Jac volunteered for the honor of digging the litter box. I proposed calling it the piss pipe but got outvoted.

As Tom and I walked back to the crash site to retrieve the raft, I asked, "Are we going to be alright?"

"We have food, shelter, and fresh water. We should be okay for a good long while. I don't know how long the fruit will last. We need to explore the island to see what else there is. There are animals here somewhere. If I had to guess, they are probably over toward the promontory on the far end." He nodded his head backward, gesturing to the giant craggy protrusion coming up out of the earth. It's a good thing we'd missed that on our way down, or we'd all have been charred chunks of debris instead of survivors trying to make do. After visualizing us as a fireball rising to meet the clouds the night we crashed, I realized Tom was still talking. "Calories are going to be a problem eventually, but that's getting ahead of ourselves."

"What if somebody gets hurt or sick?"

"That's definitely the biggest variable. Look, we've got to take this one thing at a time. No sense worrying about things that haven't happened yet, and might not happen. There's nothing we can do about it right now."

We stopped in front of the raft, both looking at the mostly submerged plane. Tom shook his head and turned his back to it. "If you have any more questions, now's the time. Once we start dragging this thing, we're going to be huffing and puffing like freight trains."

"I'm a girl. I don't huff and puff. I'm more refined than that."

He wrinkled his nose. "You don't smell very refined."

"Not nice."

"Ready?"

We picked up one side of the raft and started dragging. It didn't take me long to regret turning up my nose at piss pipe duty.

CHAPTER 14
THE HEADS OF OUR ENEMIES

OVER THE NEXT SEVERAL DAYS, nothing disastrous happened, and we settled into a routine. Every pair of people were assigned duties that rotated daily. One pair gathered coconuts, papayas, and seaweed. Another collected wood for the fire. A third was tasked with restarting the fire and boiling fresh water. The final pairing helped maintain the camp, cleared brush, added palm fronds to the shelter, or did whatever we needed to keep things in good condition.

None of this took a particularly long time, especially when you considered how much time we had in a day. With the morning chores complete, we sat down to eat what we'd gathered. For the time being, we were a functional little commune.

After doing my rounds making sure the shelters we'd built for wood, food, and ourselves were serviceable, I circled back to Tom. He smiled when he saw me coming and waved me over. When I got to him, he held up what he'd been working on.

I was confused. "Is that a pike to display the heads of our enemies on and ward off raiders?"

"Ha! No, but maybe that's a secondary use I hadn't considered."

"Okay, tell me what I'm looking at."

I didn't know if he was happier about what he'd made or the opportunity to explain it to someone.

"You know how coconuts are such a pain in the ass to open?"

I nodded. It was a hassle, and I was pretty sure someone was going to lose a hand to a machete injury.

"So we bury this end in the ground." Tom patted the butt end of the thing. "Pack it in real tight with rocks and sand. Then that'll leave about three feet sticking up out of the ground so you can slam a coconut down on it and open it up that way."

"What happens when someone misses and rams the palm of their hand through it?"

He grimaced. "Don't miss?"

"And where could you possibly put this so that somebody doesn't impale themselves on it?"

"I'll find somewhere out of the way to put it. Maybe I can make a cap for it."

"Uh-huh. I want the record to reflect that I like the idea in principle but not in execution."

"Noted," he said, his enthusiasm dissipating.

"Come on," I said, urging him to go with me to join the others around the fire.

This was a special day, but not in a good way. Today marked Day 10 of us being marooned on this island. Rather than mourn it, we'd decided the night before to celebrate it. And since celebrations everywhere involve food, we collectively agreed to use some of our masa to make tortillas. No one had a recipe, but Norman, our resident foodie, said flatbreads are the only thing he knew of that we could make with only flour and water.

When you have an entertainment deficit, it turns out that your selectivity for what you will or won't spend your time watching changes dramatically. In my case, watching Norman figure out how to make flatbread on a whim was one of the more interesting things I'd seen in the last week.

Denisha said, "Talk us through it like you're hosting a show on a food channel."

I'm not sure he'd have done it for anyone else, but I think he was starting to think of her as a daughter of sorts. The situation necessarily meant that we were all spending a lot of time around each other, but because they were paired up for chores, they got more time together working as a cohesive unit than they would have otherwise.

He smiled at her and donned his presentation voice. "We've got a special treat for those of you watching at home …" His voice cracked when he said that last word. It was unexpected. We'd all been avoiding any reminder of home. He used his shirtsleeves to wipe away the tears that had immediately formed.

Norman cleared his throat and continued. "For those of you in our studio audience, my apologies for that brief interruption. One of my lousy assistants was cutting up onions moments ago, and there's a bit of something still lingering in the air. Today, we'll be making rustic flatbread. Rustic because we'll be using one dish for both mixing and cooking, and because we won't be using any measuring devices, just playing it by feel."

He pulled the basin from the air fryer in front of him and poured in a half a bag of masa. Swirling his hand, he made a hole in the pile until it looked like the top of a volcano. "Now that we've got our flour, we are going to add water a little at a time until we have a very sticky ball of dough."

Norman used a rough-hewn ladle that Tom had carved to dip water from the suitcase that we used as a reservoir. After he poured water into the middle of his flour volcano, he worked the flour into it little by little. He did this several times until it was the consistency he was looking for, which could best be described as a gooey blob.

"Now that we've got our dough, we'll knead it just a little bit and release the gluten."

I didn't hear anyone clambering about needing a gluten-free diet. Funny what knowing you're not that far removed from starvation will do to a person.

"Does anyone have moderately clean hands?" Norman asked.

Each of us inspected our fingers and palms. Even with our adjusted expectations of what clean meant, no one qualified.

"I tell you what, we'll do this — y'all go down to the water, rinse your hands, and when you get back, we'll move to the next step."

We followed instructions like eager school children wanting the teacher's approval. Norman handed everyone a small masa ball and gave Denisha two. "One of those is mine."

With a nearby stick that he picked up, Norman scraped a heap of coals away from the fire and set the overturned air fryer basin on top of them. Then he placed a piece of coconut on top of it. When it sizzled, he used his finger to push the chunk of coconut over the surface like it was a stick of butter.

When he motioned to Rhonda, she handed him her dough ball, which he flattened with his palms into roughly the shape of a tortilla before tossing onto the modified flattop griddle. A couple of minutes later, he flipped it over. Shortly after that, he set it on a plantain leaf and gave it back to Rhonda.

Between the smell of the freshly grilled flatbread and Rhonda taking a bite as steam rolled off it, I could hardly bear it. I don't know how Norman had the fortitude to wait until last to make and eat his own. It may go down as the greatest self-restraint that I've ever witnessed.

In the *before* version of my life, a single corn tortilla would never have been an indulgence, but it was now. It also set the stage for what the rest of the day had in store.

CHAPTER 15
GNATS AND FLIES

WHEN TOM and Ryan scampered off into the woods after breakfast, they hadn't said what they were up to, and no one had asked. With some actual carbohydrates in our bellies, everyone was feeling energized. Denisha and I talked about lying on the beach, but I was already getting brown as a biscuit. Ultimately, we decided we were getting plenty of tropical sun without adding a future risk of skin cancer to the mix.

Later, as the sun reached its zenith and poured heat onto our little island, no amount of shade was sufficient to keep me comfortable. I talked the other women into going and bobbing with me in the sea. It was a lot easier to ditch my clothes and get down to my underwear when half of our contingent did it with me. Dozens of small whiting fish scattered in all directions as we hit the water.

Jac said, "If we caught some of those, we could add some meat to the menu. I mean not meat-meat, but fish-meat."

"I think we'd need to catch *all* of them to make it worth our while," Rhonda said.

"Does anybody have any safety pins?" Denisha asked. "We might be able to use it as a fishing hook."

Rhonda shook her head. "No safety pins, but I do have a

little sewing kit tucked into one of the pockets of my suitcase. I'd kind of forgotten about it."

I said, "I bet if you get the needles hot enough, you could bend them into a hook. Of course, that'd be a lot easier with pliers. Getting them in and out of the fire, then bending them? I don't know."

"I've got eyebrow tweezers." Rhonda suggested.

Jac's eyes lit up. "Oh, me too!"

I nodded a little too aggressively. "That might work."

Denisha said, "I saw a fish washed up on the beach a ways away when Norm and I were scouring for firewood this morning. That could be our bait."

Rhonda said, "Okay. Jac and I will get to work on the needles if you two will get the fish."

We made our way back to the shore, excited about our prospects. When we hit the sand, Denisha peeled off to the left. "This way."

I turned and took a couple of quick steps to catch up.

"You think this is going to work?" she asked.

"I don't know. Maybe. We fished a bunch when I was a kid. I think I remember how to tie knots that will hold."

"If not, we could always ask Ryan. He was the knot guy."

"I can't tell you how much I'd rather not. He's kind of insufferable."

Denisha frowned. "He's not so bad."

I raised an eyebrow at her.

"Not like that," she said, shoving me toward the waterline. "I just mean he's okay, you know."

"He definitely pays plenty of extra attention to you."

"Oh, I know what he wants." She stuck her chest out and strutted. "He's just going to be super disappointed about that."

Returning to the more pressing subject, I said, "If they can bend the needle, and if we don't catch anything too big, it should work. We can tie the thread to a bamboo shoot to use for a fishing pole."

"Works for me. The real question is, who's going to carry this nasty fish?"

She pointed down at a fish that had clearly been laying in the sun for the better part of a day. Gnats and flies had already made meals of its eyes. There could be no doubt that it would give off a scent that would attract … something.

"Rochambeau?" I proposed.

"Best two out of three."

Throwing paper and then scissors didn't work out for me. I got swept. Fortunately for me, the fish was hard and crusty, not still slimy, but that's me trying really hard to find the bright side of carrying a rotting animal.

We'd no sooner gotten back to camp and found Rhonda and Jac going through Jac's sewing kit when a commotion emerged from the woods. Our fishing idea was about to get lost to a much grander revelation.

Tom strode out, knife in one hand and machete in another. His hands were stained red, which was alarming for obvious reasons. I'd never seen a bigger smile on his face.

My immediate concern for Ryan and whether Tom was about to re-enact *The Shining* was short-lived. Ryan followed in his wake with a goat draped over his shoulders like a bulky shawl, which he kept in place by maintaining a grip on its legs.

"Bastards," Jac muttered, knowing Tom and Ryan had heisted her thunder right out from under her.

Ryan said, "We brought dinner."

The group erupted into questions as though this were a press conference.

"Hang on," Tom said. "Before we tell the story, we've got to skin it and build a rack so we can smoke it. Who wants to help Ryan with skinning it?"

An answer was a long time coming. Relieving an animal of its skin wasn't anyone's idea of a good time.

"I can," Denisha volunteered. "I've done plenty of deer hunting. Alex can help too. If y'all have time to make two racks, we can dry out the pelt and use it too."

"Good thinking," Tom said. "I guess, if everybody else will work with me, then. Many hands make light work and all that."

Tom's crew followed him toward a thicket of bamboo. Ryan lifted the goat off his shoulders and started to set it in the sand.

"What are you doing?" Denisha said.

"Putting it down so we can start working on it."

"Not in the sand, and not near camp." She looked tilted her head and looked at him for a couple of seconds. "Have you ever done this before?"

"No," he said in a clipped voice.

"Alright. Are you willing to take instructions?"

Ryan smirked. "A hot girl telling me what to do? Yeah, I can get behind that."

"Girl?" Denisha scowled. "This isn't high school. Y'all find a clearing away from camp and put some palm fronds or plantain leaves down so the goat isn't laying on the ground. I'll get a couple of knives."

As much I wasn't looking forward to the work at hand, I was pretty sure I was going to enjoy Ryan having to submit to Denisha.

"It's just like a fish," she said while we waited. "Except bigger and with fur and legs."

"We always released what we caught. No one wanted to clean them," I said.

"Ah, well, the good news is they already gutted it, and that's the worst part."

"I thought the worst part was peeling a sweet little goat's skin off like it's a banana."

"Have you ever smelled a perforated intestine before?" She asked.

I wrinkled my nose and shook my head.

"Ever pulled out an animal's innards with your bare hands when its heart has barely stopped pumping and they're still about a hundred degrees?"

I considered making a pun about *bear hands*, but let it go and shook my head again.

"Then you'll have to take my word for it."

CHAPTER 16
WATCH PARTY

BY DUSK, the smell of the goat that had been cooking over the fire most of the day was intoxicating, but maybe not as intoxicating as the Colombian alcohol that was being passed around. Its label said it was less potent than most other liquors, but between our state of chronic dehydration and the desire for a release from our present situation, the effect was very pronounced. It was certainly less intoxicating than the bumps of powder leaving their residue on the undersides of Ryan's and Jac's noses.

I'm a lightweight anyway, so a couple swigs were enough to have me feeling it. A couple more had me swimmy-headed, a feeling I'd never liked. I found the inability to be in total control of myself off-putting, for whatever that says about how uptight I can be. Most of my fellow castaways didn't have those same inhibitions.

When we gathered around the fire to eat, I counted only six of us. "Where are Jac and Daryl?"

Rhonda grinned, making a circle of the index finger and thumb on her left hand, and shoving her right index finger in and out of it.

"No," Denisha said with excited surprise. "Come on. Let's

go see." She jumped up and tugged at my shirtsleeve.

"I'm good."

"Come on. Please."

I was ashamed of my morbid curiosity. I'd never thought of myself as a voyeur before, but I wouldn't be able to escape the label after this. "Fine." I pushed myself to my feet.

"Where?" Denisha asked.

Rhonda pointed toward a dune a few dozen yards away. As we approached with nervous giggles, I shushed us both. We crawled up the sand to the tune of what someone could easily confuse for animal noises on the other side.

When our heads popped over the top of the dune, Daryl's nakedness greeted us with so much very white skin. He was on top of Jac in the middle of … the act, with his pants around his knees. All I could see of Jac was her head and parts of her arms and legs. It was just as well. I'd seen too much already, and I could never unsee it. Any of it.

Denisha unleashed a shrill catcall.

Daryl froze.

Jac located us and waved, then slapped Daryl's naked butt. He recommenced his grunting and rhythmic movements. I bowed out, turning around and sliding down the dune — a little nauseated and a lot regretful.

Denisha stared a little longer. I tapped at her ankle. "Come on, D. It's kind of getting weird now."

She looked down at me, wide-eyed. "You're right about the weird part. He's—"

"Nope. I don't want to know. Really."

She huffed and joined me at the bottom of the dune. "Well, that was interesting."

I shook my head. "I regret everything."

At the campfire, Tom was carving hunks of meat off the goat and passing it around. No plates, no utensils. We'd gone from one primal ritual to another. Next up, human sacrifice.

Kidding, of course. Being adults, we were well beyond a *Lord of the Flies* situation.

I gratefully accepted the piece of meat he took off a rear leg and handed to me as I rejoined the group. In my former civilized life, I generally tried not to be conscious of meat being muscle, and grease being rendered fat, but those thoughts were hard to avoid when the animal we were consuming still had teeth and eyes in its head.

When I sat down, Rhonda said, "Well?"

I nodded. It was the only acknowledgment I wanted to give what I'd witnessed. Denisha, on the other hand, was much more explicit. I focused on my chewing and tried to drown out the commentary.

Within a couple of minutes, Jac and Daryl strutted around the dune, making their way toward us. The glow of a cigarette cast a soft light on her face. Its acrid tobacco smell crowded into an already full olfactory space: meat that had been smoking for hours, the fire itself, the tanginess of the sea water, and a small contingent of musty survivors.

Daryl sat down beside Norm, who nudged him in the ribs. "That was a long time coming."

"I'll admit to having thought about it a time or two."

Apparently, Daryl was getting over his concern about what his wife was going to do to him. His shift marked an interesting turn we were all coming to terms with. With not even the faintest hint of rescue in a week-and-a-half, this may not be some temporary arrangement. Still, the thought of it sent a shiver down my spine.

Jac slid into the space beside me, a couple of ribs in one hand. With the other, she pointed at the two men on the other side of the fire. "If y'all start talking about me like I'm just some piece of tail, I'll wait until you're snoring and dreaming happy little dreams, then I'll plop one of these coals in your mouths. Comprende?"

Both men nodded vigorously.

"Now," Jac said, "where is that bottle of liquor? My brain needs to scrape a few cells away and dull its short-term memory a bit."

Rhonda held a bottle that had only one hard swallow left in it. Jac motioned for her to pass it down. As it came to me and I handed it over, I wondered how much of its remaining contents was backwash. So gross. Maybe the alcohol would kill the germs.

"Fear not, fine people," Ryan said, holding up an unopened bottle of aguardiente.

A cheer went up.

Ryan took a swig and passed the bottle to his left.

Once that bottle had been emptied, another made an appearance. With nothing but goat meat and some dried seaweed in everyone's stomachs to soak up the alcohol, it hit bloodstreams hard and fast. Temperaments made rapid evolutions, and before long, there was a frenzied edge in the air.

I yawned and looked down at my watch. It wasn't quite as late as I thought. The introverted part of me was letting me know its interaction tank was overfilled and it wanted to tap out.

"You got somewhere to be?" Tom asked.

I wrinkled my forehead. "What?"

"Checking your watch like that — you on a schedule?"

"No, Tom," I said a little defensively. "Just getting a little tired and seeing what time it is."

"Time doesn't matter anymore. Do what you want, when you want." He projected his voice more loudly than normal, his words emphatic but slurred. "You don't need permission from some watch. Look at it." He unlatched the watch from his wrist and threw it over everyone's heads toward the waterline.

The groups' heads swiveled as we peered into the darkness.

A moment later, Ryan jumped up and grabbed a branch

that had only one end sticking into the fire. He hurried in the direction Tom had thrown his watch, wielding the makeshift torch.

"Come here!" he yelled.

Tom charged after him with a whoop.

Rhonda and Denisha giggled at the uncomfortable tension in the air. Or maybe I was the only uncomfortable one. The others fell into line. I sighed and stood. It would make more of a scene not to go along with this nonsense.

Ryan held his torch down to the sand where Tom's watch was half buried. "Tom's right. Our watches don't matter. Time is an artificial construct."

Was Ryan more eloquent when drunk? That was an odd effect.

"We don't have to be burdened by these societal implements. Here." He took off his own watch and threw it down beside Tom's.

Never mind that it was a smart watch whose battery had died days ago.

Four more watches hit the ground in quick succession. Rhonda stood directly in front of me, looking at her wrist. I'd noticed over the last few days she wore a really nice chronograph. If I were a betting person, I'd lay money on it being a gift related to piloting. Maybe even a treat-yourself moment after some accomplishment.

She swore quietly and stripped off the watch.

All eyes turned to me.

"Take your watch off," Ryan commanded.

"I'm good," I said flippantly. Regardless of my feelings for the watch, I didn't like being told what to do, and I certainly didn't take well to Ryan's implicitly threatening behavior. Sweat coated my palms.

"Do it." He didn't hide his anger.

I flinched and shied away a step. Discomfort gave way to fear.

"She doesn't have to," Denisha said. "It's not a big d—"

"Shut up. Yes, she does. We do this together."

I was done with this and turned to walk away, but a hand clutched my arm hard enough that I knew there would be an imprint when the person let go. If the fingernails weren't breaking the skin, then it was held taut by a few cells.

When I whirled around, I found Jac, her jaw clenched. I yanked my arm free.

Angry, scared tears sprang to my eyes involuntarily. The combination of stark moonlight and the weak glow of the torch turned the other seven into a horde of ghouls.

"Don't be a titty baby, Alexis," Jac mocked.

We weren't beyond *Lord of the Flies* after all, but I had no intention of becoming Piggy. Rather than antagonizing the little drunk mob further, I wrenched the watch off my wrist and chucked it at Ryan's chest. So maybe I wasn't totally done antagonizing them.

I spun and stalked back toward camp. No one stopped me this time.

By the time I crawled into the lean-to and laid across the bamboo base, they'd already cranked their party back up. I thought I'd curl up and go to sleep, but sleep was far away. Instead, unexpectedly, tears returned and rolled down my cheeks.

At any other time in my life, I would've called my mom right then to tell her I'd been at a party and things had gotten out of hand. It was scary. No one stood up for me like I thought they would. But worse than any of that was that all those people were going to crawl into bed with me before too long.

I really wanted to be asleep when that happened.

CHAPTER 17
MAKING AMENDS

I MANAGED to crawl out of the shelter without disturbing anyone. The first person awake was supposed to stoke the fire, refill the water supply from the stream if necessary, and put some water on to boil. I considered shirking the responsibility. A figurative middle finger to the group so they'd know I hadn't forgiven them. Instead, I decided it would make them feel more guilty if I carried on with our morning routine like normal. My mother was fluent in passive-aggression, so I'd learned from a true expert in the field.

It was kind of nice to have the space to myself for a while. There was so little solitude at camp. I carried the air fryer basin and the basket that goes inside it over to the stream to rinse them. The water was refreshingly cool. I considered putting my feet in, but I didn't want sand clumping up on them on my walk back, so I refrained.

Once they were both reasonably clean, I realized that the return trip was going to be a little trickier than the outbound trip. Carrying the basket while transporting the basin full of water wouldn't be the easiest thing. I filled the basin first, then squatted down to snatch the basket's handle with my pinky finger.

Denisha walked up. I ignored her and continued my efforts. She reached down to pick up the basket.

"I've got it," I said.

"Don't be ridiculous. Let me help."

"Oh, like you helped last night?"

She hung her head, either in real shame or at least putting it on. "I'm sorry. I know it's not an excuse, but I was drunk and kinda scared of what was happening. It was just all of a sudden."

My cheeks got hot. I knew they were flushed. Tears welled and spilled over for a third time. "You were scared?! *You* were? I was effing terrified, D."

She whispered. "I know. I'm sorry."

"You know what? Whatever. I shouldn't have expected anything from any of y'all anyway. Every single one of you bailed after the plane crash, and you did it last night, too. It's just how things are."

I intended to storm off, having said my piece. Instead, realizing the direction I was going was toward camp and all the people I wasn't currently interested in seeing, I just awkwardly shuffled my feet a few times, making false starts. Beside me, Denisha said, "Can I ask you a question?"

I paused. That was as much permission as I was willing to give at the moment.

"This is probably terrible timing, but if anyone can appreciate that, it's you."

Now I was curious. I swiveled, my heel grinding into the sand. I would have crossed my arms to amplify my mood if I weren't carrying all this water.

Denisha smirked out of one side of her mouth. "Did you just say *effing*?"

I flushed again, with embarrassment this time. Though between the chronic sunburn and already having a red face because I was angry, it may not have been discernible. But Denisha had shattered that anger, at least as it applied to her.

I curled my toes, digging them into the sand. "I don't swear."

"Like, not at all?"

I shook my head. "Not really. Maybe occasionally if it's funny, but other than that, no."

"Is it a religious thing?"

"No. More like a manners thing."

"Huh." She couldn't have been more dumbfounded if I'd told her I had met an extraterrestrial life form. "So … are your parents going to ground you when I tell them you insinuated the f-word?"

I smiled and hugged the basin to my hip so I could free a hand to flip her off.

"Whoa!" Denisha raised her hands to her head and pulled them away quickly, like I'd blown her mind. "Who is this rebel?"

I laughed and said, "I'm going to storm off now."

"Right. Sorry. I interrupted that. Please, carry on."

I hadn't been gone long, but apparently, it was long enough for the others to regain a semblance of consciousness. They moved around like mindless zombies and did their best to avoid eye contact with me.

Breakfast around the campfire was awkward. As had been every waking moment prior to it, but at least in those moments, we weren't all gathered in one place. While I was still very much on edge, I had the satisfaction of watching a bunch of adults act like the sun was going to split their heads in two. Vampires are less fearful of its effects than these folks were. Hangovers must treat you a lot worse in mid-life (or later) than in your twenties. *Sucks to be you.*

Finally, Ryan kicked the elephant in the room. "I want to apologize about last night. Things … got out of hand."

I refrained from saying, *First of all, saying you want to apologize isn't the same as actually apologizing, and second, that's among the worst apologies I've ever heard.*

There was a murmur of assent from the others.

But he didn't stop there. He should have, but he didn't. "I just thought it would be this fun thing, where we all left our watches there and let the tide carry them off. Symbolic, you know. But you messed it up because you didn't want to participate and you were being a — I mean, I'm not blaming you. I'm just explaining what happened."

"It sure sounds a lot like you blaming me."

Tom stood up, waving his hands like he was directing traffic. "Look. Bickering isn't going to do anyone any good, so let's go down to the beach and you can get your watch. And we can put this whole thing behind us. Sound good?"

"Fine." I stood, but no one else did. "You don't have to go with me. I can get my own watch."

Tom shrugged off the suggestion. "I wanted to go down to the water anyway."

Once the group was behind us, I said, "This doesn't let you off the hook for not standing up for me last night."

Tom opened his mouth, presumably preparing to make some excuse. Then he shut it and opened it again, looking like a beached fish. "I know. I'm sorry. That was pretty gutless of me."

"I concur."

We cleared the tall grasses that separated the campsite from the beach. All we saw in front of us was white sand, littered with a few broken shells.

"Were we further down that way?" he asked, pointing to the south.

"No, we were straight out." I remembered traversing the same worn path we'd just crossed. It was kind of impressive how quickly we'd begun making lasting changes to our environment.

We walked over the powdery sand, beyond the high tide line where the sand became damp and compacted, and stopped when the waves began lapping at our feet.

Tom asked, "Do you remember how far out we were?"

I shook my head.

"Looks like the tide got 'em."

"It's taken everything else from us. Might as well have our watches, too."

I kicked the next wave just to make sure it understood my sentiments.

"Not everything," Tom said. "We still have each other."

"That's a whole lot less comforting than you intend it to be."

CHAPTER 18
HUDDLED IN THE DARKNESS

A SCREAM SHATTERED MY SLEEP. My breathing and heart-rate ramped up as the screaming continued. Everyone under the shelter was awake and sitting up now. Huddled under the purple and orange pre-dawn sky, it was impossible to tell who was missing.

When the screaming stopped, an eerie silence fell in its wake.

We piled onto the open ground outside the shelter, each of us looking at the others, counting. Six. The two missing: Ryan and Denisha.

Rhonda led the charge toward the latrine, where the scream had come from. They were her brood.

Toward the end of the trail, we found Denisha in a heap, her legs folded under her, and her face in her hands. On the far side of her was a puddle of blood. The kind of puddle you see in movies when somebody's throat has been cut. But no body was lying near the puddle. No body was within sight. In the gray light, the blood looked black as pitch.

Rhonda wrapped her arms around Denisha, cradling her. "Where's Ryan?" she asked softly. She repeated the question several times before Denisha gave any kind of response.

Even then, she only pointed. Everyone's attention shifted in the direction she indicated. Something was laying in the blood, at the puddle's edge where it had mixed with dirt to form a coagulating gruesome mud. I leaned forward but couldn't make out the object.

Tom scanned the ground around himself and picked up a stick. He stepped forward and squatted, using the stick to retrieve the object. After several tries, he got hold of it and stood up. When he turned around, blood spattered to the ground as it dripped from Ryan's watch.

A drop fell on Denisha's hand. She flung it away like it was a yellow jacket and screamed again. Rhonda hugged her tighter, shushing her and stroking her hair.

Once Denisha quieted again, four pairs of eyes traveled from the two women and settled on me.

CHAPTER 19
RISING PANIC

I DIDN'T UNDERSTAND or appreciate the stares. "What?"

Norman said, "You were fighting with him about the watch thing."

My jaw fell slack. I clenched it before responding. "What are you trying to say, Norm?"

"I'm just saying. Y'all had a fight, and now he's dead."

Rhonda let go of Denisha, spun herself upright, and shoved a finger into Norman's face. "He's not dead. We don't know that." Some of her spittle landed on his mustache.

"She's right," Daryl said. He looked toward the incrementally brightening sky in the east. "It's getting light enough now. We should go looking for him. Maybe after that, we can reconvene and talk about the finer points of how Alex got the jump on Ryan, bled him out, and carted off his body without leaving any drag marks or covering herself in gore."

I looked down at my clothes, as did most everyone else. Not clean as a whistle, because they'd been through the wear-cycle a couple of times without a proper washing, but not covered in blood either.

Tom shook his head. "With that much blood loss, he didn't

get far. Not on his own, anyway. We need to stick to groups of two or three … just in case … you know."

No one asked the obvious follow-up question. *Just in case what?* I certainly wasn't going to be the one to ask. Everyone paired off quickly. Jac and Daryl, naturally. Tom and Norman. Rhonda and Denisha. My friend of eleven days averted her gaze from me.

Before splitting the group split up, Tom said, "Everybody meet back here in ten minutes."

Jac coughed loudly, trying to cover up a bark of laughter, despite the circumstances. With a constrained voice, she said, "Exactly how are we supposed to tell how long ten minutes is?"

"Come on," one of the men said.

I looked up to find Daryl beckoning me. Beyond him, Norman let loose a string of expletives after stepping in the latrine.

When I sidled up to Jac and Daryl, he said, "Let's go inland. They all went to the water or back toward camp."

I was still seething at the absurd accusation as I fell in behind them. I almost ran into Jac, who'd stopped abruptly. "Daryl."

He turned around.

"What if it wasn't a person who got Ryan?"

I looked at her quizzically. "You think he killed himself?"

"No. What if it was an animal? Like a jaguar or something."

Daryl shook his head. "No big cats in the Caribbean islands. No big mammals at all, really."

"And just how do you know that?" Jac said.

"National Geographic. Or Discovery. Whichever one is on Disney Plus."

I asked. "How sure are you about that?"

He shrugged as he walked. "I only know what I watched.

But let's say it was some kind of animal. We would have heard it. There would have been a commotion."

"What about if it … you know." I mimicked something clamping down on a throat and tearing it out.

Daryl wasn't buying it. "Nah. There would have been a mess."

Jac scoffed. "You don't think that was a mess?"

"Different kind of mess. That was done by a person."

My blood curdled when he said it. I didn't want to entertain that notion. We were limited on options when it came to suspects.

"What person?" Jac said.

"Don't know, but it wasn't Alex. I can tell you that. The only two people big enough to carry Ryan are me and Tom, and it wasn't me."

Jac asked playfully, "Why should we believe that?"

"Because I disdain all of you equally."

"First of all, you can't verbify disdain. Second, even me?" She batted her eyelashes.

"Especially you." He smiled wryly.

I couldn't believe they were flirting when we were minutes removed from the most horrifying thing I'd ever seen. "You think it was Tom, then?"

"Not really. I don't think Tom has that in him. Besides, why would he? Ryan was like his little padawan."

Panic rose in my throat. "Who then?"

"Hell if I know. Are we sure we're alone?"

I groaned.

Jac chastised him. "That's not helpful."

"I'm not trying to be helpful. I'm trying to figure out why all that's left of Ryan is a giant puddle of blood and a watch that we all thought had been swept away by the ocean. I don't have just a whole lot of answers that make sense."

We heard voices before we saw who they belonged to. All

three of us paused, waiting and tense. My throat ached with fear.

I looked around and realized I hadn't been paying any attention to where we were. My fight-or-flight response was telling me to run like hell, but I didn't know which way to go.

When Rhonda and Denisha emerged around a copse of trees, I collapsed to my knees.

My breathing came in staccato bursts that exacerbated my panic rather than alleviating it. The cognitive part of me knew I was having an anxiety attack, but the rest of me was helpless to stop it. My hands and face were clammy with sweat.

Denisha hurried over to me and wrapped her arms around me. "Deep, slow breaths," she whispered.

I nodded my head but couldn't change my ragged breathing. My vision was getting gray.

"Just do what I'm doing."

She inhaled slowly, intentionally, her chest expanding outward as she did so. I forced myself to do as she was doing. I concentrated on her lips. It was like the piano lessons I took in elementary school, trying to make my hands do what my teacher's were doing: never quite succeeding but improving month by month. Here, though, it only took minutes for my breathing to be restored to its normal cadence and to where I didn't think about it anymore. It just happened like the commonplace miracle it was.

Denisha squeezed the backs of my arms gently. "You okay?"

"Not really, no. But I don't think I'm going to pass out any more."

"That's not nothing. Can you stand up?"

When I nodded, she stood and held her hands down to me, pulling me to my feet. Before I let go of them, I said, "I didn't do anything to Ryan."

"I know."

"Earlier you looked uncertain."

She shook her head. "I don't know what happened to him, but I believe that it wasn't you."

We joined the conversation the other three were holding, as Rhonda recounted what they'd seen. "Not much," she said. "It's not like we're trackers or anything, and we didn't want to stray too far in case … I don't know."

Jac said, "The two who've actually explored this island are Tom and Ryan. Probably about time we all get to know it a little better. That way, we're all on equal footing and know what we're dealing with."

Tom hallooed as he approached from behind us. "Y'all see anything?"

We responded with collective murmurs and head shakes.

Daryl asked, "Where's Norm?"

Tom looked over his shoulder in the direction he'd come from. "Don't know. Lost him a few minutes ago. One minute he's behind me. Next thing I know, he's not there and didn't respond to my calls."

CHAPTER 20
PENT-UP TENSION

DARYL PUSHED PAST TOM, going the direction Tom had just come from.

Jac called, "Where are you going?"

"To find Norm. Where do you think?"

"By yourself?"

"If I have to." He turned to walk away and ran smack into Norm.

Daryl's face flushed red. "Where the hell have you been?"

In his confusion, Norm didn't respond right away.

Daryl shoved him in the chest. "Where were you?"

"Easy, man. What's going on?"

"Answer the question," Jac said.

Norman sighed and looked down at his feet. As quiet as a field mouse, he said, "I was taking a poo."

Denisha snickered. I laughed nervously. A large volume of pent-up tension vanished both from me and, judging by the expressions on everyone's faces, the group of survivors at large.

Tom suggested, "Let's go back to camp and regroup. We can get a couple of bites, then maybe widen the search. I assume no one found anything?"

After everyone's obligatory negative responses, Jac said, "Nothing like some goat jerky and papaya to jump start your system."

We no longer distinguished between breakfast food and other mealtime food. We took whatever sustenance we could get in whatever form it took. It's not even that we were short on food. We weren't, but I had plenty of uncertainty about how long the island could sustain us. We hadn't used any more of the masa. We were holding it back like regular folks might stash a nice bottle of wine. Except that we didn't have any proper storage, so we probably needed to eat it relatively soon before it went bad.

The walk back to camp was quiet, with no levity to be had, and no escaping the task that remained in front of us or its greater implications. Something or, more likely, someone had soundlessly murdered Ryan and made him disappear, as best we could tell. There was no reason to think there was anyone else on this island other than the eight of us, regardless of what Daryl had said.

Granted, we'd seen neither hide nor hair of Walt since he'd vanished from the plane after the crash, but there was little doubt that he was crab food by now. Even being able to think that with no emotional response was a stark indicator of the callouses that had formed on my psyche. Faced with this much devastation, it was unavoidable. Maybe not totally unavoidable, but the alternative was to be crushed by it.

We gathered around the fire pit. In its present state, it had reduced itself to coals, but Rhonda was trying to revive it with fresh wood and acting as a human bellows. She put on a strong facade, but an occasional moan betrayed her as she exhaled. I don't know how well she knew Ryan or whether she even liked him, but they were colleagues, and that counted for something.

Before long, flames leapt off the now-orange coals, reaching for kindling. We didn't need the heat as much as we needed water. There were some chores that we couldn't abandon, no matter the circumstances. We'd started using coconuts we'd bored holes into as a kind of canteen. It was Norm's idea. Their only limitation was that they had to be rotated out every few days, or they took on a fermenty, zingy taste, like pico de gallo that's been in the fridge too long.

While Tom doled strips of goat to everybody, I took the machete and quartered two papayas. I was impressed with my improvement using the knife. My cuts were clean and mostly even.

I handed the slices out one at a time. It was only when I was left with two slices, one of which belonged to me, that I was smitten anew with our loss. I didn't know what to do with it. I just stood beside the fire like a child who'd lost a parent, holding my hand out. It felt crass to offer it to anyone, and worse still, to waste it.

"Here," Rhonda said.

I couldn't remember whether she'd said anything else the entire morning.

She picked up the machete and deftly cut the slice into seven fairly even pieces. I wished I had the kind of special acuity that would let me cut something into an odd number of chunks like that.

Once I'd downed my fruit, I took the machete down to the creek to rinse it. The water rambled from its source in the heart of the island past me and on to the sea. A dark shape appeared over my shoulder. I pushed to the left and ended up crab-walking away from it.

"Easy," Tom said.

I let myself fall on my back and put my hands over my heart. "You ought not sneak up on a girl like that ... especially when she's carrying a machete."

"That one?" He pointed to where it lay in the grass growing beside the stream.

I pushed myself to a sitting position and propped my arms behind me. "Uh-huh. Think of the damage I could've done."

"Guess I'm in luck to still be alive," he said with a smirk.

"You're darn right."

He held up the knife he'd used to parse the goat. Its blade gleamed in the morning sun. "I needed to clean mine, too."

I smacked my forehead with the palm of my hand.

"Yes?" Tom said with a curious raised eyebrow.

"Are all the knives accounted for?" I should have thought of it sooner, when I retrieved the machete.

"Yeah. All except the one Ryan carries."

"Huh. Okay. What's the plan?" I asked.

"We need to cover as much of the island as we can. It's not that big. A couple miles long from end to end and half as wide. I was thinking you, me, and Denisha could go one way. The others can go the other way, and we can walk the perimeter and meet on the far side. That'll probably take a couple hours or so."

"And then?"

"Then we'll know if there's been any coming or going from the island. If not, then Ryan's got to be here."

"If we see tracks?"

Tom held his hands up. He didn't know, and I shouldn't really expect him to. I don't think they covered this scenario in his MBA courses or survival shows.

I nodded. "Alright. Let's take it to the others and see if they have any suggestions."

As Tom turned to head back, I reached out and touched his arm. "One more thing."

He paused.

I was almost too embarrassed to ask and nearly told him to forget it. Instead, I swallowed my pride. "So I know you do MMA—"

"Brazilian jiujitsu," he corrected.

"Is there a difference?"

He looked like he was above to delve into a much longer answer before settling for a simple, "Sort of."

"Do you think you could show me some ... things? I just want to be able to defend myself a little if something ... like, you know ... happened." *This is so embarrassing I want to die.*

"Yeah, of course," he said enthusiastically. "How about we start tomorrow after chores?"

"Start?" Maybe I'd bit off more than I wanted.

"Yeah, start. It's not a one time thing. It's a practice."

He nodded at me as if he were my dad and I'd made him proud. All that was missing was him rubbing the top of my head and calling me Scout. As we walked back, I said, "Obviously, I have my knife skills to fall back on. I just need something to supplement it."

"Obviously."

CHAPTER 21
ONE MORE THING

I POINTED to what appeared to be an inlet in the rocky promontory that stood before us. "Should we go up there?"

"To what end?" Tom shrugged. "That's all handholds and toeholds. It'd be tough for any of us, and we're not even carrying a hundred-and-eighty-pound body trying to scale it in the dark."

Denisha said, "Besides, there's no blood on the rocks. Don't you think there would be?"

"Y'all." I bugged my eyes at them in frustration. "Every movie ever says if we don't go look up there, that's exactly where he's going to be."

"This isn't a movie. Actual laws of physics are in play here."

Denisha changed her tune. "She has a point. No stone unturned and all that bulls—sorry," she said with a grimace.

"It's a personal choice, not something I'm trying to impose on anyone else."

"Let's go with *hogwash*. That's what my Papaw would have said."

"What's this now?" Tom asked, clearly confused.

Denisha pointed at me. "She doesn't swear."

Tom looked at me like he'd never seen me before. "Huh. Never noticed. But whatever, if one of y'all wants to climb that, have at it." He stepped to the side and made a chivalrous, sweeping gesture.

Denisha and I exchanged glances. Neither of us was keen on it. I'd kind of been counting on Tom to climb it for us.

"Rock, paper, scissors?" I held my fist against the palm of my other hand.

Denisha grabbed her left arm and held it close to her side, grinning out of one side of her mouth. "My poor wing. I'd be in terrible shape if I re-injured it."

"Oh. My. Gosh. You're disgusting," I laughed. "Fine."

I strode up to the rock face and reached a hand up, imitating what I remembered seeing college friends do when they were bouldering. Fortunately, the pitch wasn't overly steep and there were plenty of holds. Pulling myself up the fifteen feet or so onto the shelf on the rock face brought with it a great sense of accomplishment and a degree of curiosity about why I had quit doing this with my friends. I stood up and did my best impression of Rocky Balboa at the top of the steps.

I turned back to the ledge and looked along it. "Ooh. There's a cave." I side-stepped over to the cave and looked in where it burrowed into the rock.

Tom called up. "I don't know if you should go in there."

I turned my head back toward them. "It's okay. I think it comes out on the other side." I couldn't see an opening, but light glittered off the outside wall of a bend ahead of me.

"Here," Tom yelled. A second later, there was a clattering sound behind me. "Be careful."

I picked up Tom's Spyderco pocket knife that looked more akin to a talon or grizzly claw than a regular knife. Surely, he knew I'd been kidding earlier about my knife skills. I was probably more likely to injure myself than someone else. Regardless, I opened the knife, which made a satisfying click as it locked into place.

I pressed forward, knife in one hand and the other trailing along the damp cave wall. Water dripped slowly from the ceiling, forming occasional small puddles. I passed the remnants of several birds' nests, but noted no other signs of life. I rounded the bend in the opening and saw that I'd been correct. The cave opened up on the far end. From where I stood, the vista showed sapphire ocean all the way to the horizon.

I turned and headed out the way I'd come. When it was time to descend, I remembered why rock-climbing wasn't for me. Dangling my legs off the edge and scooting backward, then blindly feeling around for a foothold wasn't my idea of a good time. Just before my eyes dropped below the edge of the shelf, I saw what appeared to be something of a trail traveling down the ledge and beyond my sight line on to the face of the promontory. I'd been too fixated on my task to see it earlier. It was just luck that I'd see a potentially easier route now that I was committed to this descent.

With some help — "A little more to the left ... no, back to the right ... now up a smidge ... there!" — I reached the ground without incident and without inadvertently reenacting our plane crash.

As I slid back over the ledge, I told them what I'd found. I tossed Tom's knife to him, which he promptly opened to inspect for new scrapes. It was his most prized possession, of which there weren't all that many anymore.

Denisha said, "Well, that was a dead end."

"Think about it more positively," Tom said. "We're eliminating possibilities."

I looked down at the scrapes covering my palms. "We've definitely eliminated the possibility of me doing that again."

"Did I tell you this is where Norm and I found the goat poop?"

"You got him to walk this far?"

Tom wagged his finger at me. "You don't give him enough credit. He's more spry than you think. More spry — is that right? Spryer?"

I shrugged.

Denisha said, "Spry is only one syllable, so I think it's spryer. But that doesn't sound right. Like funner. Maybe it's an exception."

"Either way. Norm has more life in him than you think. There's a slope around the other side where you can walk up to the top of this … what do we call it?"

Denisha craned her neck to look up. "It's not big enough to be mountain. Is it just a hill?"

"Maybe it's a volcano," I said. "And it's been lying dormant all these years, waiting for an opportunity to bury some bystanders in ash and lava."

A concerned expression passed over Denisha's face. She reached down and placed a palm against its base. "It's not hot," she said, as if that settled the issue.

I didn't know enough about volcanoes to dispute it, though I was pretty sure the litmus test for whether something was a volcano wasn't dependent on it being hot to the touch.

Something occurred to me. I whirled to face Tom. "Did I climb this thing for no reason? Could we have gone up the same way you did and gotten to this cave?"

"Nah, I don't think so. Y'all want to go up? You can see the entire island from there. Oh, and one more thing that I may have forgotten to mention — you can see the island next door to us, too."

Denisha said, "I'm sorry. What?"

CHAPTER 22
SLAVERY BY ANOTHER NAME

I CROSSED my arms and shifted my weight to one hip. Universal body language for: *You messed up and I want you to know it without having to use words.* Denisha's posture was slightly different but sending the same signal.

Despite being someone whose emotional intelligence isn't found in his strengths column, Tom picked up the cues and held out his hands in a defensive posture. "It's not a big island. Much smaller than this one. Basically just a sandbar with a few trees."

"Its size is hardly the point," I said. "How could you keep this from everyone?"

"Look, there are no secrets out here. We're around each other all the time, and everybody knows each other's business. So I had this one little harmless secret. It's not a big deal."

Denisha picked up the questioning. "Have you been over there?"

"No," Tom answered definitively. "There's a couple hundred yards of water between us. I don't know what the current is like and haven't wanted to spend the energy. Besides, there's no reason to go over there. Aside from a few coconut trees and palms, it's pretty desolate."

I looked at Denisha. "I guess we'll have to see for ourselves."

She nodded.

"Y'all are going to swim to the island?"

I gave Tom a look of consternation and pointed up. "No, we're going to climb this thing so we can see it since, I guess, we can't trust you to tell us everything anymore."

"That seems a little heavy-handed," Tom grumbled.

Denisha stepped out from in front of him. "Lead the way, Tom."

Tom sighed and began walking, circumnavigating the base of our miniature Mount Saint Helens. The sun beat down on us from high overhead as we walked around and through brush that crowded the base of the hill. As I flailed my arms in front of me for the hundredth time, vainly trying to shoo away gnats and sweat bees, I wondered how they'd subsisted so long on such a remote island. It was like they'd been placed here thousands of years ago with the promise that their ancestors would one day have us to feast on if they could just survive.

When Tom turned left and began his ascent, I followed him, and Denisha followed me. It became clear that we were on a game trail, probably a fork of the one I'd spotted earlier. Why the goats would climb this feature, I didn't know. Maybe they liked some of the sparse vegetation that grew out of the rocky crevices, and this was the only place on the island they could find it.

As we climbed the side of the hill that faced the interior of the island and rose above the canopies of the trees, I saw our island in a new way. The creek where we got our water lay about half a mile away. Camp was on the other side of it, though all we could see of it was the fire pit. We'd built the rest of it under the trees to protect from wind and exposure. Several hundred yards beyond that, resting just offshore, was an unmoving shadow: the corpse of the plane that had brought us here. Until today, I hadn't wandered beyond the boundaries of that little triangle in the last eleven days.

Denisha tapped me on the shoulder and pointed. I followed her finger, bringing my gaze back toward camp. A half-dozen small shadows patrolled the shallows. Sharks.

One of my favorite television events every year was Shark Week. Vicious predators that were all teeth, muscle, and cartilage. For that reason, I didn't want confirmation that I was occupying the same waters as them. I'd always heard rumors in Gulf Shores and Orange Beach, where my parents took us on family vacations, that helicopter pilots would say that some days as many sharks were swimming in those crystalline waters as people. I'd only seen a few in my time there, but that was enough to keep me wondering how closely I resembled a sea turtle while boogie-boarding. It sapped about a third of the fun out of it, but not enough to stop doing it. There was nothing like catching a wave just right and riding it all the way in to shore.

Denisha pulled me out of my memory. "What are you smiling about?"

"Didn't realize I was. Just thinking about vacation when I was a kid. What kind of vacations did y'all do?"

She shook her head. "That wasn't really a thing for us. My parents worked three jobs between them. Unless he was deathly ill, my dad worked every day of his life until the last of us was out of college, which wasn't optional. My people come from slaves and sharecroppers — which was slavery by another name. When my dad worked his way to plant management in both of his jobs, you could see the pride his parents had in that."

"They must think what you do is cool."

"Eh. They don't really understand it. I almost never saw anything except southern Mississippi as a kid. I even went to Southern Miss. Biggest city I'd ever seen was Gulfport, which might as well have been Manhattan compared to what I was used to. When an airline came to the career fair and promised that I could see the world, I leapt at it and never looked back."

I plastered on my cheesiest grin and mimicked the announcer from *Wheel of Fortune* as best I could. "Look at you now, on an exclusive island vacation in the exquisite Caribbean Sea."

She gave me a wan smile in return.

"If you two are done sharing personal histories like a couple on a first date, there's something you need to see."

I sighed. "You're ruining a beautiful moment, Tom."

"Well, as much as it does my heart good to see you two bonding, we have more pressing things at hand." Tom stood above us at the island's summit, using his hand as a visor to keep out the blinding sun and gesturing to the south. The hill blocked my view in that direction.

I trudged to the summit, uncertain what to expect, but definitely not expecting what I was confronted with. Denisha and I pulled up on either side of Tom, catching our first view of the neighboring island we'd only learned of a few minutes earlier. If I would have gone closer to the mouth of the cave instead of turning around, I would have seen it then, but the island was small enough that the narrower angle of view delayed the revelation until now.

He was right. It was significantly smaller than ours and only sparsely populated with trees. Several hundred feet of blue water separated it from us.

It only took a moment to recognize what had drawn and kept Tom's attention. A dark, oblong object lay at the edge of the receding tide. Water still tugged at one end of it as the waves came in.

An icy ball of fear formed in my belly, something I wish I was becoming less acclimated to. "What is it?"

Tom breathed in deeply and exhaled slowly. "I'd have to guess."

"Guess," Denisha said, not even trying to hide the panic behind her voice.

"I'd really rather not."

The three of us let the moment hang there a long time. Sweat rolled down my face and back. I wiped my palms on my pants. Gulls squawked at something that offended them.

I took a half-step forward and turned to face Tom and Denisha. "We have to go see."

Tom nodded reluctantly. "I know."

CHAPTER 23
MAKE BETTER DECISIONS

"WAIT," Denisha said, holding up a hand. "Before you two go swimming across the English Channel, I have a question." She paused until Tom looked her in the eyes. "Should we talk about your innocent secret now or after you get back?"

Tom grunted.

I said, "Let's harangue him about it afterward."

"Or hang him," she offered.

I think she was mostly kidding. "Hang. Harangue. I'm open to either. Let's see how it goes. Sure you don't want to go?"

Denisha took another step away from the water. "Someone's got to be able to tell the others what happened to y'all, and I've never seen a shark attack before. Should be interesting."

Tom huffed. Presumably, he was tired of the back-and-forth, which was mostly coming at his expense. *Make better decisions if you can't take the heat.* He strode down toward the water and began shuffling off his clothes, folding them neatly and laying them on top of his shoes. He stopped disrobing when he got to his boxer-briefs.

I still hadn't stepped away from Denisha. I didn't want to

do this, and not just because I'd have to undress again. I didn't want to swim a long way to go see what we presumed to be a corpse. I was tired and hungry and wanted all of this to stop.

Sensing my hesitation, Denisha said, "You know what my grandmother used to tell me when I needed some encouragement? 'Buck up, buttercup.'"

"Which means?"

"Quit being a sissy. That's the polite version."

I glared at her.

She was unfazed and returned my stare.

"Fine." I slid out of my shoes and pants and handed them to her. After I unbuttoned my shirt and shimmied out of it, I handed it over as well and met Tom at the water. He watched me walk toward him a little longer than I'd have liked, but he didn't say anything inappropriate, so that would have to do.

While we waded into deeper waters, Tom said, "It's kind of a long swim, so don't take off too fast. If there's a current out there, don't fight against it. Just take your time swimming out of it."

I restrained myself from telling him that I didn't need a lesson on pacing and rip tides, but that would be bad for morale. I let it go this time, knowing that he wasn't really saying it because he thought I needed to hear it, as much as he just needed to say it. My mom was the same way. It was like her brain had a certain allotment of words it needed to verbalize every day, probably as many words as the rest of the house combined. None of the rest of us — my dad, brothers, and me — had ever been confused for a Chatty Cathy. But with my mom, I'd walk into the living room where she was folding laundry and she'd be in the middle of a conversation with herself like it was the most normal thing in the world.

By the time we were halfway across the channel between the two islands, the ache in my shoulders intruded on my memory. My breathing grew labored and uneven. Fortunately, no significant current pushed us off course.

I focused my attention on a single tree, keeping myself pointed toward it so I didn't waste energy with lateral movement. I got my breathing under control too — breathe in four strokes, breathe out four strokes.

The tree got progressively closer until one of my hands dug into the sand on its downward stroke. I planted my feet and stood, looking over my shoulder to check on Tom. He'd fallen behind me a few paces and needed a minute longer until he was only knee deep as well.

My heart still banged against my ribs, not just from the exertion, but also from the constant fear that with every stroke, I would draw back a nub, courtesy of a razor-toothed shark. Based on the way Tom hunched over and grabbed his knees, I gathered he'd had much the same experience.

A couple of minutes later, he stood upright and asked, "You good?"

By then, I had my breathing under control and nodded. I turned to the old island and waved at Denisha to let her know we were alright. She returned the wave and sat down in the sand. It would be a boring wait for her, but hopefully not a long one.

Tom led the way up the embankment, cutting a path across the island rather than circumnavigating it along the waterline. The rise wasn't particularly steep, but any increase in elevation in sand is noticeable.

The sand atop the embankment was about a thousand degrees. With every step, it set the soles of my feet on fire, and I flung sun-bleached lava onto my calves and hamstrings.

We hadn't gone more than a dozen steps, when I couldn't take it anymore, did an about-face, and ran back the way we'd come. Behind me, Tom followed suit. "Oh, thank God."

I slid down to water level and splashed in. I'm fairly certain my feet sizzled. After we recovered ourselves for a minute, I suggested, "How about we go the long way around?"

Tom nodded in agreement. "The sand up there is darker. Reflects more heat."

Walking side by side, Tom and I stayed close enough to the water that the sand was packed, wet, and cool as we trekked toward something (and likely someone) neither of us wanted to talk about.

Conversation fell away as we rounded the horn of the island and came within sight of the dark object we had come to inspect. It was still some distance away. The minutes it took us to get to it felt like hours. Dread sat heavy as a weighted blanket, with all the claustrophobia and none of the comfort.

When we were no more than twenty feet away, I stopped and grabbed Tom's wrist so that he'd stop as well. The dark thing lay at the crest of the high tide line, where the sea had deposited it. The sand above it was fluffy and inviting until you saw the heat shimmers that arose from it. While below it, the sand was hard-packed by millennia of subjugation.

Several minutes passed in which nothing happened. Tom made to move forward. I squeezed the wrist that I was still seizing.

I whispered coarsely, "Hold on, Tom. It's moving."

He paused mid-step, leaning forward and squinting. "I don't think it is. I think something is moving *on* it."

Tom was right. The thing itself wasn't moving. It was in exactly the same position it had been in since we first spied it from atop our island. But its surface was teeming and wriggling.

Almost involuntarily, I crept forward, Tom alongside me, as slow and steady as the progression of the sun.

Ten feet away. It was definitely the shape of a body, but one with no definition.

All at once, the wriggling stopped.

Tom brought a hand to his face to scratch his nose.

A black cloud of flies took flight off the body. For a

second, the cloud retained the shape of a man before dispersing.

The pungent odor was immediate and overwhelming, striking with all the suddenness of a thunderclap.

I wretched into the water at my feet. The remains of a meager breakfast.

Tom put a hand on my back. "Don't look," he said as he turned away.

I couldn't not look.

Tens of thousands of maggots fed on the bloated, rotting remains of Walt.

I turned and was sick again. Mostly stomach acid this time.

CHAPTER 24
NO WAY TO DIG A HOLE

JAC BROKE the stunned silence by asking, "So, what did you do with him?"

Tom and I looked at each other and back at the group. With a grimace, I said, "Nothing."

Righteous indignation flowed out of her like a lava. "You what?!"

It wasn't a question that required a response. It wasn't really a question at all. We waited for her to come around with a follow-up. The sequence of Jac's outbursts wasn't new to anyone.

"Why did you leave Walt to fester in the sun and get eaten by animals?"

I looked at Tom, deferring to him to fall on the sword and answer the question.

He sighed, resigned to his fate. "There was nothing we could do. First, there was no way to dig a hole deep enough."

"Are you kidding me?! Have you never buried someone in the sand before?"

The rest of the group contented themselves to watch the volleys and not get involved. Preservation instincts run strong.

Tom took an extra beat before answering. "Second, he would have …" He started gesturing weirdly with his hands. "… come apart. He would have come apart. There was no way to move him."

Jac crossed her arms, dissatisfied with the answer but unwilling to press the issue. I had to imagine that Tom was one more jibe away from telling her no one was stopping her from swimming over there and burying him herself. If I were a little more assertive and wanted to make an enemy, I'd have said it.

Denisha asked the others. "Y'all find anything?"

"Nothing having to do with Ryan," Daryl said. "No sign of any kind, but we did come across the goats. If you follow our stream inland, there's a spring, and that's where they were. They were pretty skittish."

Tom nodded, "Not surprised. They were skittish, but curious, before Ryan and I caught and killed one of them. Now they have a reason to fear us."

"I know the feeling," Rhonda muttered.

Norm raised a finger in the air like it was a light bulb that had turned on. "Won't goats eat most anything?"

Denisha said, "They're not known to be picky. My grandparents have goats. Sell a lot of goat's milk to lactose intolerant folks. They've made a pretty good living that way, and all the Hispanic families come buy one for their daughters' quinceañeras."

"So … hear me out. What if whoever killed Ryan, assuming that's what happened—"

"It's what happened," Rhonda interjected flatly. She didn't pull her gaze out of the fire when she said it.

She's taken a turn from insisting he's not dead.

Norm continued, "What if whoever did it … you know?"

Denisha shook her head emphatically. "No. Not a thing. If they'd have tried to feed him to the goats, he'd still be here. They don't eat meat. I'm not saying they won't touch it. But, like, if you take them table scraps, they'll eat around it. Strictly herbivores. Now, if we were talking pigs, that'd be a different conversation."

Jac's face turned a peculiar green hue. Daryl patted her on the leg. She batted at his hand and hurried away. Something about discussing the prospect of a friend being fed to wild animals as a means of disposing of the body had turned her stomach.

"Friend" may be using the term a little loosely, but English doesn't really have a term that adequately describes our relationships with each other. German probably does, and it's likely fourteen syllables long.

Three days later, not much had changed. The scrutiny Rhonda leveled at everyone had intensified rather than subsided. She'd taken to carrying with her a spear she'd fashioned from a long, straight stick whose end she'd whittled to a point. It would be almost humorous if it weren't hazardous. She was dour and jumpy, and I was afraid that if I accidentally happened upon her when going to or from the latrine, I'd wind up unintentionally impaled. The problem with being accidentally killed is that it doesn't make you any less dead.

I spent increasing amounts of time alone, detaching myself from people. This was a coping mechanism from moving so much as a kid. It was a lot easier to move away from a town if you didn't make anything more than acquaintances while you lived there.

That said, more alone time was a relative thing, meaning that I'd gone from basically none to some. The reptilian quadrant of my brain attempted to maintain a working knowledge of everyone's location at all times so that when I was alone, my back wasn't to any of them.

As I bobbed in the chest-deep water with the mid-morning

sun warming the backs of my shoulders, Tom waded into the water and made his way toward me. It was the equivalent of my big brother entering my room without knocking, though obviously I had no claim to this space. Maybe my European heritage had me staking mental claims on land. Before Tom got to me, I started wondering what my flag would look like. *Definitely some unconventional colors. Red, white, and blue are so trite. Hot pink, on the other hand…*

"You ready for some BJJ action?"

"Excuse me?" I was about fourteen shades of confused.

"Brazilian jiujitsu. You mentioned it the other day."

"Sorry. I thought … you know what … never mind. Yes."

He smirked.

The abbreviation wasn't unintentional. Such a boy thing to do.

"Now?" I asked.

"Yeah, sure." He looked down at his wrist, where there was no longer a tan line from a watch. "Unless you've got an appointment scheduled."

I smiled somewhat wanly. "No, my agenda's pretty clear."

"Good!" He was almost giddy with excitement. Not only was he going to get to talk about martial arts for the first time in ages, he was going to teach a captive audience how to do it. This probably made the whole misadventure worthwhile for him. "Alright, let's go start your training."

He started for shore immediately.

It took a lot of restraint for me not to roll my eyes at him. Maybe that level of self-discipline meant I was ready for some 'BJJ action' after all. Now, I was smirking at myself. Smiling at, or maybe because of, your own internal dialog is a weird thing to do.

Dripping water and doing my best Daniel LaRusso crane kick pose, I said, "I think I'm ready, sensei."

Tom's demeanor changed. "This is serious, Alex. We're

not going to be out here screwing around like a bunch of teenage boys playing grab-ass."

That was unexpected. "Okay. Sorry." I tried to be serious, but the corners of my lips kept trying to turn up. You know when you were a kid getting in trouble and a laugh just jumps out of your throat, and then you were in even more trouble? This wasn't dissimilar.

As gravely as I could muster, I asked, "Are we going to be starting with kicks or punches?"

"Neither. Most everyone out here is a good bit bigger than you. Do you think you could land a kick or punch that would harm them?"

"Maybe?"

He gave me a hard look that said I needed to do some further self-assessment.

I sighed. "Probably not."

Until now, I hadn't considered the practical reality that if I were to use any of what he was teaching me, it would be on one of these eight seven people I was sharing this space with. That was a little trippy. Tom had clearly put some thought into that already. I didn't know if that was reassuring or alarming. Did that make him a threat or the deterrent of a threat?

"Probably not," he agreed. "But what if you could get them on the ground first?"

I nodded, knowing from context what the right answer was. "I'd have better odds."

"Better odds and more options."

"Like dropping the people's elbow?" I mimicked The Rock as best I could. I knew I was treading on thin ice, but he needed to lighten up.

Tom ignored me.

"We're going to start by learning some foot sweeps, but before we get into that, we have to establish a solid base and posture."

"Tom, you may not know this about me, but … I'm all about that base."

He grunted, but the tiniest whisker of a smile betrayed him. "You're not going to make this easy, are you?"

"No, I'm probably not."

CHAPTER 25
IN THE RIGHT POSITION

WE DIDN'T MAKE much headway that first day. So the next morning, when we started back to my lessons, I came into it a little aggravated. I had wanted to learn how to *do something*, but we were spending two days talking about and practicing balance. I wasn't some toddler learning how to walk.

"Here's the deal," Tom said with a bit of gravel in his voice. "If you don't have a good base to start with and can't keep your balance, none of the rest of it works."

I stood up and crossed my arms.

Without another word, he slid directly in front of me and shoved me in the chest, just below where my collarbones meet my sternum. I stumbled back two steps. "What the hell, Tom?"

"Balance. Control." His voice was smooth and collected now. "You can't have it when you're upright like that. Now, get yourself in your athletic stance."

I exhaled slowly and unclenched my jaw. I spread my feet shoulder-width apart and bent my knees. Tom walked around behind me. I resisted the urge to turn my head and see what he was doing. Everything felt like some kind of test.

"Lower."

I bent my knees a little more.

Tom put his hands on my hips and pushed down. *Down* may not be quite right. He applied a downward pressure

I jerked away and swiveled around to face him. "Hey!"

He held hands out, palms toward me, in a disarming gesture. "I'm just trying to get you in the right position. You have to lower your center of gravity. Nothing weird. You have to trust me."

"Trust you? Tom. Someone got murdered," I hissed. "You're teaching me to fight. You're basically the only one capable of killing Ryan, who we've never found, by the way. You've explored the island more than anybody, so you'd know what to do with him."

Despite his effort, he failed to mask the hurt my distrust caused. After a long minute, he said, "I will concede that all those things are true. But let me ask you this — do you think I killed him?"

I'd known Tom for a while, and nothing in any of that time had suggested that he was a straight-up killer. But how many *60 Minutes* episodes featured interviews with neighbors and lifelong friends saying, *I never would have thought....* I tempered my answer. "I don't think you'd kill anyone in cold blood. I think if you did kill someone, it would weigh pretty heavily on you."

"I can live with that," Tom said. "So with that in mind, can you trust me while we're doing this?"

"Okay."

"I'm going to have to get you in the right position, and I have to use my hands to do that, okay?"

"Can you at least give me some warning before you put your hands on my hip and make me dip, you dip, we dip?"

Tom frowned. "Are pop song lyrics going to be a big part of this for you?"

"I'm really uncomfortable. You have to let me have this."

"Fine," Tom grumbled, "but this is very unconventional."

"Oh, is learning jiujitsu while being marooned on an island with a murderer the normal state of affairs?"

One corner of his mouth turned up. "I wouldn't describe it that way, no. Get in your stance."

I resumed my stance. Knees bent, weight on my toes, though the latter was a little tricky in the sand. Tom wandered around behind me again. I got lower so he wouldn't have to do it himself. My quads burned from consecutive days of strain.

He shoved me in the middle of my back with almost an open-handed punch. I rocked forward but kept my balance.

When he moved within my peripheral vision, I braced for a side-shove.

"You see how much better your balance is when you have a low center of gravity? It's very difficult for someone to get you off your feet that way."

"Don't worry," Denisha said.

I nearly jumped out of my skin. I'd been so focused that I hadn't seen her walk up on the other side.

She continued the line she was delivering. "Someday, the right boy will come along and sweep her off her feet."

"How long have you been there?" I asked.

"Long enough to know that Tom is lucky you didn't kick like a mule when he got too handsy, and to wonder how deep your hip-hop repository is."

"I guess that's probably enough for today," Tom said a little sourly. "Same time tomorrow?"

I nodded. He grabbed his coconut canteen and headed toward the campfire.

"You his protégé now?" Denisha ribbed me.

"I don't know. I'm just trying to not get killed too easily."

"Ha. That's dark, girl. But the reason I'm here is to see if you'll stand watch while I go to the latrine to … you know."

I walked toward Denisha and looped my arms through

hers. "Why yes, I will be your protector while you take a slam."

She shook her head. "Dark *and* crass. That's going to require a very specific kind of Prince Charming."

"You have no idea. I'm kind of a basket case."

"Please, no Green Day," she pleaded.

"It's like you don't even know me. I had a boyfriend in college who rode a motorcycle, a Suzuki Boulevard. He told me once that if he died in a bike wreck, he wanted 'Boulevard of Broken Dreams' to be played at his funeral."

"Oof. I hope you dumped him."

"I did. Not strictly because of that, but it didn't help his cause."

"Good. Now, if you'll excuse me."

When Denisha stepped behind a tree, I wandered a few paces away, focusing on breakers pounding the sand so I didn't hear any unpleasant sounds of Denisha doing her business. Unfortunately, the word *pounding* reminded me of the scene involving Jac and Daryl on the night of the watch party. That madness would be seared into my memory for the rest of time, but even more curious to me was that they'd acted so normal around each other in the days since. Not lovey-dovey and not awkward. Maybe that's how grown-ups conducted themselves. I hadn't been in a real relationship since my twenties, so it was hard to know.

Denisha startled me when she touched the back of my arm.

"Jumpy much?"

I shook my head to clear it. "Lost in thought."

"About?"

"Jac and Daryl."

She wrinkled her nose like she'd encountered a foul smell. "Eww. No." Her expression changed to one of curiosity. "Or were you thinking about them in a 'I'm lonely and could use some action' kind of way? Because I bet Tom would sort you out if you pressed the issue."

My face flushed fourteen shades of red. "No. I'm not —"

"Well, Norm probably can't get it up anymore without his little blue pills, and it can't be me." She pointed at her ring finger. "Married."

"I don't—I'm not—" I was rendered incapable of finishing a thought.

Denisha smiled, clearly enjoying herself and reveling in my discomfort.

I buried my face in my hands. "Oh, my gosh."

"Did I embarrass you?" she asked with sweet innocence.

"Just a little. I come from a house of prudes. We don't talk about sex."

"What about *the talk*?"

"Oh, my mom did a lot hemming and hawing, used several clunky analogies, and eventually gave up, patting me on the knee and saying, 'In due time,' before walking out of my room. Sex ed class filled in the most pertinent gaps."

"So … have you—"

"Okay," I interrupted. "We're going to move on to literally any other subject and never revive this one."

CHAPTER 26
ABRUPT AND ALMOST IMPERCEPTIBLE

"I WOULD KILL for some toilet paper right now," Denisha said. "Not you, obviously."

"Obviously," I said.

"Would it be uncouth to discuss who I would be willing to sacrifice?"

"Uncouth," I repeated. "There's a word you don't hear very often."

We strolled back into camp as Denisha said, "I know words. Lots of them. I may not know how to pronounce all of them because I learned them while reading books instead of hearing people say them, but I know them."

"Ooh. Do you have one that's embarrassing? I once said Rene Descartes' name in front of a bunch of philosophy majors, except I pronounced Dez-car-tez because I'd never heard it said out loud before. They acted like I was a lower life form."

She smiled, knowing my pain. "I can tell you this much — hors d'oeuvres is not said whores deh oovers."

I patted her on the back. "Sympatico, chica."

"This place is a ghost town," Denisha said. "Where is everybody?"

"Chores," a voice croaked from the back of the shelter.

With the stark contrast between the bright sunlight and the deep shadows under our shanty, I couldn't make out who it was.

Denisha and I walked over and leaned in. Rhonda lay tucked into its recesses with a dark shirt wrapped around her eyes. Denisha grabbed her hand and squeezed lightly. "What's wrong?"

Rhonda flinched. "Quieter," she whispered. "Migraine. Had an aura. Nearly fell into the fire. Here now." Every word took an uncomfortable effort.

"Do you have medicine?"

Her head shake was abrupt and almost imperceptible. "Out. Forgot refill."

Denisha patted the hand she was holding.

"Would caffeine help?" I asked.

She let go of Denisha's hand and gave a thumbs up.

Denisha frowned and quietly asked, "Where are you going to get caffeine?"

"Coffee. I had a bag. A couple other people did too."

Rhonda grimaced.

"Sorry," I said. "Last question. Where's your canteen?"

She flicked her hand outward at the wrist. Not a very specific gesture, but I took it to mean it wasn't in the shelter with her.

"Come on," I whispered to Denisha.

She touched Rhonda's hand one more time. "We'll be back."

The woman didn't respond.

We followed the short trail we'd worn between the shelter and the fire pit. On arrival, we found the fire burned down to coals and the water basin mostly empty. I flipped open the suitcase nearby where we were storing water that had been boiled. There was enough in there for what we needed, but not much beyond that.

"I thought she said people were doing chores?" I grumbled.

Denisha shrugged as she worked to rekindle the fire with some nearby sticks.

"Well, they're doing a piss-poor job of it."

She grinned. "Look at you coming out with the salty language. Do you kiss your mother with that mouth?"

"Shut up," I said playfully.

She brought her hand to her chest, wincing as she did so and ruining the effect of whatever joke she was about to go for.

"Shoulder still bothering you?"

She shrugged. "Only when I move it in very particular ways. It's not that bad. Just catches me off guard sometimes." As if to test the accuracy of what she said, Denisha picked up the unwieldy suitcase and tipped one corner down to the basin, pouring most of the remaining water in. I looked around for a green coconut with an "R" etched into it.

"Will you grab some coffee from the pantry?"

I walked over to the tree line where Tom and Ryan had built an elevated platform out of bamboo around which they'd built some makeshift walls. A miniature version of our shelter. It gave us a place to protect our meager stores from the elements and nominally from any big varmints, if there were any. Though mouse droppings suggested they went where they darn well pleased and were in no way deterred by our ramshackle walls.

I snagged a bag of coffee and salivated at the prospect of smelling it. Even though my brain knows coffee smells way better that it tastes, it was excited about drinking something other than coconut milk or boiled water. A light bulb went off.

When I handed the bag over to Denisha, I asked, "Have we considered catching a momma goat so we can milk her?"

Denisha's laugh was a staccato bark. She gestured to

herself. "*We* haven't, but I will absolutely sign up for watching the goat wrangling part of the rodeo."

The mental image set me to giggling. We were both still laughing when Jac walked up, assessed us, and walked off without a word. Her obvious disapproval triggered a new round of laughter.

By the time we'd fully collected ourselves, steam danced over the surface of the coffee.

I asked, "How are we going to get that from there to in there?" I pointed from the converted air fryer basin to the quarter-sized hole in Rhonda's coconut.

Denisha pursed her lips and moved them from side-to-side, thinking. She unbuttoned her shirt, slipped it down her shoulders and off. She wrapped it around her hands, making oven mitts.

I rolled my eyes in as exaggerated a manner as I could manage. "I don't even know why you are bothering to put it back on. You're out of it as much as you're in it."

She grinned and arched her back. "When you got it, flaunt it."

What I hate most about that expression is that *got* and *flaunt* don't rhyme, and people carry one saying it like they do. Almost rhyming is an affront to my brain.

At just that moment, Daryl popped over the dune and entered the clearing. His eyes roved over before he made a U-turn and left the way he'd entered. I don't even know if he registered my presence.

"Looks like you just gave him a new deposit for the spank bank," I said.

"Eww," she said, slumping her shoulders instinctively. "Now, hold that coconut steady. You'll be lucky if I don't scald your hands on purpose after little bit of vulgarity."

Her hands were steady as an assassin's. Only a couple of small rivulets escaped the spout as the rich coffee made its way in.

I whispered mischievously, "Are you sure we have to give it to Rhonda? She'll never know."

"Maybe you're our resident sociopath. Can you account for your whereabouts the other night?"

Even as she finished her question, it was apparent that she regretted making the joke. The whole thing was still too close to home, and there'd been no closure whatsoever. Four days later, we still hadn't the slightest trace of what had become of Ryan.

I swallowed my retort about still having an indention in my hip from her booty having been planted against me most of the night. It had been a weird transition going from living alone and never having to contend with touching someone else or having my movements inhibited while sleeping to the present state of never not touching someone in bed.

Denisha set the water basin on the flat rock in the fire pit ring that served as our potholder, then put her shirt back on. After the last button slid through the hole, she reached down for the coffee-filled coconut. "I'll take this to Rhonda, since I obviously can't trust you to do it."

I hung my head in faux shame.

"If you can manage it, I left enough coffee for both of us."

When she walked back toward the shelter, I grabbed her coconut and wedged it between my feet as I sat in a butterfly position. I leaned forward and picked up the basin, held my arms out and began tipping it toward myself, thinking about how many different ways this could be catastrophic.

CHAPTER 27
ANY KIND OF CONVICTION

I PULLED the coconut away from my face. "That was not the experience I thought it would be."

"Agree," Denisha said. "I don't know if there are people who combine coffee and coconut on the regular, but if so, I don't want to associate with them."

"What?!" I said in disbelief. "That was the best thing I've had since we left Colombia. That opinion is bad and you should feel bad for having it. The only downside to this experience was wading through the grounds."

"Hard disagree. Now, help me with this suitcase so we can carry it down to the stream and fill it."

I wrinkled my nose at her. "Can I opt out since you're not my designated chore buddy?"

"You may not, if for no other reason than I haven't seen either of our chore buddies in a while, and I don't want to be the one to have left the water thing empty."

"Fine. Another question," I said.

She tilted her head. "Are you just delaying?"

"I'm not *just* delaying. I have a real question. Not that we can change it now because that would be confusing, but wouldn't it make more sense to put the clean water side nearest the fire?"

"I asked Tom about that whenever we were setting up the first time, and he made a good point. If the already-boiled water is closest, then we might contaminate it with the other water as we're taking it to the fire."

"You don't think we're contaminating it by putting it in a bin that previously held somebody's dirty underwear and socks?"

Denisha shrugged. "Control what you can. Leave the rest up to God. Now, pick up your end."

We walked awkwardly, with the large, empty suitcase banging against our hips. I asked the natural follow-up question, surprised the topic of religious beliefs hadn't been broached already. Frankly, I was mildly surprised there were any topics left to explore. "You believe in God then?"

"I do."

"Even after all this?" I gestured around us with my free hand.

"Sure. I can't go and quit believing just because something bad happened to me. That wouldn't be any kind of conviction, more of a hope for good fortune. Are you familiar with *The Problem of Pain* by C. S. Lewis?"

"I'm familiar with the problem that being in pain sucks."

She gave me a half-smile. Not my best joke, but I was super uncomfortable with these kinds of conversations and trying to defray the effect ... even though I'd started it.

"It talks about why God allows pain and suffering in the world if He loves his creation."

"And?"

"And it's complicated and I can't do it justice. You should read it, if you're interested, when we get home."

We both knew she should have said *if* instead of *when*, but neither of us wanted to bring attention to it. It killed the conversation, so we walked in silence.

The group had discovered over the last week or so — since most of us had implicitly accepted our fate that no rescue was coming — that the mention of home was the quickest way to awkwardly end any conversation. Even the formerly taboo discussion of politics was no longer off the table because it was inconsequential.

As we neared the stream, Denisha suddenly dropped her end of the suitcase. The now-free hand went to her mouth, and the other froze in the air like her software had glitched. Her eyes remained fixed ahead of her.

I set the suitcase down on my end and moved beside her so that I could see what had spooked her. At the stream's edge, something glinted in the sunlight. I couldn't make it out.

When I moved forward, she snatched my hand and gripped it like a vise.

"It's okay," I said. "I'm just going to see."

She reluctantly let my hand slide out of her own. I crept forward until the glimmering object revealed itself to be a watch. My head popped up, and I looked around in all directions, a prairie dog in search of predators. Behind me, Denisha slunk to the ground. She buried her face in her hands. *How did she make out what it was from there?*

I moved forward with an abundance of caution, to borrow a phrase from the early days of the COVID-19 pandemic. The watch wasn't the only thing on the bank. A pool of blood encompassing it leached slowly into the stream.

I didn't recognize the watch, just another leather-banded timepiece. It could be almost anyone's.

My heart raced, and a knot formed in my belly. I suddenly needed to pee. Slowly, I squatted beside the watch and reached down to touch it, but yanked my hand away, thinking that maybe I shouldn't. *Whatever. It's not like a forensic team is on its way to fingerprint the scene.*

I surveyed my surroundings again. Denisha still hadn't moved. Nothing else seemed out of place. The only two people I'd seen in the last little while were Denisha and Rhonda. One of the others could be anywhere. I reached down and pulled the watch out of the slurry of blood and mud in which it was partly embedded.

Holding it flat in my palm, I read Jack Mason on its face. I'd bought one for my last boyfriend when I was under the mistaken impression that we were more serious than apparently was the case. The real shame of it was that my last boyfriend would be my last boyfriend, and he got the distinction of sullying that too.

I flipped the watch over to expose its back. The bloody mud mixture obscured an inscription. I used the meaty part of my other hand to clear it. "With all my love, Anetta." Under the words was a date, presumably some kind of anniversary. When I remembered that Norman's wife was named Anetta, it hit me in the gut like a sucker punch.

My body sagged.

Only after Denisha wrapped an arm around me did I realize that at some point, I'd gone from squatting to slouched on the ground. Tears blurred my eyes, and my cheeks were wet where they'd been streaming. "I can't do this."

Denisha pushed herself to her feet and reached her hands down to me. I let her pull me up. She looked me directly in the face. "What choice do we have?"

I bit the inside of my lip and nodded my head. We didn't have any choices. This wasn't a newsletter that we could opt out of, or even a scary movie that we could turn off. I didn't have any idea what we *could* do, and I could barely function more than keeping myself on my feet. "What now?" I asked.

Denisha gathered herself for a minute. She was making a remarkable rebound from her state a few minutes earlier. It reminded me of my mother in a way. She moved through life meekly, but when things started getting real, she was at her most assertive and resolute. In those moments of necessity, she was unflappable. I hoped there was some of that in my DNA as well.

"We walk into that camp and start demanding answers. We're going to get to the bottom of this," Denisha said.

"And when we do?"

"Then I guess the five of us will have to figure out what to do with the one. For now, though, let's go upstream a bit and get you cleaned up."

I looked down at myself. My hands and lower legs were smeared with Norman's blood. I tightened my grasp around the watch I'd managed to hold on to. "No, let them see it."

"That-a-girl," she said.

I built my resolution one brick at a time. It felt put-on, but maybe that's what it feels like for everyone until you get used to it.

CHAPTER 28

THE COLOR OF COLD ASH

JAC HURRIED up to me and took on the role of a mother hen. "What happened? Where are you hurt?" Without giving me time to answer, she looked at Denisha and restated her questions. "What happened to her? How'd she get hurt?"

The fussing grabbed the attention of the others in camp. Rhonda roused in the shelter, sitting up and dangling her legs over the side. She planted her feet in the sand as though she were going to stand but didn't. Daryl moseyed over from the pantry.

Jac grabbed my hands and flipped them palms up, searching for signs of injury. When she observed the watch in my right hand, she flung my arms down and backed away. The color drained from her face, and she frantically checked her surroundings. "Where's Tom? Norman?"

Daryl tensed and stepped forward a few paces, his hands out in front of him.

I might as well have been holding a hand grenade whose pin had been pulled. It hadn't occurred to me that they would so quickly turn and suspect me of killing one of our number … again. But why not? Wasn't I wondering the same of each of them? Who among you are killing off the rest of us? The irony planted an ill-timed smirk on my lips.

"Something funny, Alexis?" Daryl said, a grating edge in his voice. He may have been past his prime, but he was still much larger than me. If he used physical violence, I'd be in bad shape, my single jiujitsu lesson notwithstanding.

The bemused expression fell away from my face. I fully opened my hand so they could clearly see the watch. "It's Norm's. We found it by the creek." My voice cracked.

Jac shook her head. "No. No. No." Each denial carried less conviction than the one before it. She became unsteady on her feet. I moved forward to offer my support, but she stumbled backward in an effort to keep the gap between us.

I stopped and held a hand out, like someone trying to placate an aggressive animal. In this instance, I was perceived as the predator. Did that mean the prey thought I was trying to lull it into a false sense of security? I fell back in line beside Denisha, who — along with Rhonda — hadn't said a word since we'd entered camp. For the time being, this was a family matter, and they were the cousins. Of course, the cousins had been the first to lose someone.

Daryl asked, "Why were you at the creek?"

"Getting water with D. We used the last of it making coffee for Rhonda. She had a headache."

"Were you going to bring it back one scoop at a time?" he added with a boatload of snark.

Denisha and I looked down at our hands, then at each other. We'd left the suitcase down by the water. I couldn't even remember who'd had it. "We left it." I pointed with my thumb in the direction we'd come from. "Got a little preoccupied."

He turned to Rhonda. "Can you confirm that?"

"Yep. Migraine," she whispered with a sigh, the strain of talking being almost more than she could tolerate.

Denisha glared at Daryl. "Best watch yourself and how

you handle this impromptu interrogation. The shoe will be on the other foot in a couple minutes."

"Whoa! Hold on now, missy—"

Daryl stopped himself. But it was too late. The other four people in camp were women who'd been on the receiving end of old-white-guy condescension far too many times.

He looked over his shoulder at Jac. She gazed back at him with a clenched jaw and furrowed eyebrows. He'd lost whatever backing he had.

"Look, I'm just asking some questions, trying to figure out what happened."

"Yeah," Denisha said, "that's what an interrogation is."

"Now, I have some questions for you," I said. Before he protested, I lobbed a question at him. "Where have you been this morning? I've been from the stream to the latrine and haven't seen you, except when you popped into camp for two seconds."

Daryl's mouth stayed clamped shut while he decided whether he was going to engage. I don't know what tipped the scales. Probably the fact that he had a bunch of making up to do after his derogatory comment.

"After breakfast, I was with Norm collecting firewood."

Denisha grunted. "Hmm."

It didn't mean anything, but it didn't not mean anything either.

To lend credence to his alibi, Daryl pointed at the freshly restocked pile of firewood.

"After that?" I prompted.

"After we dropped the wood off," he said, gesturing again in case anyone had missed it the first time around, "Norm said he had some personal business to attend to, so we went our separate ways."

Jac asked, "What does that mean — personal business?"

"You know."

"I don't."

"Number two. He had to go number two."

"Again? Isn't that where he was the last time he disappeared?"

Daryl shrugged. "I didn't ask a lot of questions."

Jac said, "Must be nice. I've been stopped up for days."

"Same," Rhonda croaked. Under different circumstances, it would have been comical, but there was no levity in our present situation.

Daryl tried to divert the attention away from himself and asked Rhonda, "Can you account for where you've been?"

She laid back down in the shelter, covered her eyes with a cloth, and raised a middle finger to him.

He muttered, "That's not an answer."

I continued questioning him. "After y'all split up, what did you do?"

Daryl's growing impatience showed in his face, which was increasing in the intensity of red on display. "I waited until Norman finished taking a dump, stalked him down to the creek, and stabbed him to death. Then I made him disappear. Is that what you want to hear?!"

"Is that what happened?" I coaxed him.

"No, it's not what freaking happened. I can't believe—" Angry tears slipped down his checks. I knew what that was like. When I got angry enough, my body freaked out and started crying, like it didn't know what else to do with all the emotions it was generating.

Daryl pivoted so that he faced the shelter, but he wasn't interested in the shelter or its occupant. He swung his head wildly back and forth between Jac and me. His shoulders hunched forward and tensed. His posture resembled the depictions of primitive men, the hunter-gatherers who relied more on their brawn than their brains. Not really the best look for someone trying to establish that he wasn't a murder suspect.

When neither of us gave an inch, Daryl clenched his fists,

tilted his head back, and roared in frustration. One of my nephews had once watched a *Daniel Tiger* episode about being so mad that you just want to roar.

He stalked toward the pantry and picked up a papaya. "I got more fruit for us. She knows. She saw me." He pointed at Rhonda, whose face was still covered.

Denisha said, "Rhonda?"

"Affirmative."

"Why didn't you speak up sooner?" Daryl said.

She shrugged without sitting up. "You didn't ask."

"I'm done with this! Somebody else's turn to face the inquisition."

"What's going on here?"

Everyone turned in unison toward the beach, where Tom stood in the gap we'd worn through the tall grass.

"Where the hell have you been?" Jac's voice was cold and flat.

A confused Tom repeated his question. "What's going on?"

In answer, I tossed Norman's watch to him. Instinctively, he reached out to catch it. As he inspected it, he used his thumb to wipe away some of the dirt and dried blood on its face.

Tom looked up, taking a mental accounting of everyone in camp and who was missing. By the time he discerned Norm's absence, his face was the color of cold ash.

CHAPTER 29
A GOOD EGG

TOM WORE the expression of a man who'd run face-first into a colony of pissed off yellow jackets and didn't know which way to run. If fleeing was what he had in mind, he didn't do it in time.

Jac barked at him. "Where have you been?"

I didn't want to relive a second round of the pummeling we'd given Daryl, and I could already see Tom getting his back up.

"Hang on," I said, stepping into the middle of the fray. "Just hang on. We need to regroup. Attacking everybody as they walk in isn't going to benefit anybody."

Denisha had my back. "She's right. We've still got to live together."

"Right up until somebody kills us," Jac said.

Tom disregarded the sniping. "Was it like Ryan?"

I looked to Denisha to answer since she'd happened upon the scene with Ryan, and I'd only gotten there with the rest of the crew.

"Pretty much," she breathed. "But less …"

Her throat constricted. She couldn't finish the sentence.

She didn't have to. Everybody got the gist. The first site looked like every last drop had been wrung out of Ryan. This one was a mess, but not that. Not by a country mile.

"Where?" Tom asked.

"Where we get water."

Tom broke into a trot, headed that direction. The rest of us fell in behind him. I wasn't eager to revisit it, but I wasn't keen on being left behind either. Even Rhonda made her way from the shelter, slowly and unsteadily bringing up the rear. An unenviable position.

When I was in college, a small band of us went hiking in the Smokies. Hiking was nothing new to us, but this particular trail was, and we didn't get started until late afternoon. We fancied ourselves as adventurers but we weren't; we just had the unfailing confidence of youth that doesn't allow you to recognize that you're more likely to be on the news for having been rescued by Park Rangers than for some kind of trail-blazing feat. After it got dark, we left the trail thinking we knew a shortcut back toward the car. We didn't.

Instead, we wandered through the woods until we were fully immersed in darkness. After a couple of hours, we stumbled upon a mostly dry, boulder-ridden creek bed. We'd crossed a creek on the outbound trek. Surely, this was the same one. My roommate's boyfriend took the point position. The bigger question was who was going to be the caboose, making sure no one got left behind.

With a half-moon hanging low in the sky, my roommate's boyfriend nominated his best friend. He wasn't eager for the task, but he wasn't going to balk and show his cowardice either. He waited until we started picking our way among the rocks in the direction we thought we'd come to reveal his true nature. Several minutes in, he wordlessly slunk past me, transposing our places in line.

The pit that I already had in my stomach, from the combination of both lack of food and water and an excess of fear, grew exponentially. Now, I could be snatched by a bear or cougar or deranged serial-killing hillbilly, and no one would be the wiser for some time, because you could be darn sure that the best friend wasn't checking his six.

Even in the light of morning, Rhonda's position didn't feel altogether different. Until Denisha fell back to walk beside her and steady her.

A good egg, that one.

Ahead of me, Tom stopped. The others, Daryl and Jac, fanned out beside him. He'd brought himself to a halt behind the forsaken suitcase as if it were the Rubicon. Beyond it, footsteps crisscrossed over each other, leading toward a rust-colored patch of sand at the water's edge. The puddle was gone, having either run off into the stream or been soaked up.

After a few minutes of taking in the scene, Tom asked, "Where was his watch?"

I pointed. "Just kind of in the middle there."

"Did you search the area around it?"

"No?" I intended it to be a statement, but it came out as a question.

Sensing my confusion, Jac said, "Sherlock here thinks he's going to inspect the scene for clues."

Tom ignored the derision. He entered the tall grasses to the left of the trail, moving forward one painstakingly slow step at a time. He pushed the grasses in front of him aside before moving, making sure there was nothing to be found at its base.

Daryl followed suit on the right side. They combed the small area until they met at the bank, neither apparently having turned up either a weapon or any other kind of evidence.

Tom said, "I feel like we're missing something."

"Footsteps." Rhonda was squinting and shielding her eyes with one hand.

"Yes." Tom pointed at her for emphasis. "He went somewhere afterward. There should be evidence of that."

We scoured the ground around us. Of course, it was littered with footprints and divots of all kinds, both from today and every day for the past couple of weeks.

"I'm not any kind of tracker," Daryl said, "but there should be a blood trail, too. I haven't seen a drop other than where that one puddle was." Receiving nods all around, he continued. "The only way that can possibly be is if they went either upstream or downstream afterward, staying in the water."

Denisha said, "All that's downstream is ocean."

If you stepped into the middle of the stream and looked east, you could see beyond the grass that leaned over into its waters and past where it cut through the dunes to the sea.

"Hang tight," Tom said, splashing into the water and striding downstream. He was never quite out of sight, but it still made me nervous. I wasn't sure I'd ever be comfortable again with anyone leaving the group. Not only because people had a sudden propensity for getting killed when they went off on their own, but also because I was that only one I could totally rule out as doing the killing.

"Nothing," he said when he returned. "That leaves us only one choice."

"Go in there?" Jac nodded toward where the cool waters disappeared into the undergrowth and shadows?

"Yep."

"Like hell I am."

"You don't have to go," Tom said, then more broadly to everyone. "Nobody has to go."

"Well, I'm not staying here and getting murdered. I can tell you that," said Jac.

Tom stepped out of the stream, making sure to take a big enough stride to miss the remains of the blood puddle. "I'm going to grab a couple of bites and get my canteen, then I'm going to find Norm. Anybody who wants to join me can, but I won't begrudge anybody who doesn't."

We learned in the next couple of minutes that there wasn't a soul amongst us who was ready to have anyone else outside of their sight lines.

CHAPTER 30
BREACH THE SILENCE

DARYL PULLED up beside me as we walked from camp back to the stream. He said nothing at first, but just kind of lurked. There was clearly something on his mind, but I was going to make him breach the silence. I can't even say why, maybe just general orneriness, or maybe it's because he didn't have a good enough alibi that I could cross him off the list.

"I'm the only one who got questioned."

"Tom did, too."

He shook his head. "He pivoted the conversation right away and turned it into a crime scene investigation."

I played the scene back in my head. "Huh. You're right."

"What are you going to do about it?"

I nearly objected, asking why it was me who needed to do something about it. But with a bit of introspection, I knew I *wanted* to be the one to do it. It was written into my DNA. So instead of going all Nancy Kerrigan, I asked, *Why not me?*, and didn't have an answer.

I won't say I was eager for it, but whatever the word is that means eager-and-anxious-and-scared all at the same time, that's a pretty good descriptor for how I felt. "I guess I'm going to rectify it."

The response seemed to surprise Daryl, who'd probably expected to have to do some convincing. "How?"

"I don't know yet, but not city-hall-meeting style, I can tell you that. There's a reason that cops don't do their investigations out in the open."

"What about congressional hearings?"

"Come on. I may be young—"

He raised an eyebrow at me.

"—ish. Youngish, at least compared to the rest of y'all. My only knowledge of politics comes from watching MSNBC on election nights, but even I know congressional hearings are just for show. All the actual work has already been done behind the scenes. Here's what I know." I looked around to make sure no one had dropped back to listen to us as we walked. "As best I can tell, I'm the only one that can fully corroborate my whereabouts all morning because I was with other people — first Tom, then D."

Daryl pursed his lips and didn't make eye contact with me when he said, "Awfully convenient that the person looking into the murders has already ruled out herself as a suspect."

I shrugged and held my hand out palm up. "I invite you to get anyone else to do this."

"Nah. I trust you."

Instead of pointing out the inconsistency in his back-to-back statements, I grabbed his wrist. "You shouldn't. None of us can afford to blindly trust anyone right now. You should check with Tom and with Denisha to see if what I'm telling you is actually true."

Daryl looked uncomfortable. "Why are you telling me to check up on you?"

"Because it's what I'm going to do to every one of you. Besides, who watches the watchers?"

"Trust but verify, huh?"

"Yep. It's like the TSA says ..."

He looked at me quizzically.

"If you see something, say something."

"Ah."

It was hard to know where to take the conversation after that, so we fell into a lull that coincided with us approaching the place where Norman had been killed. Murdered.

Each of us stepped around the rust-colored patch of ground, splashed into the water, and headed upstream. The foliage closed in around us. The air grew denser and the light more refracted. It reminded me of *Heart of Darkness*—actually, that's not true. That's me trying to sound impressive. We were supposed to read it in high school, and while I was very much a rule follower, that didn't really seem like a good time to me. Instead, I watched *Apocalypse Now*. Turns out that wasn't a good time either, so the truth is that us heading into the jungle chasing after some unknown evil was ominous as hell, and it reminded me of Martin Sheen trying to find Marlon Brando.

My shirt clung to me. Fear and humidity made for a sticky combination. I couldn't see my smell because I'm not a cartoon, but it was very nearly to that point. Based on the number of mosquitoes and biting flies whose attention I had captured, I gathered I was pretty pungent. The others slapped at themselves incessantly as well.

I spent most of the trek through the steamy jungle figuring out how to handle what I'd just agreed to. Fortunately (if that's the right way to look at it), HR gives you plenty of experience tackling uncomfortable topics with people.

The stream narrowed the further we followed it, to where instead of two people being able to walk abreast in it, we fell into a single file line. At its source, in what I assumed was approximately the midpoint of the island, water burbled up out of the ground and began its journey toward the sea.

We found no sign of Norm or whomever or whatever had taken him. It was as if he and Ryan had just vanished. I didn't believe in the supernatural or paranormal, but if this continued inexplicably, I wasn't certain I could maintain my disbelief. I was certainly becoming doubtful about the involvement of anyone in the camp. The complete disappearance of bodies was truly baffling. Maybe that's too obvious to even need saying.

The walk back to camp was grimmer even than the outbound voyage. Whatever we'd collectively hoped to see, finding nothing had a devastating effect on morale.

Tom went to the campfire and stoked it. When no one else followed, I joined him, sitting upwind of the smoke.

Several minutes of silence passed.

"You never said where you were," I said.

"I didn't kill Norm. Or Ryan, for that matter."

"I know. But still …"

"I can tell you, but it won't give you any answers."

I shrugged as if to say, *Let's hear it.*

"I went up the beach a ways to have some alone time and read a book."

"What book?" I was trying really hard to keep my voice conversational and not sound investigatory. I'd not had to think about the tone of my voice while talking earlier.

His lip turned up in one corner. "*One Hundred Years of Solitude.* Picked it up at a bookstore in Colombia."

"Huh." That kind of stumped me.

"You know *Encanto*? It's rooted in the same magical realism that Marquez—"

I waved him off. "I know about magical realism. Don't try to explain it to me because you're just now getting into it."

"Sorry." I felt bad that I deflated him a bit, but I didn't need a lesson about the basics of Gabriel García Márquez.

I knew how to perk him back up. "Are we still going to do my jiujitsu lessons?"

Right on cue, Tom's posture improved, and his demeanor did a one-eighty. "Of course." He added tentatively, "I wasn't sure you'd want to?"

I wasn't accustomed to this unconfident Tom. If that's not a word, it should be. "Why?"

He looked at the ground. "Because I don't have an alibi."

"Tom." I used his name, so he'd look up at me. I wanted him to see me say this. "Whatever is happening, I know you're not the one doing it." I mostly believed that, but he needed to hear that I was committed to it.

Tom nodded, then launched into his ideas about my training. "We'll start with leg sweeps. That's something that can help negate a size advantage and is important since you're smaller than most people. I can teach you five sweeps. Maybe we'll work on one a day."

"That's all well and good, but what am I supposed to do with somebody once they're on the ground?"

"We'll get there. Patience, grasshopper."

"Okay, David Carradine."

"Well, actually …"

He couldn't help himself, and I would have to endure the explanation about how my retort had gone wrong.

CHAPTER 31
WHEN THE WEATHER TURNS

I STUMBLED to the fire like a zombie and plopped down beside Denisha, who always made an effort to be put together and presentable while the rest of us looked like … we'd been marooned on a deserted island. Of course that begs the question, is it deserted if it was never inhabited?

"G'morning, sunshine."

"Are you really this chipper, or are you in flight attendant mode?"

"I'm actually feeling pretty good. And if all goes well, nobody will die today. Wouldn't that be nice?"

"Well, I don't think I slept a wink last night."

Denisha gave me a sideways look. "If that's true, I have some concerns about why you'd snore like that while awake."

"Deception." I grinned even through my grogginess. "Besides, the snoring was this morning. I said I didn't sleep *last night.*"

"The point remains," she said haughtily. "I was the last to bed and the first up. You were sawing full-size redwoods."

"Whatever. Did you sit up all night?"

"Just had some things on my mind." Denisha shook her head, as if to clear out some leftover thoughts. "Who do you think snuggled with you and kept you warm during the night? You know it wasn't one of the dudes, or you'd have felt them probing you with—"

"Nope. Don't. Gross." I gave an exaggerated shiver to emphasize my point. "Also, if I haven't said so, you're an exceptional snuggler. I've never been someone who wants someone touching me while I sleep. I mean, I think of those couples who spoon all night and have to wake the other person up when they want to turn over and swap the spoons, and it's horrifying. There's something deeply wrong with those people. That said, you're very toasty."

"I know."

"What are we going to do when the weather turns, though?"

"Don't worry," Denisha said. "We'll all be dead and gone by then."

My jaw fell open. If it could have fallen to the ground like I was one of the Looney Tunes, it would have. When the surprise wore off, I said, "Geez Louise, D, there can't be two of us spitting out gallows humor. You're encroaching on my space."

"Who said anything about being humorous?"

Having nothing to say in response, I let my focus get lost in the fire dancing along the wood that someone had added. Having had my fill, I asked, "You really think it's one of us?"

"As opposed to?"

"What if there's something else out there?"

"Like what? It's not an animal. This isn't how animals work. I hope you're not about to tell me you believe in ghosts or some other craziness."

I'd never felt so sheepish and absurd in my life. "Not ghosts exactly, but I think there are things we don't understand. Like paranormal things." I peeked over at Denisha to see how she was taking it. She raised an eyebrow at me. I sighed. "Did you ever see *Predator*?"

"You think aliens are abducting us?!" She was alarmingly loud.

"Shut up," I growled. "Keep your voice down."

"You're damn right *keep my voice down*. If these people hear you talk like that, they're going to think you cracked. Maybe you have. Have you?"

I shook my head.

"Hey. Look at me."

Reluctantly, I swung my head toward her.

"Are you losing it?"

I shook my head again.

"Say it. I'm not losing it."

"I'm not losing it."

She held my gaze for a long minute, assessing me. I wasn't losing it. Not really. Maybe a little bit, but mostly not. I was just really hurting for something to attribute two missing people to. The only thing possible was the unfathomable. I wanted to rule it out, but then there was nothing left except goblins and extra-terrestrials, neither of whom had proven themselves to exist.

That left one of the six of us. It was time to get to work testing alibis and eliminating options.

Tom had no alibi. He was by himself.

Daryl was alone, too.

I didn't do it. Obviously.

"Okay. So, if it wasn't Casper or Marvin the Martian, then it was one of us, right?"

"I think that's the page we were on five minutes ago before you brought out your tinfoil hat."

"Just a blip. A bit of denial. And hope."

"Okay," she said with enough reservation to make sure I knew she was still somewhat disturbed by the episode. "If that's all it was."

I nodded.

"How do we start?" Denisha asked.

It was my first murder investigation, but it wasn't my first time looking into an incident. Thanks to all those (mind-numbingly boring and slide-deck intensive) continuing education courses, I had a playbook for this kind of thing. "We start by asking questions."

"To eliminate people?"

"I like to gather as much information as I can before I start drawing conclusions."

"Well, I think we should focus on the men and take the women off the table for now."

Obviously, we had different philosophies about how to attack this. "Why is that?"

"None of the women could have carted off either of those two guys on their own. They would have had to drag them and that would've left a trail."

I didn't think that was necessarily true.

Denisha crossed her arms. "Say it."

"What?"

"Whatever it is you have to say. You're working that lower lip like a cow chewing its cud. So say whatever you're not saying."

Old habit. I ran my tongue across my bottom lip and found it raw and irritated. I'd worked really hard to break it, but getting pummeled with a bunch of stressors must have caused a regression. "When I was a kid, I could always tell when my dad was really fixated on a problem or anxious about something because he would clench his jaw, and you could see the muscles in his cheeks working. He said he'd ground his molars flat doing it."

"Mine had a vein that popped out of his forehead. Looked like a rope tucked under his skin." Despite sharing the memory, her tone hadn't let up. "But maybe that's enough reminiscing. Say it."

I sighed. "On that first morning, you were carrying

around airplane parts like they were nothing. You're probably the strongest woman I know."

"So you think I killed a couple of dudes and carried them away and made them disappear?"

The forehead vein must have been a genetic trait. Denisha had one that ran from her hairline to her eyebrow, and it was nearly throbbing.

"I think you *could*. Like you're physically capable of it."

She asked in a clipped tone, "But do you think I *did*?"

"Not really, but I'll feel more assured about that if you'll tell me where you were before you met up with me."

Denisha broke off her eye contact with me and looked off into the foliage that surrounded us. "I was skipping chores. I was supposed to be getting coconuts and papayas, but I didn't."

"Because …?"

"Because she was lying out topless on the beach like we're at some resort vacation." Denisha and I spun to see Jac grinning like the Cheshire Cat. "Norm and Daryl saw her, too. Saw and lingered … for a while. It wasn't drift*wood* they were gathering; I can tell you that."

"Eww." Denisha instinctively covered herself.

To turn the table a few degrees, I asked Jac, "And what were you doing that morning?"

She presented her middle finger and stalked off in the direction she'd come from.

CHAPTER 32
THE SLIGHTEST IMPROPRIETY

AFTER DINNER, the entire group of us went to the beach to watch the heat lightning play in the ocean off to the east. Calling it dinner was a misnomer by any account, comprising as it did of the last bits of dried goat and some seaweed.

The lightning reminded me of the summer weeks I spent in the Texas panhandle with my cousins. Everything was so flat that you could see for a thousand miles in any direction. When the wind blew just right (or wrong, depending on your perspective), you could smell all the cattle down in Hereford. Every time, my uncle would say, "Alex, that there is the smell of money." He said it my whole life, and probably says it to his grandkids now.

Daryl said, "We're going to need more meat." He ripped an extraordinarily loud fart as an exclamation mark.

No one begrudged it. The nights we ate seaweed were a noisy affair for some time afterward on account of the pronounced flatulent effect. Good manners just led to bloating and gas pain. We were all better off letting them go. It embarrassed me every time and simultaneously made me miss my brothers, who could be disgusting in every possible way. But the moment I showed the slightest impropriety, they made sure I got lectured about manners and being a Southern lady.

"I don't mind getting us another goat, but I can't do it by myself," Tom said.

Jac sat forward. "I told the girls about an idea I had for fishing and using a sewing needle to make a hook."

"That's a great idea," Tom said.

Never mind that it was my idea to convert the needle into a hook. She could have her moment.

"It's not like we can't do both," Rhonda said, still leaning back, propped up by her elbows. "There's not much chance of us having too much food."

"What are you doing?" Jac asked Daryl, who was looking at his wrist.

"It's driving me nuts not to have my watch. Wore one every day since I was a kid," he complained.

"What, are you taking medicine?"

"Actually, yes. But who knows? Maybe this new island diet won't clog my heart up. Still, I'd kill to have that watch back."

Again, he didn't catch himself until it was too late. Daryl couldn't help but shove his entire foot into his mouth on a regular basis.

"Figuratively, not literally. Obviously," he added. The golden hour light just before sunset did nothing to hide the crimson that had rushed to his cheeks.

"I think you've got it wrong there, big guy," Jac said. "You have to *be killed* to get it back."

I grinned but knew better than to laugh out loud at that. I turned my head away to hide my reaction. Denisha nudged me in the ribs, knowingly. The nudge jostled an idea loose. I felt stupid for not thinking of it sooner, but no one else had mentioned it, so at least we were collectively stupid.

Whoever was making us disappear had to have a cache of watches. If I could find the watches, there was a pretty good chance I could identify the culprit.

I sat upright, readying myself to make an exit, but realized that I would need an excuse. I didn't want to draw suspicion and certainly didn't want to end up with any company. My earlier reminiscing had been making me sad. If I could tug on that string for a minute (despite my eagerness), a couple of tears would be good cover for me bailing on our little kumbaya moment to go play the role of sleuth.

High school drama class had taught me I'm not much of an actor, but in my moment of need, my body came through. There was no sobbing and no free-flowing tears. I managed just enough mistiness to be convincing, like what happens when you have to pee super bad for a long time and finally get to go right before your bladder bursts.

Once my eyes welled up enough, I put on my gloomiest face and looked down the line of survivors/suspects. When I stood up, everyone looked my way. Neither Daryl nor Tom said anything. Men never know what to say when a woman's upset.

Denisha reached up and held my hand. "Are you okay?"

I nodded and wiped my eyes with the back of my other hand. "Just need a minute."

As I turned back toward camp, Tom said as gently as he could muster, "Take somebody with you. Don't go off by yourself."

I had no intention of including anyone else in this endeavor. "I'll be fine, *Dad* ... unless one of y'all comes and murders me. So, how about we agree to no murdering instead?"

There was some light laughter, and no one got up to join me. Denisha raised her eyebrows, asking if she should come with, but I shook her off.

It really was a heck of a performance. Ms. Higginbotham would have been proud.

Everyone's suitcases were clustered around the shelter. I started on the far side so it would give me some cover from folks at the beach. However, that also meant I couldn't see anyone approaching. I'd cross that bridge if I came to it — my usual approach to problems that hadn't arisen yet. Sometimes, it worked out better than others.

Fortune seemed to shine down on me that evening. The suitcases of the three people whose whereabouts I hadn't fully been able to corroborate — Tom, Daryl, and Jac — sat side-by-side.

My stomach became queasy at the prospect of invading everyone's privacy and trust, particularly when there was so little of one and a steadily decreasing amount of the other. I thought I might be sick. That would be great. *Hey, by the way, I was searching your bag for our watches and threw up on your clothes. M'kay, bye now.*

I pushed open the lid to Tom's suitcase. It was like getting a glimpse into his brain. Pants, shirts, socks — all his clothes were packed away into their own separate bags. There was little chance of me moving anything around without it being noticeable. I was about as subtle as a hippo.

I chanced partly opening the top zipper, just in case there was a secret stash of watches tucked away innside ... presumably in their own bag. Things shifted in the lid as I unzipped. If I kept at it, they'd tumble out, so I settled for tugging at the flap and peeking inside. It was getting too dark to make much out. The trees that stood as sentinels over the shelter also dispersed the light as it filtered its way down to us.

With a couple of zips and a quick pat, I slid over to Daryl's bag, which was also a window into his chaotic soul. Instead of stacks, he had loosely jumbled his belongings into mounds. This was something I could dig my hands into — not that I particularly wanted to — without any possibility of it being noticed.

"Just what do you think you're doing?!"

CHAPTER 33
TAKE A LITTLE HEAT

I SLAMMED the luggage closed and looked up with widened eyes like a deer in headlights. Rhonda loomed over. I must have stayed hunched there for an eternity when she yelled again. "I said, 'Just what do you think you're doing?'"

The commotion brought the rest of the group around the side of the shelter. They'd decided to return to camp at a really unfortunate time, and super quietly. The din of insects chirping and welcoming the evening provided background noise that shielded their approach, but that was now replaced by the sound of blood rushing in my ears and my panicked heart banging against my ribs.

I stammered the same syllable a half-dozen times while trying to come up with some explanation for what I was doing. When nothing arrived, I stood up. If I were going to be mute, at least I wouldn't be cowering too.

The moment I got to my feet, Rhonda stepped forward and shoved me in the chest. My heels hit something, and I fell backward against a tree, landing with a thud and a grunt. A surge of adrenaline rushed up from my toes, but it was tempered by the air being expelled from my lungs.

I heard sounds of protest, and Denisha rushed to my side.

Undeterred, Rhonda skulked toward me. When she came within range of my legs, I kicked out ineffectually. She easily dodged the impotent gesture.

"What's going on?" Tom demanded as he stepped forward and grabbed Rhonda by the arm.

She yanked loose and pointed down at me. "She was going through everybody's stuff."

Tom's brow furrowed. "Is that true?" The disbelief in his voice was that of a principal who can't believe one of his star students is being accused of plagiarism.

Denisha got me under the armpits and pulled me to my feet. She nudged me a couple of steps to the left to create some space.

I nodded as tears fell down my cheeks. Real ones this time. Anger, fear, and embarrassment were quite a combo.

"I told her to do it." Daryl walked between Tom and Rhonda, shouldering them aside as he passed through. He turned to face them and Jac, who was still in the background.

"You what?" Tom said incredulously.

Rhonda fell silent for the time being.

"I told her to go through people's bags. We've got two people missing, and we don't know what's going on, so I told her to do it."

Jac stepped up beside Tom. "You told her to look in your bag?" The skepticism in her voice was thick.

Daryl looked over his shoulder at me and shrugged. "I didn't tell her not to. I'm not any less a suspect than anybody else."

Denisha mumbled something under her breath that could have been, "You got that right." It was hard to be certain.

"So we're all *suspects*, then?" Jac said.

"Well, yeah," he said. "Unless anyone has a different explanation."

"Except her?" Rhonda's voice dripped with venom. She didn't care who had ordered the actions. The invasion of privacy — never mind that I hadn't gotten to her bag — was unforgivable.

Denisha said, "Look, I don't like it any more than anybody else, but it makes sense. How about this? Can we at least look in Ryan's and Norman's bags?"

While rifling through live people's things felt wrong (even if it was justifiable), going through the luggage of people who were presumably dead was on another level. No one jumped at the idea, and I certainly couldn't be the person to advocate for it, but no one outright dismissed it either. A quiet uneasiness fell over us, an unspoken concession that we were going to do something distasteful.

Daryl sighed and mumbled something vulgar that sounded as though it was meant for the entire group. He shouldered his way out of the makeshift circle, picked up Norman's suitcase, and toted it to the campfire. We no longer had enough light to see.

Tom looked at Jac with a question on his face. She shrugged, then turned and followed Daryl. He went with her. Rhonda strode to Ryan's bag and carried it toward the fire as well.

Before I fell in after her, Denisha grabbed my upper arm. "Were you going to search my bag too?"

I evaded the question. "I hadn't gotten that far."

"But?"

"I would have." There was no use lying about it.

Her lips twitched, and she nodded once. She followed in the others' wake, leaving me standing alone on the outskirts of an island jungle that was swallowing us up one at a time. I hurried to the fire to see whether my disastrous mission would turn up anything useful.

It didn't.

Well, mostly not.

Norman had squirreled away a bag of chocolate-covered coffee beans that became community property. Beyond that, it was mostly soiled clothes and a few miscellaneous personal items.

Part of my brain told me there were several people's suitcases that remained unchecked. I had to let it go. If I got caught pulling that stunt again, there was a fair chance they would exile me to the other island with Walt's rotting corpse.

Just when I started to wonder if they might exile me regardless, Tom wandered over.

"You decide to forgive me?" I asked.

"Nothing to forgive, as far as I'm concerned. It was a good idea … just poorly executed."

"Ha. Yeah, you're not kidding."

He leaned in close to me, reminding me of what some execs and upper management used to do when they'd had a few drinks at an event. Feeling less inhibited and unencumbered by their better judgment, they'd find a way to "inadvertently" brush against you.

But that wasn't Tom's motive here. He left an air gap between us and said quietly, "You should have used the idiot sweep."

"What?" Lost in uncomfortable memories, I was only half paying attention.

"When she knocked you on your ass, you should have used the idiot sweep we worked on this morning. Hook the ankles, and push her backward at the hips. Not that flailing kicking thing."

"Oh, yeah. Didn't think about it. I was kind of caught off guard."

He nodded. "That's why we're training — to develop that muscle memory so your brain doesn't have to think. Your body just knows how to respond in a situation. Anyway, I think I'm going to turn in." He patted my shoulder and gave it a squeeze as he walked past me.

I looked around and saw Daryl standing by himself with his back to the fire. I joined him, watching the ghostly breakers rolling onto the beach. The moon had risen out of the sea and begun its ascent.

"Why did you do that?" I asked.

"Just because."

"That's not an answer."

He looked down at me and glowered, even though he didn't really mean it. "Any chance you're going to let this go?"

I grinned as broadly as I could muster to counter his glumness. "I think you know me better than that."

He looked back out at the water. "You're the only person who's been genuinely kind to me out here. Not that I didn't deserve the rocky start. I did."

"What about Jac? Y'all seem to be getting on pretty well."

"That's not kindness. That's … something else. And I'm not sure it's all that good for either of us."

There was a deep sadness in his voice that I hadn't heard before.

"Still, you didn't have to say anything. I would have been okay."

"It's fine," he said dismissively, clearly ready to be done with a conversation where he was at risk of exposing his humanity. "Everybody already thinks I'm a bad guy, so I figured I'd take a little heat off of you."

CHAPTER 34
A REGRETTABLE LAPSE

JAC SLAPPED her legs in frustration. I just wanted her to sit still so she'd shade me from the early morning sun. Instead, I was having to bob like a Weeble to keep the glare out of my eyes.

"All I'm saying," she was half yelling at this point, "is it's not a good idea for us to be splitting up into pairs and going off together."

"We can't go around like a herd of cattle," Tom said. "We'll never get anything done."

"SOMEONE IS KILLING EVERYONE ELSE." Jac roared at full volume. She gestured at me. "And Inspector Gadget here isn't any closer to figuring anything out."

Her being so amped up this early had me wondering how much of that cocaine I would have found left in her bag.

I'd been hoping to stay out of the conversation, but that option had been yanked away from me. "As evidenced by my assault last night, people get real … sensitive about me investigating, so it's been tough sledding."

I sensed something looming over me, despite being able to see the other five members of the group. With a little foreboding, I hinged at the waist, looking back and up. A bank of gunmetal gray clouds flew over us from the west. We'd had pretty good weather to this point … aside from the storm that had crashed us into this island in the first place. And then the deluge a couple of days later. And a few afternoon showers here and there. Okay, so it hadn't been great, but nothing to write home about.

A bolt of lightning reached back in the direction it had come from. My eyes followed its path and saw a sheet of rain bearing down on us. We all jumped up nearly in unison and dashed for the shelter.

We learned in very short order that our shelter could only be called that in the best of circumstances. It effectively did nothing to ward off the torrent of water that pummeled it. With the mostly good weather — well, that and the frequent missing persons that had necessarily captured so much of our attention — we'd gotten somewhat complacent about our housing and hadn't replaced the dried and shrinking fronds with fresh ones. A regrettable lapse.

With as much water as was pouring into the hut, it was hard to tell whether we were any better off inside. In theory, at least, the bamboo sides shielded us from some of the wind. I kept moving from one soggy spot to another, trying to find a not-already-occupied space with the least drippage. It wasn't dissimilar from going back and forth between two checkout lines at the grocery store only to see the one you just vacated move faster.

I gave up and laid down, curling up as tightly as I could squeeze myself, pulling my shirt over my folded legs.

"I'm jealous you can still do that," Daryl said. "If I even gave it a thought, my knees would never forgive me."

Tom said, "Give her a few years. She'll be as decrepit as the rest of us."

"Speak for y'all's selves," Denisha protested. "I'm spry."

For once, Daryl didn't say anything objectionable. I chalked it up as a real growth moment for him. With as cold as we all were and as sopping wet as her blouse was, there were a half dozen comments right there for the taking, and he didn't touch one of them. Or her, for that matter. Like I said, growth.

Rhonda sat in the corner, scowling at everyone. I was trying not to harbor any ill will about the night before. We were all under a tremendous amount of stress. It was pretty much a given that someone was going to come unraveled if things didn't change, but I wanted to avoid being the person who escalated it.

The temperature fell slowly but steadily, and the rain didn't let up. I started shivering not long after, and Denisha laid down between the wall and my back, mashing herself against me like the outside spoon and taking the brunt of the wind and intruding water.

"You don't have to do that," I whispered.

"Hush."

You watch a show like *Survivor* where virtual strangers are cuddling up together at night and think how improbable that seems. You tell yourself that you would never. You're wrong. I was wrong. Necessity drives forced contact. It's not even intimate like it might be under normal circumstances. At least, it doesn't start that way. But when you sleep with half of yourself in contact with someone else for enough consecutive nights, you form a bond that isn't easily broken and isn't quite like anything else. It's weird, and you won't believe me unless you've been in this situation.

With no watches and no sun to cast shadows, it was hard to know how long we stayed under the shelter waiting for the storm to pass. It was probably six or seven eternities before the lightning passed, but the downpour persisted.

Tom sat upright. "I'm going hunting for a goat."

"In this?" I said, pointing outside as if it wasn't abundantly clear what *this* meant.

He shrugged. "I'm no less cold, wet, and miserable in here than I will be out there. Might as well be doing something."

It made a certain kind of sense. Still, it seemed unnecessarily risky. I wasn't his mother, so I let it go, though not without pointing out one more obvious point. "We don't even have a fire anymore." I hadn't seen the fire pit in the last few hours, but I could imagine the coals and ash were a sodden mess that had been stripped of all their warmth.

"We will," he said, as if that settled the issue, and pushed himself out into the weather.

Rhonda looked around at us and called after Tom. "Wait up."

I didn't know whether it was an indictment of me personally or us collectively that she'd rather go on a rain-soaked goat rodeo with Tom than stay in the safety of the leaky hut with us. After the events of last night, though, I had a guess.

Jac fidgeted for a few minutes. She seemed on the edge of bursting. "I'm going to get some fruit. We're running low. Come on, Papi. You're going with me."

Denisha mouthed "Papi?" in my ear, and I nearly burst with laughter. I forced myself to cough several times, trying to cover it. Jac's glare indicated she wasn't buying the facade.

Daryl's grunt was only a superficial resistance. He did as instructed. Seconds later, they disappeared into the gloom.

The thing about being stranded on an island with a bunch of executives is that they're intrinsically incapable of inaction. They've spent their entire adult lives grinding so hard that relaxing is more stressful to them than work. If it's not a diagnosable dysfunction, it should be.

The problem is, it's contagious, if for no other reason than that you start to see yourself as slothful in comparison.

When I made the first movement away from Denisha and toward the front of the shelter, she put her hand on my hip. "Stay. Please. There's nothing to do now that we can't do later."

The words were compelling, but the gesture made my stomach clench with anxiety. I had always been bad at interpreting the intention between contact with other people, frequently making more of it than was intended. Or not? I don't know. It's not like you can ask.

I rocked back into my spot. She didn't move her hand. Not for a minute.

When she took her hand off my hip, she patted me awkwardly, perhaps realizing the peculiar moment she'd created. Then, with one more emphatic pat, she said, "Ooh! I was wrong!"

I rolled away so that I could face her and see what was causing the sudden excitement. "About?"

"About not doing anything now that can't be done later. Everybody is gone. We can check their stuff now."

I groaned and covered my face. She was right, of course, but there would be hell to pay if I got caught … again.

CHAPTER 35
CLEAR LINES OF SIGHT

DARYL DUMPED an armful of wet driftwood onto the pile and shot a glance at Denisha and me under the shelter. "You know, you two could be doing something to help."

If only he knew. We'd been helping in a much more enduring way than bringing something back to camp to burn. Never mind that our search hadn't turned up anything damning.

"You're doing great, Daryl!" Denisha cheered with feigned enthusiasm.

I cackled with laughter.

He scowled and stormed back off into the sodden jungle. While the rain had lightened up, there was still a steady downpour.

"They're not staying together like they're supposed to," I said.

"Okay, Mom." Denisha elbowed me.

"I'm just saying ... what if something happens?"

Denisha shrugged in a not-my-problem kind of way.

When Jac entered camp a minute later with a load of papayas, I cheered with a big "Woohoo! Go Jac!" Denisha whistled so loudly that my ear rang.

Jac didn't look our way or even acknowledge our existence. That was as funny as if she'd reacted poorly. I hadn't acted this obnoxious since I was a teenager. Jac lowered her arms and let gravity pull all the fruit into the food shelter. One papaya missed the mark and rolled out onto her foot. She reached down to pick it up, then swiveled like a shortstop and launched it at us. Denisha and I dove in opposite directions. The papaya sailed between us and out the back of the shelter, leaving a hole in its wake.

I pushed myself upright in time to see Jac give a self-satisfied nod and wipe her hands on her pants before striding back out of camp. Denisha and I gaped at each other with wide eyes. We fell backwards onto our bamboo bed, howling with laughter.

When the laughter ran out and I caught my breath, Denisha sat up, holding her lower abdomen. "Ooh. Got to go." She pushed herself to the edge of the shelter.

"I'll come with."

"No," she said. "You don't want to be there for what I'm about to do."

"Gross." I frowned. "We're not supposed to be alone." I didn't point out that the last time she'd gone off to the bathroom alone, she'd found all that was left of Ryan.

She looked at me intently, all the joy of the previous few minutes swiped from her face. "Nothing's going to happen."

Trying to retain a bit of lightness, I said, "Famous last words."

She smirked. "Fine. If I turn up dead, you can say, 'I told you so.' Deal?"

I nodded.

I was worried as she followed the muddy footpath to the latrine.

Instead of sitting around fretting, I made myself useful and retrieved the papaya that Jac had attempted to bury in my chest. It was laying a few yards behind the shelter, near a tree that it appeared to have struck. A ripe papaya would have burst with that kind of impact, but this one had only a scrape to show for its trouble. My chest isn't nearly as hard as a palm tree. When thinking about the effect the fruit would have had if it had connected, the immortal words of *Tommy Boy* leapt into my mind. "That's gonna leave a mark."

I dropped off the papaya with the other food as the rain slackened to little more than a sprinkle. Off to the west, the sky made an appearance. Before long, the sun would turn this whole island into a sauna as it began the process of drying us off.

The fire pit was a slurry of sopping sand, ash, and charred wood. I grabbed the chunk of bark we'd been using as a shovel and started digging it out. The mixture was thick as wet concrete and no less heavy. After several sweat-inducing minutes of removing the wettest sand, I dug down into the middle of the fire ring. My knuckles and the backs of my hands told me the mixture here was warmer than the top layer I'd removed. Not long after, I uncovered gray coals, and the tiniest hisses rose up to me as the last remnants of the storm waltzed down from the clouds.

Despite my already burning arms, I redoubled my efforts to shovel out more of the sand that had served as an incubator for the nest of coals at the center of the fire pit. They needed some attention now to rekindle a flame, but nursing them back to life would be a far easier task than having to start from scratch.

When Denisha walked up, I gestured with my chin to another piece of bark. "Give me a hand, yeah?"

"Can't. Got poo on my feet."

I paused my work and rocked myself into a squatting position. I looked up at Denisha, my face an open question.

"The latrine overflowed while I was … going. I mean, I didn't make it overflow. It just happened to because of the rain while I was there."

"Uh-huh." I poured as much skepticism as I could into those two syllables.

"Shut up. I'm going to wash off my feet in the str—" Denisha cut herself off. As sudden as a car wreck, her demeanor changed from disgusted to dour. She cleared her throat. "At the beach."

No one had used the old path to the stream in the couple of days since Norm disappeared. We hadn't openly discussed the topic, but it was a place no one wanted to revisit. We forged a new path southwest of camp, through the jungle rather than through the grasses. The route was longer and inconvenient, but a less immediate reminder of our friend's death.

"Hello?! Help! Hello!"

I stood up and whirled around.

Tom was in front of the shelter, running blood-stained hands through his disheveled hair. What was normally salt and pepper now had a red sheen. His hands and forearms weren't the only parts of him that had become crimson. The front of his shirt and pants were splashed with generous amounts of blood, too.

The knife he'd carried on his goat hunt was secured to his hip by his belt. An odd and unnecessarily risky choice when he could have closed and pocketed it. The blade left hard lines of blood on his shirt and pants.

When I stood up, he saw me and took a step in my direction. His eyes were frantic and erratic. Even though I was more than a dozen yards away, I took a step back. I should have checked where I was going first. I tripped on the stones surrounding the fire pit and nearly fell in.

As I recovered myself, Denisha hurried down the path from the latrine and brought herself up short, keeping plenty of ground between herself and Tom.

Coconuts made a clattering noise as they hit the ground to Denisha's right. Jac froze, looking like someone whose fight-

or-flight response was glitching, leaving her precariously exposed.

"Help!" Tom bellowed, showing us his palms.

Denisha asked cautiously, "Are you hurt?"

He looked at her like she'd asked a ridiculous question.

She hadn't. Given his appearance, it was a perfectly reasonable question.

"No. Rhonda's missing. She's just … gone. Vanished."

Something crashed through the brush in the jungle behind the shelter. My view was obscured for the moment, but Denisha and Jac had clear lines of sight. Their faces told a horror story.

CHAPTER 36
LIKE A LIGHTNING STRIKE

RHONDA STUMBLED INTO CAMP. A gaping wound in her chest pumped blood out with every heartbeat.

I covered my mouth to stifle a scream.

Everything about Rhonda was wild and chaotic. With every step, she was on the verge of falling. Something in her open mouth glittered in the sunlight.

She spied Tom and raised an arm toward him, one crooked finger outstretched as she careened in his direction and crashed to the ground. Whatever had been in her mouth spilled out beside her.

Rhonda's heart beat weakly a couple more times, spewing her blood into the dirt before growing still.

I swallowed the terror that was building up inside me and hurried to her side. Since she was face down, positioning my fingers to check for a pulse was awkward. I ended up kneeling on one side of her and reaching over her to check her pulse on the other side. I didn't detect any heartbeat.

Jac yelled, "Get back!" She stepped toward Rhonda and me.

I shied away, but she wasn't hollering at me. She was looking past me.

On my other side, Tom had moved toward us, presumably to help. Jac wasn't having it.

He stopped in his tracks and raised his hands, palms out.

I turned my head back to Jac, feeling like a court-side spectator at a tennis match. Behind her, Denisha bowed on the ground. Her legs were folded under her, and she lay forward over them. If this were a church service back home, I'd have made judgy assumptions that she was working out some issues, but this was the furthest thing from church.

"Why did she point at you, Tom?" asked Jac. Despite the phrasing, it was an accusation, not a question.

Tom gaped at her.

"Answer the question," she roared, a mama bear protecting her cubs.

Tom set his jaw, anger stretching across his face. "She wasn't pointing *at* me. She was reaching *for* me."

"The hell she was," Jac said.

When I had checked Rhonda's pulse, the back of my hand brushed against something near her face. I reached over her again, knowing Tom and Jac were too engaged in their standoff to pay me any mind. I fumbled around in the sand until I found it.

Jac was repetitively accusing Tom, who was still defending himself. As expected, neither had noticed my movements. I latched onto the found object — which was chunky and metal — and drew my arm back to me. Once I had it safely tucked close, I opened my grasp. It was a fancy Tissot chronograph.

The latent panic that I'd set aside earlier burst out like a lightning strike, running roughshod over every nerve ending. I clenched my hand into a fist again.

In addition to the clamor of voices above me, my ears rang violently. My surroundings turned gray. Pain built itself up deep within my chest.

When I realized I hadn't breathed in a while, I expelled the air I'd been holding and dragged in a fresh breath. Color returned, and the pain receded. Once I felt steady enough, I stood up. The duo hardly noticed me.

I was pretty sure the watch was Rhonda's. Why else would someone have shoved it into her mouth like that? The brutality of that made me shiver, but I needed confirmation.

I walked over to Denisha and knelt beside her, setting a hand on her back. Her entire body was trembling.

"D," I said as gently as I could muster.

The trembling intensified, a self-contained earthquake.

"It's me. I need your help."

She shook her head without looking up.

I switched tactics. "Hey. Get yourself together." Harsh this time. "We can't do anything about what happened to Rhonda, but we can figure out if it's the same thing that happened to the others. I need to know if this is hers."

I didn't know much about caring for people who were in crisis, but this probably wasn't the best thing for them. We'd have to deal with that later, though. It was imperative that I confirmed whether Rhonda belonged to the watch.

I peeled Denisha's hand away from her arm and shoved the watch into her palm. Long seconds passed before she moved voluntarily. In the interim, Jac continued barking at Tom, demanding that he tell her where he'd been and what he'd done. Tom offered a variety of answers, none of which she found satisfactory. "You *know* me. I wouldn't do this." "I told you where I was. We were hunting a goat, and after I killed it and while I was field dressing it, she stepped off to go pee. When she didn't come back, I got worried and came here." "I'm not answering the same questions again. My answers aren't going to change." He became unexpectedly calmer the more excitable Jac acted.

When Denisha moved, it was with all the urgency of a desert tortoise coming out of hibernation. She unfolded, bringing herself upright and pulling her hands into her lap.

She looked straight ahead, perhaps gathering the courage to look at the object her fingers were wrapped around.

Denisha opened the hand holding the watch and absently scraped away the sand that clung to it, made sticky by spit and blood. In my hurry, I hadn't thought to wipe it off.

My stomach clenched. Acid rose in the back of my throat. I pushed it down.

Focus.

Her hands grew still again when the watch was as clean as her fingers could make it.

I put a hand on her knee. Softly. "You have to look at it."

She bowed her head as if in prayer. The watch, now cupped in her hands, the offering. A blood sacrifice? Sunday School lessons about Abraham and Isaac flooded my brain. We had most of the elements here. We substituted a goat instead of a ram. Supposedly, it was dead in the jungle somewhere. Maybe the rest of its herd was mourning its death much the same as we were doing. What we were missing was God intervening to stop the human sacrifice and offer up a goat as an alternative.

I couldn't believe those words came back to me. It had been at least fifteen years since I'd been in a youth group where I would have heard them and almost as long since I'd been in any church.

Denisha nodded. "Hers." It was barely audible.

I reached for the watch. She closed her fingers around it in silent protest.

"It's okay," I whispered. Slowly, she relinquished the watch. I stood, dusting the sand off my knees and shins before returning to the fray that was Jac and Tom's battleground. At this point, it looked more like a staring contest.

I positioned myself equidistant from both of them. They both turned their gazes to me. Neither asked who I was going to side with, not using words anyway.

Immediately before I started spitting out words, not really

knowing where I was going with it because everything felt too surreal to be certain of anything, a new voice asked, "What's going on?"

Not a new voice.

A familiar voice.

But new to this conversation.

Daryl.

I had totally forgotten he wasn't with us.

CHAPTER 37
THE ENSUING SILENCE

EVEN DENISHA CAME out of her funk to gawk at Daryl. I scoured him from his balding head to the soles of his shoes, inspecting him for any hint of blood spatter. I didn't see anything, but I was far enough away that it wouldn't be difficult to miss something small.

Jac pointed at the obvious and said angrily, "Rhonda's dead."

Daryl nodded once. "I gathered that."

"Does that come as a surprise to you?"

Something like bemusement crossed his face, but he recovered quickly. "It does."

Daryl was being far more careful than usual. Maybe the snafu after Norm's disappearance and the other dozen times he'd drawn people's ire out here from running his mouth had finally made an impression.

Jac crossed her arms and cocked a hip out. To know Jac was to know this posture meant she was conjuring all the saltiness at her disposal. "Did you kill her, Daryl?"

He shoved his hands in his pants pockets, offsetting her interrogation with a casual air he certainly didn't feel. "I didn't."

"Maybe you did it," Denisha said, "because you touched her in a way she didn't want, and she said no. So you felt weak and rejected, and decided to show her how strong you are."

Okay. Wow. So we haven't let that go, obviously.

Daryl's face ran a deep red. "No," he said emphatically. "That didn't happen."

"Do you have an alibi?" Tom asked.

That seemed awfully bold coming from a guy slathered in steadily drying blood.

"I do."

Maybe Tom should have asked that question in a more open-ended way, but Daryl could have been more forthcoming. What had seemed several questions ago to have been caution was now becoming obnoxious.

"Well?"

Daryl shifted his gaze to Jac, who stared him down.

I thought I knew where this was going. Are you familiar with Georgia's minor league hockey team, the Macon Whoopee?

"Jac and I were together for a while, gathering wood and fruit."

His tone insinuated there was a lot being left unsaid. I decided to see if a little prompting would provide the encouragement he needed. "And?"

"And she wanted to fool around. So we did. We were, you know, making out — I have scratch marks to prove it." He gestured to his back.

Eww. But also, those could have come from Rhonda fighting for her life, too.

Jac stood still as a statue. Fury boiled off of her.

Daryl continued. Now that he was talking, he was going to tell all. "But then — look, man, I've been feeling guilty about … everything … and Gabriela, you know. So I stopped it. Jac got pissed and left."

Tom let the ensuing silence hang in the air for a minute. He prompted, "Jac?"

"What?!"

"Can you vouch for him?"

"Never happened. None of it's true. He's a lying liar who lies."

If this were an episode of *Animaniacs* instead of real life, several of our jaws would have fallen open to the ground, and we would have had to reel them back up with some kind of gear mechanism thing. I'm not an engineer. I don't know what it's called.

Not Daryl, though. He wasn't the least bit surprised. He grinned wryly, unable to suppress the expression.

Tom said, "Jac, it's really important that you tell us what happened."

She wordlessly stormed toward the beach, roughly bumping shoulders with Daryl as she passed him.

The old axiom, *Hell hath no fury like a woman scorned*, may be a gender-reinforcing stereotype, but as applied to Jacqueline, there was a strong argument to be made that in her present disposition, she'd prevail over Hell or any other opponent.

With a lull in the goings-on, I noticed flies had landed on Rhonda. I hurried over to her suitcase and grabbed her captain's jacket and several other articles of clothing. As I walked back to her, I watched the others. Denisha was still shellshocked despite the line she'd hurled at Daryl. The two men were doing literally nothing.

Even when I got back to Rhonda, shooed the flies away, and covered her, none of them stepped forward to help. I know everyone copes with loss differently, but that doesn't mean it's not a little frustrating. Still, I tried to be graceful about it. My meltdown was probably coming. I just had to hope that when it barged in, there'd be someone present who was inclined to act in my stead.

Although I would've rather had everyone here for the next

bit of conversation, I wasn't inclined to chase down Jac. I stepped into what was more-or-less the middle of our dwindling congregation, directing everyone's attention to me. I was usually more prepared in these kinds of situations, with slide decks, hours of rehearsals, and preparation for questions no one would ever ask. But not now. I shot from the hip. "This was in Rhonda's mouth when she died." I held my hand palm up, displaying the watch, then corrected myself. "When she was killed."

Tom and Daryl drew toward it like dogs to a treat. Denisha didn't move off her spot.

Tom picked it up and examined it. "You're sure it's hers? I mean, I guess, obviously, it is. Whose else would it be? I'm just asking."

"Yes. It was Rhonda's"

Tom offered the watch to Daryl, who declined. Instead, he asked, "So whoever made Ryan and Norm disappear also killed Rhonda?"

I nodded. "Seems that way."

Tom asked, "But why not make her disappear too? Instead of, you know?" He glanced over at the cloth-covered corpse.

"Maybe she got away?" I didn't really believe that, but I couldn't get anything else to make sense.

"OW!" Daryl yelled.

Denisha stood behind him with a sharp stick that she had used to poke him. She jabbed it at Tom, but he scurried away like a crab, stopping only when he bumped into Rhonda. Denisha's eyes narrowed with anger. Sand and grime streaked her cheeks. "Maybe you two should start answering questions instead of asking them." She thrust the makeshift weapon out menacingly at no one in particular. "Since you're the only ones who could've been killing all of us."

After being stuck the first time, Daryl rolled into a sitting position and scooted away from Denisha. "It wasn't me," he protested.

She swung her gaze and stick to Tom.

"Well, I didn't do it."

"STOP LYING!" Denisha stalked toward Tom, turning the stick in her hand so she could stab down with it.

Tom was stuck in a sitting position, wedged against Rhonda. He could only move laterally and not quickly, but he didn't do that. He waited on her to advance, legs drawn in like springs. When she closed within a few feet, he struck out with one leg, hooking her behind the ankles, and jerked. She crashed to the sand on her belly. The short spear flew away from Denisha as she fell.

Tom pounced on Denisha. He bear-hugged her torso, pinching her arms against her sides, then rolled over so that she was on top of him and locked his ankles against the insides of her thighs.

"DON'T TOUCH ME!" All but immobilized, she head-butted his shoulder repeatedly.

Tom craned his neck away so she couldn't make direct contact with his face.

"LET! ME! GO!"

He didn't. The chords of Tom's muscles held taut as his blood vessels popped out with the strain.

Denisha's demands devolved into unintelligible screams and from there into sobs, which continued long after she stopped writhing. Her face remained buried against Tom. He unlocked his ankles, and the restrictive bear hug became an embrace.

CHAPTER 38
ACCUMULATED WISDOM

DECIDING where to bury Rhonda was more difficult than I would've expected. Once we arrived at our decision, it seemed the obvious choice. Some combination of physical fatigue and emotional exhaustion prevented us from arriving at it quickly.

Tom set her body down in the soft, dry sand just below the dunes that were overgrown with sea oats and morning glories. Directly out to sea lay the shell of the mostly submerged jet that had brought us here.

When I backpacked in Ireland with a couple of friends after college, we spent a few days on the northwestern coast in a little town called Sligo. There's a mountain nearby, Knocknarea, with a giant cairn on top. Legend has it that about two thousand years ago, they had a queen named Maeve, who was both beautiful and vicious. In an act of vengeance, her nephew assassinated her, but she didn't die immediately. Her dying demand — it wasn't a request; she wasn't that kind of girl — was that she be buried atop Knocknarea so she could watch over her kingdom even after her death. Her subjects complied, but no one forgot her brutality. Everyone who's gone up that mountain for the last two thousand years has carried a stone with them to add to the cairn and make sure she didn't rise from the grave.

Rhonda's burial place reminded me of that. Not because she was evil. Mostly because I thought she'd like that we were laying her to rest in sight of her plane.

I can't even believe I said *laying her to rest*. It's such garbage. Her last minutes on earth were terrifying and painful. Maybe she's getting some relief in whatever life follows this one, but then again, maybe she's not. I read a book once by C. S. Lewis or George MacDonald — I can't remember who for sure, and it's not like I can look it up. The idea was that for people who go to heaven, their life on earth was their version of hell, and vice versa. Hopefully for her, this would be the worst part of her existence.

Rhonda's death had me in a funk. Only a few hours ago, she'd been strong and … whole. Her murder was unlike the others' disappearances. Their deaths still felt theoretical, intangible, whereas hers was as visceral as it gets.

"Over my dead body."

Jac's voice brought me back to the present. She stood beside Denisha, whose feet were planted shoulder width apart with her hands braced to her hips. She gave off strong Wonder Woman vibes. Both of them stood between the men and Rhonda.

Tom reasoned, "It's going to take you twice as long if you don't let us help."

Denisha was quiet and fierce. "I don't care if it takes ten times as long. Her murderer will not bury her."

It seemed like a bad time to mention that lots of people had been buried by their murderers. Younger me would have said it without thinking. In fact, I'm kind of surprised Daryl didn't blurt it out. Present me had accumulated enough wisdom to keep my mouth shut, at least this time. Present me was also still enough of a dumb-ass to run off at the mouth next time.

Daryl held up a finger. *Here it comes.* "If you want my two cents—"

"We don't," Denisha said.

He smirked and tilted his head before continuing, "We—you shouldn't bury her. Put her on the raft and give her a Viking funeral as the tide goes out."

"I don't know what that means," Denisha said.

I thought maybe she did but didn't want to reckon with the idea.

Jac gave her the answer, regardless. "He means set it on fire and send it out to sea."

"We are not setting her on fire."

Daryl threw up his hands. "Fine. Put her in the ground where the bugs and crabs will get her, as if that's somehow better. I couldn't possibly care less." He stormed off toward camp, leaving heavy footprints in the sand.

"You might as well go with him," Jac said to Tom, but with less tenacity than before.

Tom shrugged and followed Daryl. Something about being called a murderer *again* made him disinclined to stick around and argue the point about helping. Hard to blame him for that, I guess. "Y'all don't actually think one of them is killing the others, do you?"

Denisha said, "*The others* is going to be you and me soon enough. The numbers are getting awfully thin around here. Besides, who else? It's not one of us. It's not possible."

It was easy for her to say. She'd only known them a couple of weeks in pretty bizarre circumstances. Jac, on the other hand, had known them for more than a decade. She would be less hasty about reaching that conclusion. "Jac?"

She knelt in the sand and started shoveling it to the side with her hands. "I don't want to think either of them is capable of it. But do you ever really know someone? Like truly?"

"Yes," I said, flabbergasted. "You can know someone well enough to know whether they're a serial killer."

"You willing to stake your life on that?" Jac said.

That's where the rubber met the road. Was I? One of my college professors told us once that he'd been in Young Republicans with Ted Bundy, who'd been the nicest, most charismatic guy, unless you were one of the college girls he raped, murdered, and mutilated.

I kept digging, as did Denisha and Jac. We got through the sunbaked, dry sand and into the perpetually wet layer, where our efforts slowed and heart rates increased. The ends of my fingers weren't quite raw yet, but they would be as the sand tore away layers of skin. Burying people in the sand used to be more fun than this.

Sweat made my hair stick to my face and neck, and ran into my eyes.

Jac said, "Well?"

I didn't have an answer. There was literally no other alternative that wasn't supernatural or extraterrestrial, and those weren't viable. "I don't know. I guess not."

Once the hole was about three feet deep, we figured that would be good enough to keep scavengers away and prevent any erosion from allowing Rhonda to surface. Denisha and I crawled out of the grave.

We lowered Rhonda in as gently as we could, covering her with several articles of clothing.

I asked, "Anyone want to say any words?" Neither woman offered, and I had nothing to say. "Maybe just a moment of silence, then."

The breeze blew gently, and the evening sun stared at us while we were presumably reflecting on the life Rhonda had lived. Instead, I was trying to recall how tall the waves normally were. Right then, they were about head high, and that struck me as unusual.

After what seemed like a sufficient time, we began

covering her with sand. Everyone waited as long as possible to cover her face. I don't know why that felt different, like we were going to smother her. I kind of wanted to reach down and shake her by the shoulder, *Rhonda, are you sure you're dead? Just want to make sure so we don't, you know, bury you alive.* I refrained. She was for sure dead. The flies and already-accruing death stench were all the affirmation I needed.

When we'd finished heaping sand onto Rhonda, Denisha asked, "So what's the plan?

Jac said, "I have something in mind."

CHAPTER 39
A HALF-HATCHED PLAN

FIRE BLAZED over a bed of glowing coals. Despite my suspicion that he might be involved in killing us, I couldn't help but be grateful that Daryl had rescued enough coals to get the fire going again. I assumed he'd have to start from scratch.

He sat in the sand, reclining on arms that propped him up. He barely flicked his eyes toward us as we entered camp. "Y'all look like hell."

No one even acknowledged it.

Jac went to the shelter. Instead of going in, she walked around its perimeter and returned to where I was standing. She showed me that she was palming a length of vines she'd braided into a thin rope. "This isn't what I had in mind for it, but ...." She shrugged.

Daryl asked, "Can one of y'all get me some more firewood?"

I felt bad ignoring the request, but I was about to feel worse. Being rude would be the least of my concerns.

The other two women disregarded Daryl's question, too.

He looked up from the fire, expecting one of us to have gone to get the wood. He nodded his head, grumbled some profanities, then pushed himself onto all fours before getting to his feet. One of his hips popped as he got upright.

As soon as he turned his back to us and cleared the fire pit, Jac propelled herself forward and tackled Daryl. Her form was as good as any linebacker. Daryl arched backward as Jac's forward momentum drove them into the sand.

He thrashed violently, trying to get free. I jumped on his legs and grabbed hold with both arms above his knees. He pummeled me with his heels. Sand invaded my eyes and mouth as we rolled and fought.

Jac yelled at Denisha to grab his arms.

This wouldn't work if they couldn't bind his wrists.

Daryl roared as he fought. His tree-trunk legs broke my grip several times. I regained my hold on him, but it was tenuous.

My eyes watered, trying to rid themselves of the sand that blinded me.

Denisha screamed in pain.

My muscles strained.

Fighting was exhausting.

Daryl yanked a foot free and kicked me in the neck. Fire flashed down my right side. I lost all feeling in my arm.

Daryl's other foot slid out from under me. Jac thudded to the ground beside me with a grunt. Daryl was free.

With my watery vision obscured, I got to my knees, waving my arms in front of my face to ward off any blows that might come my way.

"I'm not—" His breaths came in loud draughts. "Not going to hit you. Sonofab—" Daryl was too breathless even to finish swearing at us.

I felt to my left. Jac was gulping air. When I touched her shoulder, she swung out wildly and backhanded me in the mouth.

"Hey!" Blood trickled from my lip.

She fumbled for me and grabbed hold of my shirt. "Sorry. Sorry."

"It's okay." I dabbed at my mouth with the back of my hand.

Daryl hunched over still with his hands on his knees. "That's what you're sorry for?"

"D?" I looked around for her. She was huddled behind me, favoring the arm she'd hurt in the crash. "You okay?"

She nodded, but tears filled her eyes. She wasn't doing well. On any level.

Apparently, Daryl had recovered both his breath and his bravado. He stood up, hands on his hips, feet shoulder width apart. A tubby, older Superman. "If y'all would've just asked first, I'd have told you I don't have the prowess for a foursome. Probably not even a threesome, if we're being honest with ourselves. But I'm definitely not into bondage."

When no one responded, he grunted in amusement and resumed his trash talking. "The next time I hear about gender equality — and I presume it won't be from any of you — we'll revisit this little episode." He made a twirling gesture with his finger. "Where a fat bastard fended off three women who ambushed him like Nazi Germany blitzkrieging Poland. You know what, I'm proud of that last line. Normally, I wouldn't have thought of it until hours later, then regretted not having been witty in the moment."

We had that in common, at least.

He wasn't done. "You embarrass yourselves. Not just yourselves, your whole gender. In fact, I'm embarrassed for you."

I was done, though. It was enough to have lost, but to sit here and listen to his blathering was intolerable. I stood up and shuffled over to Denisha. I realized I had feeling again in my right arm, and it wasn't a good one. A swarm of bees buzzed up and down my nerves, stinging at random.

I reached down to Denisha to pull her up by the armpits.

She twitched at the contact, but at least she didn't smack me in the face.

My belly grumbled at me, letting me know it was starving. At least figuratively, possibly literally. I was losing weight. My hip bones jutted out more than usual. But I didn't have the energy to deal with a coconut right now, and with the way Denisha was holding her arm immobilized, I didn't think she'd be up for it either.

I guided us toward the shelter. Jac could fend for herself. She'd made her bed with Daryl. Now, she could lie in it.

"Don't go now," he called to us. "You're going to make things awkward."

Something occurred to me far, far later than it should have. I stopped walking and turned back to Daryl. "Where's Tom?"

There was silence while he decided whether he was going to participate in an actual conversation. "Went to get the goat, so it doesn't spoil."

Denisha mumbled, "Or to destroy the evidence."

"How long's he been gone?"

Daryl looked at his wrist out of lifelong habit and scoffed to himself. "Guess I won't be getting that back until I don't need it anymore. A while. He's been gone a while."

I craned my neck to look through the foliage at the gathering darkness.

CHAPTER 40
RESIGNED TO A FATE

"WE NEED to go look for Tom," I said, sitting cross-legged under the shelter. The dark of night had fully swallowed everything now, but the moon was well into its arc across the sky and provided some light.

"Let's be clear," Jac said. "He's one of two people who could be killing everyone — no offense." She flashed a smile at Daryl.

"Some taken, actually."

"Anyway, he might be killing us one by one, and you think it's a good idea to go wander around in the darkness looking for him? Hard pass."

I turned to Denisha, pleading with my eyes. She only briefly met them before casting her gaze back to the ground. I didn't think there was going to be any counting on Denisha for much of anything anymore. Something had broken. The phrase *minimal viable human* leapt into my brain but felt really mean.

Daryl stared at me, daring me to ask him for help. I couldn't bring myself to do it. To his credit, he tried to soften the lingering effects of our failed offensive. "Look, I understand why you did it. Don't get me wrong. It was stupid and misguided and ineffective, but, like, I get it. That said, I'm not going out there at night looking for him. I know I'm not the one doing the killing — even if y'all have a hard time accepting it — which pretty much leaves him. Check with me in the morning. I may be more amenable then."

He laid down and rolled onto his side so that his back was to us. He was being more gracious about the whole being attacked thing than I expected or than we had any right to. Was that suspicious behavior? It was hard to know. My brain had devolved into a pile of mush from fatigue and strain.

I sighed, not wanting to be a fear-monger, but also feeling compelled to use all the cards in my hand. "Y'all know he could be waiting out there for us to go to sleep, right?" I didn't actually believe that and couldn't buy into the idea of Tom being the killer, but they seemed to. So I had to turn it to my advantage if I could.

Jac said, "That's a good point. We'll sleep in shifts, two at a time. And, Alex, no one's stopping you if you want to go out there."

That didn't work out the way I'd wanted. "Fine, I will." I shimmied my way to the edge of the shelter, hesitated after dangling my legs off, and pushed out into the night. I was committed now.

The moon gave me enough light to find the trail that led out of camp into our island jungle. My mind immediately embarked on new trains of thought like, "Remember all the weird stuff that happened in the woods in *The Girl Who Met Tom Gordon?*" A topic best avoided. I counted my steps to give myself something to focus on.

I got to 214 steps before something happened. Every bird stopped its night song. All the insects withheld their chirping, as though they didn't want to reveal their location, or even their existence. I stopped and crouched. The only sound in all the jungle was my heartbeat.

I breathed in deeply, attempting to smell what I could not

see or hear. The scent of earth and decay filled my senses, but nothing more.

If you've never run through a jungle at night, it's not a great idea. There are a lot of things to trip over and even more that slap at your arms and face. Still, that seemed like a better idea than sticking around or moving slowly. I took many fewer steps getting back to the shelter.

I broke into our clearing, breathless and terrified. When I clambered into the shelter, I snuggled up to Denisha, who was already lying on the bamboo. She put an arm around me. It was a long time before sleep came.

When Jac tugged at me a few hours later for Denisha's and my shift, I hadn't had nearly as much sleep as I would have preferred. I also didn't stay awake for much of my shift. Instead, I suffered the fitful sleep of one who is sitting up and knows they're supposed to be staying awake but mostly can't. Every time I roused enough to be aware of my surrounds, I found Denisha staring straight ahead into the darkness. I'd never seen someone who looked more resigned to a fate they assumed was theirs.

Denisha woke me up when the other two started stirring. To the east, purple and red patches blotted the sky.

"No sign of Tom?" I asked.

She shook her head.

"We have to try to find him."

She nodded, but it was only perfunctory.

"I'm going to get the fire going." I didn't have any particular reason for it other than needing something to do. We had plenty of fresh(ish) water and no food to cook. It was mostly a matter of routine and busyness.

By the time Jac and Daryl ambled out to the fire several

minutes later, there was plenty of color in the sky, and the sun had already greeted us.

"Gah! I'm sore. Feel like I got in a fight."

"Har-har," Jac said, punching him lightly in the ribs.

I guess they'd made whatever reparations they needed to. I wasn't sure whether that applied to the rest of us.

"What's for breakfast?" Jac asked.

Daryl said, "I could go for a corned beef hash, a scrambled egg, bacon, and maybe a biscuit or two."

"I thought we agreed not to do this with food."

He shrugged and patted his belly. "The heart wants what it wants."

"Sounds like what your heart should really want is a cure for coronary artery disease," said Jac.

"I can tell you I'm not a big fan of this diet I've been on lately. Man may not be able to live on bread alone, but as rapidly as I'm disappearing, I don't think he can survive on fruit and seaweed either."

I couldn't take any more of this banter that served no function other than to avoid the real issue. "What are we going to do about Tom?"

"We'll go look for him," Daryl said. "As soon as it's light enough."

I squinted toward the sun. It seemed bright enough to me. The whole giant ball had risen above the horizon, but a few minutes wasn't worth picking an argument. Honestly, what were the odds we were going to find him anyway?

CHAPTER 41
APPETITE FOR RISK

NO ONE WANTED to split up. Sure, it would have let us cover more ground in the search for Tom, but our group had dwindled from ten down to four — well, five at the moment, I guess. Tom was like Schrödinger's cat. Anyway, when you and your group survive a plane crash only to disappear one by one on a remote island, you lose your appetite for risk.

As we traipsed through the already sticky jungle that was abuzz with critters, I asked Daryl, "Do you know where he killed the goat?"

"Roughly, but not specifically, no."

"How roughly?" Jac prodded.

"Pretty rough. I know what … uh … hemisphere it's on."

I swatted a mosquito the size of a small bird, and a smear of blood appeared on my arm. The gross part was that it was way too much blood for it all to have been mine.

Jac sighed in exasperation. "Well, *I* know what hemisphere we're on. What good is that?"

Daryl paused the trek and turned around. "Not hemisphere of the Earth, dummy. I know what half of the island we're supposed to be on. Second, no you don't. The only people who would've known whether we'd crossed the

Equator are the pilots, and in case you've forgotten, they're dead."

"I've got bad news for you, you big gaslighting galoot. We never crossed the Equator."

Daryl looked at me for confirmation.

"No idea," I said. "Geography wasn't really my thing."

We could have asked Denisha. Maybe she would've known, but all the evidence I saw that morning showed that she was retreating further into herself.

Time for a diversion from any bickering that was about to ensue. "Did y'all know no recorded hurricane has ever crossed the Equator?"

"Uhh … okay." Jac's voice boiled with sarcasm. "Thanks for that invaluable contribution."

As we followed the game trail the goats had been taking for … how long? Hundreds of years? Probably ever since some Spaniard's ship crashed and at least two of the animals were fortunate enough to wash ashore.

I tried to keep my bearings, but the dense foliage and winding path made that a chore. When we'd started, the promontory had been to my left. Now, though? Only God in Heaven knew, and maybe only Him if His omniscience could permeate the canopy.

All I knew for a certainty is that if I walked in a straight line long enough in any direction, I'd hit water within a couple of miles. And from there, I could make my way back to camp … eventually… probably. It all worked in theory, but I'd rather not have to test it.

Every few seconds, I could hear someone slapping their skin. A futile war against the insect horde. Our scents attracted them in droves, and we were putting off gobs of odor.

"Hold up," Daryl said, holding his fist up in imitation of every Vietnam War movie he'd ever seen. "What's that?"

Jac peered around him to the right. I moved over to his left side. Denisha stayed behind me, entirely disinterested in whatever was happening.

A body lay in the path ahead of us, but at this distance and in the relative dimness, I couldn't tell whether it belonged to a man or an animal.

The wind gently nudged the trees and shifted the light. I glimpsed blue on the body. Not a color found in nature. "It's Tom." I started toward him right away, but I hadn't gotten far when I realized the body was far too small and not the right shape to be Tom.

The blue cloth I'd seen hadn't been a trick of the light. A tattered remnant of Tom's shirt had fallen on the goat. All around it, grasses were trampled and small plants were broken. The area was a disheveled mess.

Flies landed on the goat by the dozens, crawling in and out of the incision Tom had made to remove its organs so the meat wouldn't spoil. I turned around to warn Denisha to stay back, but I needn't have bothered. She hadn't followed.

Lying in the dirt beside the goat was the Garmin smart watch that Tom touted to anyone who would listen in his constant proselytizing of all things anti-Apple. Jac bent down to pick the watch up by its leather band. Tom liked to say it was "both classy and utilitarian. Bougtilitarian, if you will." No one would. It was a monstrosity of a word.

She handed the watch to me. It was definitely Tom's. I tapped the screen. I don't know why.

The watch came to life. Displaying the time and date. MON, SEP 4. 10:04. Tears shone in my eyes. It was a weird reaction, and there's no accounting for it. The watch displayed other information around the perimeter of its face. NOW 83° | ALT 4. Alt? Altitude. I fumbled and nearly dropped the watch in my excitement over the revelation. "Look! It knows where we are."

Jac and Daryl crowded around me. Even Denisha stepped up to look over my shoulder.

BARO 1010▾ | BATT 5

Daryl asked, "Anyone know anything about barometric pressure?"

"Low is bad." That's all I remembered from reading *Isaac's Storm* by Eric Larson years ago.

"Is 1010 low or normal? Or high?"

Denisha's voice was husky when she spoke. "Falling barometric pressure means a storm is approaching."

The three of us looked at her in unison. Her cheeks pinked, and she stared at the ground. Even as we stood there, BATT dropped from 5 to 4.

Tom had always bragged about the battery life on this watch, but it appeared we were nearing the end of even its prolonged cycle.

"Click on GPS," Jac said, pointing.

I touched the screen, which changed to an image that it took me a second to figure out — . Around it, a series of roving dots showed it was thinking. BATT 3.

Using the GPS must drain it more quickly. Literally a race against the clock.

A map appeared. Central America was on the far left. Cuba and the tip of Florida at the top. There were other, smaller islands as well, but the text was too small to read. Colombia and Venezuela bordered the bottom of the screen. The watch began zooming in on an entirely blue area.

BATT 2.

It took a long time before any brown or green was to be seen among the water. When the map stopped magnifying the image, our island and its smaller neighbor were little more than debris.

BATT 1.

I made a pinching motion on the screen, trying to see what was there to be seen. Whether there were any other islands, preferably inhabited, in our vicinity. Nothing. Blue in all directions. The Caribbean had always seemed so small. It was, relative to other major bodies of water, but that didn't mean it wasn't large enough for a tiny plane with a small crew and passenger manifest to get lost in it.

The screen winked to black.

"At least we know," Daryl said.

And with the knowledge we'd gained, all the hope we'd been reserving was dashed.

CHAPTER 42
LAY DOWN AND QUIT

THE DEAD WATCH brought our attention back around to its likely dead owner and the dead goat that cluttered the game trail in front of us. In that moment, I wanted to lie down right there and die along with everything else. What was the point of doing otherwise? To borrow from the writers for Star Trek, "Resistance is futile."

Even if I managed not to get murdered by some sociopath serial killer, I was going to die here. On this island. In the middle of nowhere. Maybe not tomorrow or next week. But eventually. The first time I got sick and needed medication. When I got a cut that turned gangrenous. When my body decided I wasn't consuming enough calories and started cannibalizing itself. It didn't matter when or how. It would happen here.

Why not lie down and quit now just to be done with it?

I wallowed in self-pity for about as long as I could get away with it before my pragmatic side kicked in.

So, I'll tell you why not.

I'm incapable of letting questions go unanswered.

It's why Sunday School teachers got exasperated with me.

It's why, when I was a senior in high school, I got called

into the principal's office and was told to stop asking questions I knew the physics teacher couldn't answer.

Frankly, it's probably why none of my relationships stood the test of time either. Of course, that problem had been resolved for me. As had the matter of presumptuous great-aunts at family gatherings asking when I was going to settle down and get married.

Island living has a few perks. They are just heavily outweighed by all the murder and mayhem.

"Daryl's right," I said. "We know with more specificity what we already knew to some degree. Nothing is close. Not that it would matter if something were relatively close. We have no means of communication or transportation. We haven't seen a ship or plane in nearly three weeks. Whatever happens here is up to us to deal with. It's up to us to keep ourselves alive."

Jac pursed her lips. "It's also up to whoever's killing everyone to stop doing that. It would go a long way to helping us stay alive."

She had a point. "It would probably help if we quit putting ourselves in vulnerable positions. Everyone who's died was killed when they were alone."

Daryl crossed his arms. "I can't be around y'all every minute of the day. I need space, or I'm going to lose it."

"Since you brought it up," Jac said, "you were the only person who was alone when Tom ... you know." She flicked her hand toward the empty space where we found his watch.

Daryl huffed and balled his hands into fists. "Are we fu—are we really doing this again?! Have we not already ruled me out?"

That's not exactly how I remembered it. *Inconclusive* is where I think I landed with Daryl.

Jac shrugged. "All I know is the three of us were together ... uhh ... plotting against y'all. You and Tom were off by yourselves."

Her reminder of the attempted coup did nothing to assuage his frustration. "Fine. Let's look at this realistically. You see all these smashed up plants? There was clearly a struggle. Feel free to raise your hand if you think I came out here, got in a fight with Tom, won, killed him, got rid of his body — however I would even do that — got back to camp without a scratch to show for it all, *and* had enough left in the tank to fight off the three of you."

He stared intently at Jac, then me, waiting for a response. There was no need to engage Denisha.

"That's what I thought." He crossed his arms. "So, let's be done with this garbage about me killing anybody. I've had enough of it."

It was either a great argument or a convincing front. I should have been taking notes all along so I could keep everything straight. It was all running together. I couldn't remember where everyone was when each of the killings happened. There were too many moving parts.

One question stood out more prominently than any other. How was it that you could have four murders happen in the span of a week on a tiny island with only one body and no viable suspects?

The critters that had quieted during Daryl's tirade picked up their chirping again.

"But who then?" I asked quietly.

Jac gave an answer that displayed an unusual level of resignation. "I don't know. It doesn't make sense. None of it makes sense." In the next breath, she followed up with her customary level of feistiness. "Whoever it is better know that if they come for me, there will be hell to pay."

I had no doubt that Jac would give as good as she got, but I also wouldn't have expected anyone to get the best of Tom. So what did I know?

Daryl pointed behind us. I turned as quick as a hiccup,

expecting the worst. When I didn't see anything, I jerked my head back toward him.

"Jumpy much?"

Uhh … yeah. Kinda.

"The trail splits back there. Either of y'all remember which way we came in?"

I returned my attention to the trail. A lot had happened in the last little while, and I couldn't recall whether we'd come in on a right curve or left. Besides, the landscape looked a little different now. The shadows were murkier, and the clouds that passed persistently over the sun made everything look like it was moving.

"Just pick one," Jac said. "It's an island. It's not like we can get too lost."

"The goat?" Daryl asked.

I said, "Probably spoiled by now."

He nodded in agreement.

Daryl chose a path, and we followed. It was not the right path.

CHAPTER 43
BETTER THAN DROWNING

THE COMBINATION OF HEAT, humidity, and obnoxious mosquitoes was no less unrelenting on the wrong path. What changed was the sound. We kept walking long after we knew we were going the wrong way, and after a while, I noticed something new. I think it had been present for a while before my conscious brain noted it.

I called out, "Stop." I needed to hear it without the rhythmic trampling of our feet. In front of me, Jac and Daryl halted. Because I was holding Denisha's hand so we didn't lose her, she stopped with me.

For several seconds, we were all but statues, listening to the persistent crashing of artillery in the distance. My feet vibrated with the force of the exploding shells.

"It's every seven seconds," Jac said.

With the next thud, I began counting. *One Mississippi, two Mississippi ... Seven Missis—*

She was right.

The deep bass that resonated all around us made it difficult to determine what direction the sound was coming from. As best I could tell, though, our path was carrying us toward it.

"Keep going?" Daryl asked.

I shrugged.

Jac sighed. "Yes, keep going. What else would we do? Pretend whatever this is isn't happening on our island."

Yes didn't seem like the correct answer to her rhetorical question, but it's the answer I wanted to give. I was pretty sure that any further terrible surprises would be the straw that irreparably broke what remained of my mental and emotional well-being.

Another few minutes made it undeniably clear that we were approaching the concussions with their unfaltering rhythm. A short time after that, the sky made itself visible through the trees ahead of us. Daryl stopped before following the slender game trail out of the jungle and onto open ground.

"It's okay," Jac prodded gently.

"Easy for you to say."

He took a deep breath, exhaled slowly, and walked out of the jungle.

I stepped forward, planning to follow in his wake. I nearly slammed into Jac, who hadn't moved and held out an arm.

"What?" I asked.

"Hang on. No sense in all of us getting killed."

I shook my head. "Savage."

She shrugged.

From beyond the brush, I heard, "Whoa." The expression was quiet, almost reverent. Not a descriptor that I was accustomed to applying to Daryl.

I pushed past Jac into the sand and open air. After squinting and shielding my eyes with my hand, I saw what had captured Daryl's attention.

The beach wasn't being bombarded with shells, but with waves that were more than twice my height. Each pummeled the earth with ferocity before withdrawing to make room for its successor. Wispy strands of clouds reached over us like talons. They were linked to an arm that extended back to the horizon, where the body of clouds was much more substantial.

"That can't be good," I said.

Beside me, Denisha said in a husky voice, "Hurricane."

Chills ran from the base of my skull down to my fingers. My daddy would have said, *Did a possum run over your grave?*

Jac asked, "You sure?"

Denisha nodded.

Her pallor had been bad before. It was worse now, but in some ways, it felt like an improvement. There was fear in her eyes now; a replacement for the emptiness they'd held until a moment ago.

Daryl said, "How do you know?" It didn't come across like the challenge it might have been in other circumstances.

"We're from Biloxi. People still talk about Camille. I was there for Katrina. There've been plenty of others." She jutted her chin out toward the oncoming storm that was still beyond the horizon. "This is what it looks like."

Jac suggested, "Maybe it's just a tropical storm?"

Denisha shrugged.

A distinction without a difference, as far as I was concerned. We were on an island with no proper shelter. If the wind and debris didn't kill us, the storm surge would sweep us out to sea. And that would be that.

I looped my arm through the crook of Denisha's. I needed a little human touch. "How much time do we have?"

Several waves thundered into the island while she considered the question. "Tomorrow. Sometime tomorrow."

Even as we stood there, hypnotized by the rhythmic pounding and awed by the force of the swells, the tendrils of the clouds reached beyond our island. They were harbingers traveling ahead of the storm.

Daryl turned to us. "Any ideas for surviving a hurricane?"

I pivoted, facing the island. To my right, the rocky promontory rose above the trees. Hope sprung up in my chest. It was more fleeting than eternal, but I clung to it with everything I could muster. "There's our high ground."

Three heads turned in unison.

"There's a cave," I added. "Actually, it's more like a tunnel because it runs all the way through. We checked it out a couple of weeks ago. It can probably fit all four of us and our stuff. It'll be snug and uncomfortable, but …" I didn't even know how to finish that sentence, so it just kind of meandered into nothing.

"But it's better than drowning," Jac said.

Yeah, that was the right ending.

Daryl asked, "How far is it from camp?"

"Less than a mile." I turned my head to find Denisha, hoping she'd chime in. She was still staring out at the horizon and appeared to have withdrawn back into her shell. "About a ten-minute walk."

"Realistically, how much stuff can we get in there?"

I thought back to the few minutes I'd spent in there. It seemed like such a long time ago. "Whatever we need. Food and water. Suitcases. The real problem is one of the openings faces that way. You can kind of see it from here." I pointed even though we were already looking that direction. "Fortunately, the tunnel kind of bends, so we won't catch the brunt of it head on."

Daryl shrugged, as if to say, *What other choice do we have?*

The answer, not that he'd asked, was none. We had none. I envisioned a flickering blue hologram of Princess Leia beckoning, *Help me, little cave. You're my only hope.*

"I'm sorry," Jac said. "I've been holding this in as long as I can, and I can't take it anymore."

I braced myself.

Daryl, too, was grimacing.

This was a terrible time for a revelation.

"Has anyone else noticed that coconut water tastes like suntan lotion? It's disgusting, and don't even get me started on cucumber water. I'd rather drink pickle juice."

I laughed. A genuine laugh I didn't know still resided in me.

CHAPTER 44
THE GATHERING STORM

THE HURRICANE BEARING down on us could have done us the small mercy of cooling the temperature before its arrival, but it didn't. The overcast sky should have given some relief. Instead, it made things more oppressive. Even the wind, laden with humidity, was stifling. This is how the inside of a convection oven must feel.

There was so much wind. Not gusts, but sustained, driving winds. One of my brothers, who lived in Oklahoma for a while, told a story about how during one of their storms one night, the wind pushed around planes that were parked outside of hangars and on the tarmac. We weren't quite there yet, I didn't think, but it was coming.

I looked to the west, but thousands of trees, all waving their limbs and leaves in distress, cut off my view of the gathering storm. All the fronds in the palm trees fluttered in one direction. Fluttered is the wrong word. It doesn't have the right connotation. They clung for their lives. I had bad news for them: this was just the beginning.

I had to extend the bad news delivery to myself as well. After only two trips of dragging suitcases across the sand to the higher ground at the base of the promontory, I was already exhausted. Sand spattered every inch of me, chafing places I didn't even know touched each other.

"Are you alright?" Daryl asked as he and Jac trudged in the opposite direction as me.

I was glad to see our failed arrest hadn't taken too much shine off their relationship. Neither had him spurning her, I guess. Maybe they saw themselves as even now, or maybe their bond was deeper than the surface-level attraction I inferred it to be.

I paused and used a gritty forearm to wipe away the sweat that was about to drip into my eyes. "I'm okay."

"Denisha?" Jac said.

I waved my hand behind me without looking back. "Coming."

"I thought we agreed on a buddy system?" She had to raise her voice over the sound of the wind even though we were only a few feet apart.

"I can't get anything done if I wait on her. She's a mess."

They nodded in concession and resumed their trek to gather another load of stuff. I reached back around behind myself with both hands, grabbed the handle of the suitcase, and leaned forward like the good oxen that I was. My rotator cuffs were taking bets on which would be the first to go. The right was heavily favored. Years of volleyball and softball had contributed more wear and tear to it.

I wondered if I would be better off if the luggage didn't have these stupid, tiny wheels. They seemed to contribute more drag than anything else. The volume of cussing that I let loose — both in decibels and quantity — while struggling was kind of impressive.

Despite everything, I smiled at a memory that it jostled loose. An elementary school version of me with front teeth that were several sizes too large for my little face. Getting my avatar killed in Zelda for the six-hundredth time. Running together strings of curse words that were both nonsensical and emphatic in their delivery. I had very little experience with swearing and wasn't very good at it. The ineptitude led to further frustration and me throwing a controller that narrowly missed the TV and shattered against a bookshelf. My parents were going to ground me, but realized they didn't even have to bother with the formality because I'd broken my last controller. Experience eventually taught me that the gratification you get when you break something while pitching a fit doesn't last as long as the regret.

As I pulled myself out of my memory well, I noticed something peculiar. The beach was much larger than it had been before. The water had receded well below the normal low tide line. I remembered seeing a video of this with the hurricane that hit Tampa a couple of years ago. The wind was literally pushing the water away from this side of the island. I imagined the reverse was occurring over on the west side. Whatever marked the usual high tide was either under water or in the process of being obliterated.

Fish who'd been unfortunate enough not to keep up with the recession flopped in the previously unexposed sand. It was entirely possible the storm would deal me a similarly unceremonious end. It might, but I wasn't ready to concede anything.

With a grunt, I leaned forward and dragged the bag to the base of our new rocky lair, the home of earth's most remote lost luggage depot. Though while none of our bags were actually lost, most of them were now orphaned.

We weren't out of the woods just because a hurricane was arriving, either. I'd seen enough suspense movies to know that storms make great cover for murders, so there was that to look forward to.

I shoved the bag I'd been lugging against the base of the rocky swell and plopped down on top of it. I leaned back, determined that my makeshift recliner wasn't all that uncomfortable, and closed my eyes for a couple of minutes.

Maybe more than a couple.

"Comfy?"

I jerked forward.

Jac stood at my feet, staring down at me. Behind her, Daryl was huffing and puffing the last few steps. His splotchy, red face gave me cause for concern. If he'd been wearing his smart watch, it would have been blaring a warning at him. *Hey, it looks like your heart rate is nearing 200bpm, at which point your heart may decide to combust. Just thought you should know.*

"Sat down for a sec. I must've fallen asleep."

I expected a sharp retort from her but got only a nod. None of us had been sleeping well. Three murders in four days would do that to you.

She gestured to the cave entrance. "What are we taking up?"

"All of it? What we don't take may get blown away or swept off, depending on the storm surge."

Jac nodded in resigned agreement.

Daryl wiped his sweat-soaked face with the front of his shirt, exposing a belly hairy enough to look like a wool under-shirt. "You said the other opening was south-facing?"

"Yup."

"You think we could block it up with some of the suitcases?"

"Yeah, that should help," I said. "Some wind and rain will still get through, but at least we won't be totally exposed. We probably want to get the cloth ones so they have some give and won't crack."

Jac nodded. "And we can fill in the gaps with clothes and stuff."

That meant going through our dead friends' possessions. It didn't feel right, but no one objected. If it were my stuff, I'd want us to use it … to the extent you can want anything when you're dead.

"Alright," Daryl said. "We'll handle this end of things. Why don't you go check on Denisha?"

"What's wrong with her?"

Jac answered. "She wasn't in camp when we went back."

"Did you look for her?"

"Kind of. We checked the creek and the latrine. Hollered for her a few times. She didn't answer."

Daryl said, "Which doesn't necessarily mean anything since she's like two-thirds zombie now anyway. No. What do you call it when people aren't in a coma but they don't respond, like that kid in *Ferris Bueller* pretended to be while Ferris' girlfriend changed in front of him?"

"Catatonic," Jac said.

He snapped his fingers and pointed to her. "That's it." This was the most animated he'd been in days.

I knew he wasn't trying to be mean-spirited, but it sure came across as insensitive, at the very least. Instead of making a whole thing about it, I said, "I'll go get her."

"Want me to go with you?" Jac offered.

"Nah, I'll be fine."

As I took off back toward camp with my shirt snapping in the wind, I wondered if I would regret turning down that offer.

CHAPTER 45
FRAGILE AND FRACTURED

DENISHA WASN'T at the latrine (where she'd been the one to find what was left of Ryan's remains). She wasn't at the stream (where she and I had found what was left of Norman), which was losing its way in the sand now that it suddenly and oddly had a much longer journey to the sea. She wasn't in camp (where Rhonda had died in front of us).

There were so many places she could be, but so few places that she actually would be. If I were Denisha in her fragile and fractured state of mind, where would I be? Likely somewhere that gave me comfort or peace. Those places were in short supply on the island, so maybe a better question was, where was the last place she was comfortable?

That sparked an idea. I strode out of camp and hung a left when I hit the beach. A few hundred yards away, the jet that had been mostly submerged now more closely resembled a beached whale with wings.

Wind whipped sand all around me, pricking and stinging my skin. Despite keeping my mouth shut, grit found its way in, scraping against my gums and teeth. I kept my eyes squinted, blessing my daddy for the long lashes that my mother was always jealous of. Behind me, my footprints were swept away or filled in within minutes of me leaving them. The storm was remaking the world anew before it arrived and destroyed its creation.

Something dark snagged my attention in the sand ahead of me. My breath caught in my throat. I stopped walking and squatted down, bracing myself with one hand.

Quit! I fussed at myself. *You don't even know what it is, you big baby.*

I do, though. Maybe not exactly, but close enough.

When I'd gathered enough fortitude, I wiped away the tears that had gathered so the sand wouldn't stick to my face and stood up. One agonizing step at a time, I forced myself toward the dark object in the sand, which eventually became several dark objects as I got closer.

Written in driftwood and stones were an S, an O, and an incomplete third letter that would never be the S that Denisha had intended it to become. Her watch lay within the O, not in the middle like some kind of bullseye, but haphazardly off-center where it had been unceremoniously dumped.

I considered leaving it. The storm would carry it off or bury it soon enough. Maybe it would cleanse the island of all of us. A baptism of sorts. Ultimately, I reached down and snagged it. The other two would want more than my word for it.

Turning my back to the distress signal and the driving wind, I faced the sea, the now-elongated beach, and the wrecked plane that had been Denisha's solace. My eyes blurred with tears again as I considered our unexpected friendship. I let myself marinate in my feelings for a few minutes, knowing that I'd soon have to become more analytical and go back into survival mode.

I discovered a set of divots in the sand in front of me that I don't think I would have noticed if the light hadn't shifted. I looked up and over my shoulder. The diffuse lighting of the overcast skies grew dimmer in the late afternoon light.

Finding the divots again, my eyes followed a whole column of them leading from where I was out to the jet. Some had been lost to the wind or water, but they were clearly footsteps.

Not that long ago, I wouldn't have been able to tell you that those steps showed me they were leading away from me, as opposed to toward. After three weeks of living on the sand, though, you can't help but pick up a few things. The toes make a tiny cliff wall on the down-step and kick out sand behind them on the up-step. Even in their deteriorated condition, the pattern was visible. The packed sand had preserved them just enough, though with the weather being what it was, they would have been erased entirely within a few more minutes.

I lost the trail when they hit the waterline a dozen yards from the plane. It was clear, though, that they made a direct path for its door. What had she been doing? Even though I held her watch in my hand, I thought for a moment that she might be on that plane right now. Longing burst into my chest until I thought about the condition that our departed CEO's body would be in now, which made my stomach clench.

It was then I noticed another set of divots leading in an arch back toward me, away from the plane. Whatever she'd done, she came back. Maybe she shouldn't have. There was a predator lying in wait for her here.

I swirled around, having convinced myself someone or something was about to pounce on me, camouflaged atop the dunes by the sea oats. There was no one and nothing, except for Rhonda's grave, which I hadn't spotted or thought of until now. Whatever happened here had been done within a stone's throw of where we buried her.

A revelation dropped me to my knees. I know that sounds like hyperbole, but it literally swept my feet out from under me. I collapsed under my own weight, which seemed suddenly excessive.

It was Jac or Daryl. Or both. That seemed ... improbable?

Not a strong enough word. Impossible. I *knew* these people. They weren't capable of murder, and not just murder, but the extermination of all of us.

I was on all fours, panting like an overheated dog. Hyperventilating and trembling.

I thought I'd ruled out one or both of them. I couldn't think clearly. The wind was too loud. My vision dimmed.

I couldn't pass out. Lying here helpless and exposed might mean I'd never wake up.

I slowed my breathing, becoming intentional about it.

Once the world around me regained its color, and my heart stopped redlining, I stood up. I gave myself another minute to take in the incomplete S.O.S., a more dire cry for help than she even knew she needed. The last work of Denisha's hands.

My brain only allowed me three-and-a-half steps before reminding me of a Sunday School lesson. Daniel and the lion's den. The Old Testament prophet was to be fed to lions for disobeying the king's law that no one pray to anyone other than him.

There was a difference, though.

Daniel had to be forced into the den. I was walking in voluntarily.

Not only that, I was helping to build the den we'd be trapped in together until the storm passed.

CHAPTER 46
IN THE LIONS' DEN

WE HAD GROWN SO accustomed to sleeping outdoors — yes, I still consider a three-walled and frond-roofed shelter as being outdoors — that spending the night in the gloomy tunnel stood in stark contrast. My fingers told me the puffiness under my eyes was pronounced. I didn't need a mirror for confirmation. The intersection of mourning Denisha (as abbreviated as it had to be), refusing to allow myself to fall into a deep sleep, and alerting at the slightest movement that might mean my untimely death, was wreaking havoc on my skin care.

When we eventually retreated for the night, I positioned myself nearest the cave entrance. No one asked why or argued the point. I'd prepared a couple of lines about claustrophobia in case they asked questions. If I wanted to expose myself to the elements, Jac and Daryl wouldn't impede it. They were probably hoping that Mother Nature would send along a tree to bash out my brains and save them the trouble.

Daybreak hardly bothered to announce itself, though the hurricane wasn't at all shy about its introduction. The world outside our cave revealed itself in incremental shades of blue. It was hardly recognizable, what we could see of it anyway. Jac and Daryl crowded me when we got as close as we dared to the entrance. It took a conscious effort not to flinch at every touch.

The wind literally howled. It had at least doubled in strength since sunset. No shortage of debris filled the air.

"What was that?!" Jac said. By the time she pointed, whatever it had been was long gone. The storm appeared to be stripping from the island every small thing that wasn't rooted to the earth.

Looking further out at the water, Daryl said, "The seas were angry that day, my friends." He immediately looked back to make sure we'd caught the reference.

Seinfeld was on almost constantly in my house during my formative years, so I hadn't missed the reference.

"What?" Jac said. "Was that some kind of impression?"

Daryl looked insulted. "George Costanza. *Seinfeld*. The whale and the golf ball episode."

She shook her head. "Didn't watch *Seinfeld*. I was a *Friends* girl."

"So the thing about television is that things have different time slots, so you don't have to choose one to the exclusion of the other. You can actually watch both." When she showed him the bird, Daryl doubled down. "And the miracle of streaming services is that you can watch nearly anything anytime you want."

"I didn't like it. All the characters are assholes."

"Yeah, but that's part of the bit. They don't hide it and pretend they're not. As opposed to *Friends*, where they're all selfish jerks you're supposed to think are cool."

I had decided during the night that I wasn't going to engage with them, but my resolution didn't hold. It was impractical. I chimed in. "I prefer *It's Always Sunny*."

"What's that?" Jac asked.

Daryl said, "A show. It has the guy in it who owns the

soccer team with Ryan Reynolds. You'd hate it. It makes the people on *Seinfeld* and *Friends* look like saints."

"You've watched it?" That genuinely surprised me.

"I gave it a go, but there's so much yelling. Charlie Day was almost funny enough to keep me attached to it, but not quite."

"Fair enough."

The rain that pummeled the ground had arrived during the night and become relentless. George Costanza had been wrong about his seas being angry. Those seas had been mildly irritated at best. What I saw looking out of our aperture now was unbridled fury. The waves were no longer organized, just foamy swells that crashed on top of each other.

After Daryl grew bored with the destruction, he went to the back of the tunnel to check on his plug, as he'd taken to calling it. He came back impressed with his work. "I did good."

"Well," Jac corrected him. "You did well."

He rolled his eyes. "I'm about to get killed by a hurricane. Grammar is the least of my concerns."

"Weren't you just bragging that your handiwork was going to save us all?"

He shrugged. "I'm only one man fending off an angry planet. I can only do so much."

It was difficult to believe these people were plotting my death. If they were, why wait? And why would Jac have led the attack against Daryl just a couple of days ago? Was he acting alone? But when would he have had time to kill Denisha and hide her body without Jac knowing?

Jac said, "What are you hiding behind your back?"

Daryl grinned, then brought his hand around.

I was more than half expecting a knife.

He had a deck of cards.

"Where'd you get that?" I asked.

"Rhonda's bag."

Jac scrunched her face. "Were you sniffing her underwear again?"

"I — what are — that's not true." He looked at me with wide eyes. "I didn't do that."

"I believe you."

The relief on his face was as palpable as the disappointment on Jac's that I didn't play along.

Obviously, I didn't ask the most pressing question. *Are you going to kill me?* It's not that I didn't want to ask, but more that I didn't want to provoke it.

"The reason I was in her luggage," Daryl said, feeling the need to justify himself, "was that I was using clothes to fill in the gaps between the bags and the tunnel walls, or else wind and rain would spray in here the whole time. This way—"

Jac sighed, exasperated. "I get it. Also, I don't care. I was just messing with you."

"Rummy?" I suggested.

Jac held out her hand, and Daryl obediently transferred the deck. We sat in a triangle. Jac shuffled, making a bridge that I was jealous of. I'd never gotten the hang of it. Maybe I could get her to teach me. It's not like we had anything else to do.

A dozen games later, Daryl jumped up and danced around frantically like a character in a video game that was glitching.

"What?" Jac asked.

"My heart medicine. I forgot it."

"It's not in your bag?"

"No," he said. "I keep it wedged between two bamboo shoots beside where I sleep."

Jac shoved her hand toward the tunnel entrance, where the current squall had cut visibility down to a few dozen yards.

"You can't go out in that. You'll just have to wait and hope it's still there."

Daryl shook his head adamantly. "I have to. I'm not going to have a stroke out here."

Jac stood up and folded her arms across her chest.

I stood too, because it was weird to be the only person still sitting. "Aren't you going to run out soon, anyway?"

"I've got like three weeks' worth left. I've been only taking half a pill a day since we got here."

"Hey!" Even in the diffuse light of the storm, Jac's distress and anger were evident on her face. "You're not going to have a stroke. You'll be fine."

"The doctor said—"

"No. You *might* have a stroke if you don't take your blood thinners. Fine. But you're *definitely* going to die if you go out in a hurricane."

I recognized the look on his face. He was done talking about it. If he'd had a rain jacket, this is the moment he would have cinched it around himself. Instead, he just brushed past Jac on his way out of the tunnel. Even before he began sidling along the ledge, the gale whipped at his clothes and overly long hair.

Jac raised her hands to the sides of her head and clenched fistfuls of hair. After several minutes, and not knowing what else to do, I put a hand on her back.

Slowly, she released her hair and lowered her hands. "That's the last time we're going to see him alive."

I inhaled sharply in surprise. "Jac, don't say that."

She was right, though … mostly. If past results indicated future performance, we wouldn't see him after his death, either.

CHAPTER 47

INTO THE STORM

"I'M GOING TO FIND DARYL," Jac said.

"You can't." I rushed forward to where she stood near the cave entrance and grabbed her hand. The storm was deafeningly loud. I shouted so she could hear me. "You won't come back."

"I'll be back." She patted the top of my hand. "I have to try."

There was no stopping her. I knew that. For most of the last several hours, she'd been pacing like a caged tiger. Still, I had to try. She would be walking out to her own death, just like Daryl. At least he'd done it under the guise of some muddled form of self-preservation.

She was doing it for … love? Lust? Friendship? It was a messy relationship, and it didn't matter what the motivation was. Short of calf roping her, I couldn't stop her. Not that I didn't try one more time. "He's gone, Jac. There's no way to find him in this."

She jerked her hand away from mine and bolted into the mayhem outside. Normally, I'd say she stormed off, but that seems a little heavy-handed, all things considered.

Jac would be lucky if she didn't get blown off the rock by

the gales that occasionally carried small trees past us now. I wondered if storms like this were the reason why the Caribbean Islands shared so many common plants. It seemed like a stretch to suggest they were a net positive, though. Even if it helped distribute seeds, how much more did it kill? How would that poor little herd of goats survive this? I wouldn't have been totally surprised if they decided to bunk with me. I wouldn't have been upset about it either. Sure, they'd smell terrible and leave goat turds everywhere, but at least I wouldn't have been alone.

This was the first time I'd been alone in any real sense since we left for Colombia … how long ago? A month? A lifetime? Twenty days here on the island. A week in South America before that.

Alone doesn't adequately describe the sudden, oppressive isolation that beset me. I was cut off from everything beyond the couple hundred square feet of cave the hurricane had confined me to. Fear and claustrophobia clawed at me.

Sitting as near as I dared to the dry ground closest to the entrance, with my arms wrapped around my legs, I leaned my head against my knees and sobbed. Three weeks of pent-up fear, anxiety, and mourning poured out in undammed emotion, unfettered by other obligations or social pressure. I cried until my chest hurt and my throat was raw.

When I was done, I felt … not better, certainly. I'd just been abandoned, regardless of Jac's and Daryl's good intentions. I still considered it abandonment even though I had recently thought they might kill me, which seemed unlikely now.

Relief. That's what I felt. It was a weird sensation. Not relief from my circumstances, which were admittedly dire, but relief from a burden I'd been carrying. With that set aside, it was time to do something productive.

At home, when I needed to do something to keep me from spinning out of control, I'd clean my apartment. I don't especially like cleaning. I would rather have been weeding in a flower garden, but I couldn't justify home ownership based on preferring one chore over another as a means of therapy.

While there weren't any showers to be scrubbed or floors to be mopped in the cave, there were definitely things I could do to delay thinking while I waited on Jac's hopeful return.

We had piled the meager food stores in the middle of the tunnel. I separated them into categories and lined them up neatly. Coconuts and papayas beside each other. A partial bag of masa. An empty suitcase to serve as a water basin, though there wasn't a practical way to refill it right now that wouldn't result in it being transformed into a UFO.

After that, the luggage. Stacked according to shape and made into miniature ziggurats. I even pilfered Jac's and Daryl's bag, laying out dry sets of clothes for when they got back. Not clean sets. None of us had those anymore. Dry would have to do.

It's possible that I also rummaged through their stuff for evidence that would betray them — my watch, a knife, a letter confessing to being a serial killer. No such luck.

When Jac's arms rose over the lip of the ledge and clawed at the ground, I rushed out to help her. I didn't know why she was scaling the promontory instead of using the trail we found, but it hardly seemed like the time to ask.

Sideways torrents of rain buffeted us. I grabbed her by the armpits and hauled her up, the fronts of her legs scraping against the stone. As soon as we cleared the edge, she bucked against me and wrangled herself free.

Somewhat bewildered by the reception, I took several steps backward and saw what I hadn't initially observed.

A deep laceration on Jac's left arm poured blood.

My instinct was to grab something to wrap around the

arm to apply pressure. I quickly checked myself, which resulted in me staring at her like a calf looking at a new gate. Doing nothing.

She reached into her pocket. I flinched. Even though it was involuntary, I was mad at myself for the reaction.

Jac flung Daryl's stainless-steel watch down in front of me. It made a clatter that I heard over the din of the storm. I had no idea why he wore a watch that heavy. It seemed unnecessarily cumbersome.

This was a much different presentation than how I'd shown them Denisha's watch about this same time the day before.

My blood felt cold. Every nerve dialed itself up to eleven.

"What happened?" I pointed at her arm.

She looked down at it. "Tree branch flying at me. I blocked it. Thought it was broken at first, but I think it's okay."

Maybe that was true, and maybe it wasn't.

"We need to close that up," I said.

The light outside was growing weak. Daryl's watch said it was only early evening, but very few waves of light found themselves able to permeate the storm.

Jac pointed at her suitcase. "The divider flap thing in the middle. There's a pocket. My sewing kit's inside it."

I stepped over to the bag without turning my back to her. It sat atop one of the stacks I'd made, her dry clothes laid out on top of it. "I set out some clothes for you. Hope you don't mind."

She nodded.

I set them aside and opened the lid. I found the sewing kit and made my way back to Jac, trying not to show how wary I was. I gathered she was as on edge as I was by the way she narrowed her eyes at me and consistently turned to keep me in front of her.

"We never did get to use this for fishing," I said.

She let a quick half-smile pass over her lips. "No."

"It was a good idea, though."

"Yeah."

"Here, sit down," I suggested.

She didn't move.

I sat first, with my back at an angle to the entrance, so that when she sat, her arm would face the light. She followed her cue, though not without obvious reservation.

Her clothes were soaked and soiled, and she shivered despite the warm air.

"I'll go get one of your blazers and something to wipe off this arm."

She nodded, but her gaze never left me as I retrieved both things. I draped the jacket over her shoulders. After I sat beside Jac again, I laid her arm over my knees. I dabbed at the jagged cut. She winced. The water on her arm had thinned the blood and made it look worse than it was. Still, the wound was long, but not as deep as I'd thought.

Pulling the needle, thread, and tiny scissors from their pouch, I licked the end of the thread and threaded it through the needle on the first try. A minor miracle unto itself.

I steeled myself for what I was about to do. I hardly liked handling raw meat when I was cooking. Now, I was going to sew someone's arm up.

I readied the sewing needle. "This is going to hurt like hell."

"Hang on. Daryl's bag." Her voice cracked when she said his name. "There's a bottle of that liquor."

That would help take the edge off for her.

When I gave it to her and she pulled the cork with her teeth, she poured the contents over the wound. Then she took the swig I was expecting.

CHAPTER 48
A SOUND THAT WAS LOST

IMPOSSIBLY, the hurricane continued to increase in intensity long after darkness blanketed us. The darkness was all encompassing. As jarring as lightning would have been, at least it would have broken the monotony, but there was none: only brutal wind that regularly smashed objects against our stone prison trying to crack it open to get to us.

The rain was effectively a waterfall. There were no drops, and describing it as a sheet would be inadequate, because a sheet has no depth. It was like the water had replaced the air. Except in our cave, where, against all odds, Daryl's dam of luggage and clothing held. Regardless, the water found ways to intrude, forming lakes and rivers that ran the length of the tunnel. These prevented us from lying down. There wasn't a single dry space large enough for it.

Jac and I were isolated on our separate islands of high ground. We occupied the same time and space, but it was nearly possible to forget the other person was there. I could sense nothing beyond what was touching me. A total displacement of any proprioception.

I had no trouble filling in the gaps with visions of every

horror I'd ever seen in a movie, and some that I came up with on my own.

Maybe I had died, and this was hell. If so, I'd expected the lake of fire to be much less wet and temperate.

Something touched my arm.

I screamed.

A sound that was lost in the storm.

When the touch became a pat, I realized it was Jac. I patted her hand in return. She grabbed onto my hand and held on.

We stayed that way for a long time. Hours maybe. Or just a few minutes. I don't know.

Until something changed. Something I couldn't immediately identify.

The deafening roar of the hurricane muted. Imagine being by the stage at the loudest concert you've ever been to and someone just turns off the sound. That's what this was.

"Jac?" I said, entirely too loudly.

"Shh. Look." She pointed at the end of the tunnel.

I saw her point. I could see Jac. Light!

We both stood. My stiff, aching joints required a minute before they let me get fully upright. I was a living depiction of the evolution of humankind, going from chimps on all fours to fully upright homo sapiens. Jac took even longer.

Warily edging our way to the end of the tunnel, what awaited us there was awesome. I know it's kind of a trite word now, but I mean it in the most literal sense.

The air that greeted us was sticky and dense. Chaotic waves smashed into the base of the rocky promontory. The water was a seething mass. Walls of thick clouds surrounded us on all sides, extending tens of thousands of feet into the air. Above them, a display of stars like I had never experienced. I've seen pictures of the Milky Way splashed as millions of pinpoints of light streaking across the sky, but until that moment, I didn't know the naked eye could pick it out.

I didn't have to show Jac. She craned her neck like mine.

We didn't speak during those few minutes of reprieve.

The southern wall of clouds migrated toward us at a faster rate than was obvious in the relative darkness. Rain soon spat in our faces, and the sound of the gale announced that our waking nightmare was only half over.

It had something new in store for us.

We retreated to the relative safety of the cave before the eye of the hurricane passed fully over us. When the storm hit, it did so with all the force that had been abrading us before, but now the wind came from the opposite direction.

We were not prepared for that.

The squall blew in sideways through the open end of the tunnel. If we'd been thinking clearly, we'd have realized this eventuality was about to beset us. We were now on the other side of the hurricane's counterclockwise rotation.

"Jac, where are you?"

"Right here," she shouted.

She was close. "Keep talking."

Like a broken recording, she put herself on repeat, saying, "My name is Jac, and I'm right here."

I groped along the tunnel wall, making my way to her. I didn't want to lose contact with the wall and stumble out of the cave and to my death below. In the process of feeling my way around, I felt up Jac, which stopped her recording mid-sentence. I grabbed her hand and turned around, keeping my opposite hand to the wall now.

In absolute darkness, Jac and I fled to the cave's barricaded end, but not before it soaked us to our cores.

The distance wasn't enough to escape the deluge. Even though the rain spattered against the cave walls and fell to the floor long before it got toward the back, we still had the flooding to contend with as water poured into the cave and piled up against the luggage.

"We've got to move this," I hollered, patting the luggage loudly. "It's damming everything up."

We were ankle-deep already.

I found the handle at the bottom of the bag nearest me and tugged. It didn't budge at all. After more than twelve hours of torrential rain, it was completely waterlogged.

"We're going to have to take it down from the top."

"Okay," Jac said.

"You start on the other side. Move them behind us to make a half wall. Two across instead of three, so the water can get out. If we can. We might not have to lift them."

"Got it." She splashed the few feet to the opposite wall.

Her grunts told me she immediately got to work.

I tugged at the top bag, which inched its way off the suitcase it sat on until gravity brought it crashing to the floor, flinging water all over me. Not that it made any difference. A furious wind ripped through the cave now that it had an exit point.

The swearing that followed a heavy thud to my left suggested Jac was finding the work as taxing and frustrating as I was. Several seconds later, I heard a zipping noise and things plopping into the water.

That's why she got paid the big bucks.

I unzipped the bag I was working with and yanked out articles of clothing, several shoes, and a toiletry bag, then tilted the bag forward to dump out the standing water. Suddenly, it was much more manageable, but it developed a new problem. It was so light now that it floated. I rummaged around in the ankle-deep water for the clothing I'd discarded, rung it out, and tossed it back in.

"Where you at, J?"

"I've moved my first one. Put yours beside it."

I followed the sound of her voice and did as instructed. We used the same approach with the second set of bags but met with resistance for the luggage sitting on the ground.

Between the weight and accumulated water that pushed against it, I couldn't pull it in.

"Just push it over the cliff," Jac yelled.

That might work.

"What if it's mine, though?"

"It's not. Yours is in the middle stack."

Later, I would wonder how she knew that since we still couldn't see anything. Maybe she was humoring me so I'd let it go and move on.

"You're sure?"

"Yeah. Sure."

I sat down in front of the bag, put my feet up against it, and kicked. The water sucked me forward like a toy toward a bathtub drain. I was suddenly yanked to the left by my shirt collar and bra strap. I fell and lodged against the middle pile of luggage.

Jac hovered over me. "Didn't think that through, did you?"

My legs had turned to jello and my toes tingled from the post-adrenaline rush. "Huh-uh. How did you know to grab me?"

"Thought you might do it that way."

"How did you do it?"

"Didn't. I'm going to open it and empty it before I move it."

I could hear the smirk on her face. A face I would've liked to punch just then.

CHAPTER 49

HUNKERED DOWN

WE PASSED A DREADFULLY long night hunkered down behind our barricade. I spent much of it trying to remember how far down it was to the rocks at the bottom of the world's newest waterfall. That gave rise to wondering if Jac had been tempted to let me go. I didn't ask that part out loud.

With the first gray light of morning, I saw that my hands had turned to prunes. My feet were likely worse. Being able to see again felt like one of the wonders of the world. Jac had dozed off despite being wet and cold.

I got up slowly so as not to wake her.

Though the wind had given up some of its intensity, the rain still blew in squalls. The sea was no less a horror show than it had been at last light.

The sliver of island that served as our neighbor to the south had been stripped almost bare of foliage, but it was no longer the final resting place of our venerable CFO. Whatever was left of him had been carried off and delivered to the salt-water scavengers.

I shuffled through the cave, feeling like the undead. Two nights in the cave were taking a heavy toll. I stopped before I got to the north entrance because of the bursts of rain blowing in with such force that I leaned into the wind for support.

Even with the limited field of vision, it was clear the hurricane had left behind a wasteland. I was Noah peeking out of the ark, hoping for dry land. With nothing habitable in sight, I wandered back to Jac, who stirred when I sat down.

"How was it?" she asked.

"A mess." I took off my shoes one at a time. Blanched and wrinkled feet glared back at me. If I didn't figure out a way to dry them out soon, I'd develop a problem, and the last thing I needed was infected feet. Make that the second to last thing — being murdered on this island was the last thing ... though it would resolve the foot issue.

The late afternoon didn't bring any sunshine, but there were notable improvements in our situation. The rain blew itself out, and the low ceiling of clouds broke apart so that everything felt significantly less claustrophobic, except inside the cave. If anything, those walls seemed even more intrusive after I'd been confined within them for nearly two whole days.

"Should we go see what's left?" Jac asked.

I nodded. I didn't really want to see the remnants of our island home. It was incredible that I'd come to think of something so primitive in those terms, but when that's all you have, you take what you can get. But I also felt a compulsion to go.

The last time I'd been on the beach, we could walk out a couple hundred yards before meeting the water. Now, though, we picked our way across the undulating terrain of the dunes because most of what had been beach was carved away. The tide, which was still irregular due to wind that would have been considered heavy under normal circumstances, lapped at the dunes in many places.

Looking inland, the jungle was a hellscape. What had once been lush was stripped bare. Surviving here would be nearly impossible without a constant source of fruit. There weren't enough calories to sustain us.

I said, "How do you think the goats fared?"

"I expect they would've bunked with us except for a strong sense of self-preservation."

I didn't follow. "Huh?"

"What do you think I mean? We've killed a couple of their kind and all but two of our own. They figured they're better off taking their chances with a hurricane."

That was an awfully surly response. It was also curious that she said *we've killed*. I could only speak for myself, but I hadn't killed anyone.

As for Jac, there were people she couldn't have killed, like Tom and Rhonda, if I remembered correctly. But she definitely had an opportunity with Denisha and Daryl. Was this a multi-person effort? Someone else started it, but she finished it. That didn't feel right, either.

What felt right hardly mattered, though. I had to be unfailingly aware of her. Starting at that moment. I slowed my pace slightly so she would walk ahead of me. She slowed hers to match. Perhaps we were equally wary of each other, which made sense.

The stream that marked our near-arrival to camp foretold what we were to expect. It was becoming a pond as its path to the sea had been obscured by reorganized sand dunes and debris that littered its path. I'd have to fix that, or it would eventually flood our clearing.

As for camp, the fire pit was filled in. Only a few stones remained to mark its place. The food storage hut was gone entirely, though the stake we used to break open coconuts remained. I saved looking at the shelter for last and was surprised to see it had held together better than expected. Some ribs were conspicuously absent, but the raised floor held together. The only thing missing entirely were the fronds that comprised the roof.

That cheered my heart a little. A repair should be easier than a rebuild. It was hard to celebrate, though, when I was worried that the only other survivor of our venture might try to murder me.

Unless … and this hadn't even occurred to me until now. What if the "murders" were some kind of elaborate hoax that I wasn't in on? I mean, the only body I'd actually seen had been Rhonda's. Maybe her disappearance had just gone wrong. Everyone else was off hiding somewhere else on the island, waiting for the game to play out.

"Jac?"

She paused, clearing off the bamboo base of the shelter. I'm not sure why she thought that was a sensible thing to do. With no roof and the wind still blowing like crazy, stuff was going to fall back onto it. But, whatever.

"Hmm?" she answered.

"Do you think … forget it. Never mind." It was too absurd an idea to say out loud.

"Not 'never mind.' Ask."

I decided on a different question. "Where did you find Daryl's watch?"

That was a mistake.

Jac's face reddened, and her eyes flushed with tears. She clenched her fists. "As if you don't know."

I had no idea how I was supposed to know. But I didn't have a chance to ask, because Jac was already storming into the jungle. I said to her retreating back, "I'm going to break up the dam at the stream."

Before unclogging the drain, I got into the pond, even though the water was murkier than I would have preferred. Several days' worth of ocean spray and cave grime begged to be washed away. I accommodated.

By the time I got to the middle, I was in over my knees.

Almost impulsively, I sat in the water. I hadn't been immersed in freshwater in a long time. Fresh being relative only to salt-water and not indicative of cleanliness.

I slid down and tilted my head back, feeling the water crawl up my scalp as my hair floated around my shoulders. Finally, I let myself go all the way under. I wasn't going to walk around with all of me having been baptized except my face.

While I was under, I opened my eyes. I don't know why.

I thought I saw Jac hunched over me, arms extended, ready to hold me under.

I gasped, taking in a half gallon of pond water, and thrashed around. When I surfaced, I flung myself to the far bank. Coughing and half blind with fear.

Jac stood on the other bank, her head tilted as she watched me. Her clothes dry except for the sweat marks. She waited while I coughed up all the water I'd inhaled. When I was more or less finished, she said, "If you're about done with your spa day, I could use a hand."

There was a lot of acid in that tone.

I had something clever to say in response, but my effort to speak led to another bout of coughing and sputtering. I nodded my head, and Jac strode back to camp.

I didn't want to comply immediately (because I occasion-ally need to act out like a petulant child). So I squatted down by the dam of bramble and debris that had wedged itself against the backs of the dunes, gumming up the works.

After several minutes of disentangling things and tossing them toward camp to use for our eventual fire that I hoped we could figure out how to make, there was a satisfying gush of water. The pond began transforming back into a stream.

CHAPTER 50
OPPOSING FORCES

AT CAMP, Jac had made significant progress in getting it to look habitable again. She hadn't touched any of the structures yet, but she had cleared out all the stuff littering the ground and made it into a tidy brush pile.

"We need to get some bamboo to replace the broken or missing ones in the shelter. Have you seen the machete?"

I hadn't and said so. Jac huffed like it was somehow my fault that something went missing while we'd been beset with a hurricane.

"Maybe some bamboo fell during the storm," I suggested. "We can look for the knife while harvesting it."

"Harvesting? What are you, a farmer?"

This was fun.

"I think that's probably about all I'm going to have energy for today, and the afternoon's getting late. We'll probably need to wait to bring over the luggage until tomorrow."

Jac sighed and dropped the palm fronds she was carrying so she could cross her arms. "It wouldn't take as long if you hadn't stop to take a bath."

Being passive-aggressive is my go-to move in these kinds of

situations, but I decided on a more direct approach. "Do we have a problem?"

"I don't know. Do we?"

I stalked off toward the closest grove of bamboo to see if I could find something useful. "I'm spending the night in the cave again," I said over my shoulder. "You can sleep wherever you want."

Surly Jac was a miserable experience. I'd rather she just kill me now than torture me first. I told my brain that if she came back to the tunnel, I needed to stay awake, at least until she fell asleep.

I woke from a dream that I was choking. The weight on my chest made me think I was having a heart attack. The pain and crushing pressure on my throat ripped me out of my confusion.

The low-slung moon slipped out from behind a cloud to reveal a sneering Jac hovering over me, strangling me.

I clawed at her face.

She arched backward, which relieved some of the pressure on my throat.

I shifted my hips and dumped her off me before she could recover. I scrambled to my feet and retreated, trying to breathe. While I hunched over, Jac rushed me. I stuck out a fist. It wasn't even a punch, more like a stiff-arm. She ran right into it and grunted as it expelled some of the air from her lungs.

I circled away from her without turning my back. In moments like this, all your thoughts are more impressions than fully formed ideas. But I got the fleeting notion she hadn't been in a fight before, notwithstanding our failed attack on Daryl. Not that I was an expert, but I'd at least had older brothers and their friends to fend off, and whatever Tom had tried to teach me.

When I'd caught my breath, I croaked, "What the hell, Jac?"

With her hands on her knees, she spat at me. "I don't know how you did it or why, but I'm not going to let you kill me, too."

I was dumbstruck. Her comments earlier in the day fell into place. "I don't know what you're talking about."

"Liar!" she screamed. "There's only two of us left."

"I thought it was you."

"No!" she shrieked and charged me again. Her hands were outstretched like talons, one of which caught me across the face when I backed into a wall. She took several layers of skin with her as her momentum carried her away from me. I trailed after her and shoved, sending her sprawling.

She sprung to her feet and swiveled, like she expected me to be on top of her. I wasn't. I still wanted to talk my way out of the situation. "Jac. Let's talk about this."

I couldn't see her very well. The moon must have gone behind another cloud. I heard a click come from her direction. The sound of Tom's pocket knife locking.

I had no intention of being stabbed to death by a madwoman.

The south entrance of the cave was behind Jac. There was no going out that way. All that waited out that exit was a sharp drop to jagged rocks and maybe water if I could get far enough out.

My only chance was to get to the farthest exit before Jac and get far enough down the goat trail to stay out of arm's reach long enough to disappear into the jungle. I was pretty sure I could outrun her, so I spun and took off, staying low so I didn't bang my head.

I was wrong.

A couple of yards before I got to the exit, Jac caught my heel. I went skittering headlong toward the cliff I had first scaled a little more than a week ago. My chin and palms scraped against the stone. I flipped onto my back in time to see Jac pouncing on me, knife raised high over her head in both hands. I loaded up my legs like a springboard and exploded outward as her weight landed on me. My body groaned with the opposing forces, but I sent Jac flying sideways.

She landed on her hip, but when she put her hand down to brace, she disappeared over the side of the cliff.

I jumped to my feet, startled at the suddenness of it. And waited. For something to happen. Anything.

When several minutes passed in which no sounds came from below and no hand reached up over the ledge, I crept to the edge of the cliff.

The moon came out again. It, too, wanted to see what became of Jac. I hesitated before looking over. I didn't want to look, but I had to know. It wasn't even curiosity, just necessity. When someone is trying to kill you, you're obligated to keep up with their whereabouts.

I pulled in a half-dozen slow deep breaths and took the time to check my wounds. My chin was bleeding, but my hands were only scraped. Based on feel, the claw marks on my face would leave a mark for a few days but shouldn't have me looking like a supervillain.

Having worked up the nerve, I looked over the edge and immediately rocked back on my heels. I sat down, hoping to avoid passing out or throwing up. Or both.

Jac's body was piled on top of her head, which was bent so far back that her heels nearly touched it.

When I tried to stand up, my legs were wobbly. I had to check again. My stomach roiled at the idea of it. I could be sick if I had to, but there was no avoiding checking again. I laid prostrate and pulled myself forward, using all my restraint to force my eyes to stay open.

Jac's broken figure stood out in stark contrast to the dark rock around her. She hadn't moved and wouldn't move again.

I wriggled backward and rested my head on my arm.

CHAPTER 51
STEP OUTSIDE AND ROAR

I DIDN'T LIE THERE LONG on the side of that cliff. Even calling it a cliff was doing a disservice to actual cliffs. No matter the extremity of my sudden and overwhelming exhaustion, I could not stay in that place. Not with Jac dead below me.

I killed her. Sure, anyone would say it was justified. But that didn't make her not dead, and it didn't make me not a killer. *Her* killer.

Her attempt to kill me might also have been justifiable, thinking as she did that I murdered everyone else.

But she couldn't honestly believe that. Not if she was the one who was murdering everyone. Honestly, that seemed increasingly implausible, even though it was the only sensible explanation. I couldn't try to solve that right now. It might break my brain, which was in a fragile enough state anyway.

I hurried into the cave where I collapsed onto a nest I'd made among some of the softer bags. My arms and legs were jittery, and my heart raced. I lay as still as possible to settle myself down. When I closed my eyes, Jac's twisted body raced toward me, sending my heart rate through the roof again. If I died of a heart attack now, there would have been some irony to that. Was that irony? The word is so misused; I can never remember its correct usage.

I jumped up, jerking my head back and forth. When I thought I heard something, I roared in sudden, inexplicable rage. The noise reverberated all around me. Even my feet vibrated with it.

It took me a while to identify what I was angry about. Maybe it's something I didn't figure out in the moment, but only in retrospect. Things are still kind of tangled up. Jac. I was so mad at her. She could have fallen a hundred different ways and survived any of them, most without serious injury. But landing throat first with your body coming down on top of you isn't a recipe for survival.

In the darkness, my mind projected the scene on repeat. It could have played out so many other ways.

Also, a part of me — not one I'm keen to admit to — was jealous of Jac. This was Day 22, assuming the clock had passed midnight. For Jac, and for everyone else who'd been on that plane, the nightmare was over, while I was stuck living it.

My body ached with the effort of being awake, but there was no way sleep was going to find me in that cave. You can do a lot of things and immediately follow it up with sleep. For me at least, killing someone wasn't among them. Maybe that was for the best.

I scanned the darkness to figure out if I needed anything to take with me. Nothing presented itself, and it's not like I was leaving it behind forever. Besides, I wanted both hands free to navigate the rocky trail by moonlight.

I grabbed a spare shirt from the bag nearest me and tucked it into the waistband at the small of my back. When I ventured out of the tunnel again, a pit formed in my belly. I knew I had to check the situation on the ground again. I wouldn't let this turn into one of those things where the person doesn't make sure the other one's dead, and then — surprise! — knife to the throat.

I leaned out. Jac was still dead.

The moon and stars glittered overhead, showing off after several days of being obscured by layers of clouds. The trail leading across and down the promontory was a subtly lighter ribbon of gray than the rock that generations of wild goats had worn down. I picked my way carefully and slowly. I was in poor shape, both physically and emotionally, to do anything in a hurry.

At the intersection between the trail and the ground, which I reached without incident, relief poured over me. It didn't last. I came to a decision that replaced my relief with icy dread. While Rhonda's was the first dead body I'd handled, I was about to add Jac to the index.

I followed the promontory's curve back to Jac's location and brought myself to a stop several feet short of where she had landed. There wasn't a good way to do this. At least, there wasn't a gentle or gracious way to do it.

In my other life, where I could waste thirty minutes … sometimes more — don't judge me — scrolling through Instagram videos, I came across a stand-up comic who talked about a summer when he was a lifeguard. After a man had a heart attack and died at the top of a water slide, they had a long discussion about how to get him down. There was the awkward and hazardous method of carrying him down the ladder. Or there was the other way.

I straddled Jac's torso, squatted to get under her armpits, and lifted. Her head lolled grotesquely under her. I hugged her closer with one arm so I could cradle her head with the other and lay her down. Then, I moved down to her legs and disentangled them.

Kneeling beside her, I pulled out the extra shirt I brought with me and covered her face. I tucked the shirt under the back of her head so the wind wouldn't blow it away.

"I'm sorry," I whispered before walking away.

Our footprints in the dunes from earlier presented themselves in the moonlight. I followed them back to camp without incident. When I arrived, I made directly for the shelter and crawled onto the bamboo slats. I curled up, wishing right away that I had something to cover her with, as much for my physical comfort as for alleviating the feeling of being exposed.

I pulled my legs up tight to my chest and brought my shirt down over them. In my head, my mother scolded a childhood version of myself. *"You're gonna stretch that out, and I ain't buying you another one. You hear me?"*

That's when the tears fell again. They carried on for a long time, and at some point along the way, I drifted off to sleep.

When I awoke, the western sky was already a middling shade of blue. My nose tingled with a sharp smell. Smoke rose from the fire pit, where someone squatted. They turned to look at me and waved.

CHAPTER 52
A TROPHY OF SORTS

I BOLTED TO MY FEET, disbelieving what I was seeing. Not only *what*, but *whom*. After getting upright, I didn't know what to do. I stood there gaping.

Ryan raised his eyebrows and held an amused smirk on his lips. "I've got some breakfast going. Be just a couple more minutes." He turned his attention back to the fire and used a knife to poke at whatever he had cooking.

"You're dead."

Without looking at me again, he put the knife against his left forearm and sliced. A cut appeared. Blood dripped down his arm into the sand. "Not dead. We can talk about it when you're ready. I understand this is a bit much."

The weight of the revelation landed on me. "It was you? The … everybody … you?"

"Well, to be fair, not *everybody*." He gestured as though he were putting off praise and feigning some kind of absurd modesty. "You did a number on Jacqueline over there. Saved me the trouble."

My hands went to my mouth. Ryan's appearance had been such a shock to the system that I hadn't even thought of Jac since waking up. "It was an accident."

"Umm … that's not the way I saw it. But who am I to judge?"

He was obviously amused with this whole thing, while I seethed with fury and confusion. I couldn't not ask follow-up questions to the comments he left dangling. That was by design, of course. I was a cat swiping at a laser, even though I knew I was being toyed with. "But why?"

"In due time. After breakfast maybe. It's ready, by the way."

Ryan slid a fish fillet from the air fryer basin onto one of the stones comprising the restored fire pit.

My stomach growled. I couldn't believe it's betrayal.

I approached cautiously, trying to sense whether this was some kind of trap. He didn't pounce as I closed the gap between us. I couldn't find any animosity in his demeanor at all. I noticed his arm had stopped actively bleeding.

When I got to my modified plate, I reached for the fish but stopped abruptly and retracted my arm.

"It's not poisoned, if that's what you're thinking. Not my style."

"Please don't make light of it."

He shrugged.

Even though steam rose off the flaky white fish, I pinched off a piece and shoveled it into my mouth. Easily one of the best things I've ever eaten. I hadn't had fresh meat in a while and had eaten hardly anything in the last few days.

"Pompano," he said. "They love the northwest end of the island … where y'all never go, by the way."

"We searched for you."

He held his arms out, knife still in one hand. "Not very well. Jacqueline and Daryl were too busy trying to get in each other's pants like horny teenagers. Norman and Rhonda were inept. It wasn't any trouble to stay hidden, then stalk them as they walked the perimeter of the beach. I could've done any of you any time I wanted, you know."

"But why?"

"Why not?" he said indifferently. "Y'all weren't the first, and if I can figure out a way off this island, you won't be the last."

I stopped eating. My stomach turned at the admissions. He was a monster; a casual, callous monster.

"You know the great thing about flying rich people in private jets around the world?" When I didn't answer, he continued. "I'm in a city for a few days at a time. Long enough to get the lay of the land, tend to my particular needs, and leave, never to return. That's not why I got into flying, but it's worked out pretty well for me."

I wanted to punch him in his smug face, and I really wanted him to stop talking — it was obvious he desperately wanted to brag about all this to someone. But I also had questions. So many questions. "You faked your death, then?"

"I did. Had to sacrifice one of those poor goats, but it was for a good cause."

"How'd you get the watches?"

"I already had a plan by then to rid myself of all y'all. But when Tom pitched his watch behind him, this total moment of inspiration — like a real light bulb moment — struck me. I came up with the watch party thing right there on the spot." He was so proud of himself. It was disgusting. "Once everybody went to bed that night, I crept out to the beach and got the watches. Just in time, too. The tide was coming in. I thought it would make for a trophy of sorts, or a memorial or whatever, to leave where I took someone."

I stood up and walked away from him, heading for the beach. As far as I knew, I'd never been in the presence of a murderer before. And I'd certainly never had someone confess murder to me. It was too much.

"Take your time," he said to my back.

I stopped at the top of the dune, having forgotten there was no beach right here. The hurricane had raked it away. I made my way north toward the plane, where some remnant of a beach had withstood the storm. The aircraft itself looked to have taken a beating too. It lay askew, rotated ninety degrees so that the tail stuck out like a peacock's facing the island. The driver's side wing — I know there's not a driver's side and a passenger's side in planes, but I couldn't help but think of it that way — looked to have broken and lodged in the sand, so that the opposing wing rose steeply into the air.

It was a distressing sight, though I couldn't say exactly why. It's not like I'd stored up any hope in that plane. In fact, I was here because of it. It didn't do what it should have. Didn't withstand a lightning strike like it ought to, was made to. Anger surged through me. An accumulation of disappointment and heartache. I felt it bubbling to the surface, readying itself to pour out.

I pushed it back down. Now was not the time. Not yet. And if things went poorly, maybe never.

Ryan was back at camp, and he fully intended to kill me. He hadn't said that explicitly, but I certainly inferred it from the context.

I tried to come up with a plan so I wasn't only reacting. Because he definitely had a vision for how this would go. I couldn't overpower him. I got the impression I wasn't likely to outwit him. Maybe I could seduce him? I looked down and pushed up my battered bra. Gah. I'd rather be dead that let him touch me. Besides, I didn't trust myself to pull off something like that. It wasn't really in my bag of tools.

My feet carried me back to camp. I'd have to improvise and hope for the best.

CHAPTER 53
NOTHING TO RUN TO

"WHERE ARE THEY? Where are the bodies?"

Ryan perked up. "Okay. We're just going to jump right into this? I'm intrigued. Honestly, I saved you for last because I'm kind of tired and thought you might be the easiest to deal with." He pointed his finger at me and waggled it playfully. "I think I misjudged you. You've got gumption."

The human mind is a weird thing. While he was talking, I underwent a weird progression. I went from offended that Ryan had decided to kill me last to proud of having gumption to being disgusted with myself for caring what a serial killer thinks of me.

Focus. "You didn't answer the question."

He raised his hands above his shoulders, conceding that he wasn't going to distract me. He returned his attention to the fire he was piddling with, then waved dismissively toward the water that we could hear, but not see, from where we were. "You didn't see them?"

Instinctively, I looked, even though there was nothing to be seen. Turning back to him, I said flatly, "No."

"Oh, you saw them. You just didn't know it."

I couldn't imagine what he was talking about. "This is a fun game."

"The plane. They're all in the plane. Except Rhonda — that one went sideways. And Jac, of course. She's yours to dispose of. Well, I mean, she would be if … you know … but I don't want to put a damper on things."

It didn't take Detective Poirot to deduce what that meant.

"So Tom, Denisha, everybody? You stashed them all in the jet?"

"That's what I just said. Buckled them into their seats and everything. Daryl was tricky. It's kinda dicey out there now. Had to wait until the waves settled down after the hurricane. By then he was getting …" He puffed out his cheeks instead of using words to describe the bloating and then held his nose to indicate the smell.

Somehow, he was a monster with an adolescent's sense of humor. It was super creepy.

I needed to keep him talking, and the best way to do that was to let him feel impressive and in control, while I tried desperately to figure out a way to turn the table. "How'd you survive the storm?"

He shook his head. "It wasn't good. I thought I wouldn't make it."

It was the first time he'd displayed anything other than verbose arrogance.

Could I prod him into some kind of funk? "Where did you get shelter?"

He shook his head again, more emphatically. "I don't want to talk about it."

I poked again, talking to him like I would a scared child. "It must have been really scary. Did you get hurt?"

He burst into an angry fit, standing up and looming over me. "I said no. Leave it alone." Just as suddenly, he sat back down and ran a hand through his hair before returning his attention to the fire.

"Okay. I'm sorry," I coaxed, holding my hands out in front of me and hanging on to any semblance of control I'd gained. "How'd you keep us from seeing the smoke from your fire?"

"So inquisitive. You don't know how gratifying it is to talk about all this." His voice was relaxed again. "It was pretty easy, actually. Only burn dry wood — wet wood gives off more smoke. I only made fires at night and under the jungle canopy so it would dissipate any smoke." He grinned broadly at me, the other self re-emerging. His sinister smile held no joy.

"What?"

"Just remembered." He reached into his pocket and retrieved something. "You deserve to have this. Do whatever you want with it." He tossed the object to me. It glittered in the morning light.

I caught it and looked down. A gold wristwatch. I'd seen it hundreds of times. Jac's.

I threw it back at him as hard as I could. I caught him off guard for the first time. He raised his hands, but too late. The watch struck him in the face, right on the bone under his eye, leaving a small cut.

He bared his teeth. He looked vicious, like something right out of a horror movie.

"We were getting along so well."

I may have made a mistake.

"Let's get to it, shall we?" Ryan stood slowly. He was certain of the outcome. He did not rush.

I backed away.

He leapt over the fire, landing right in front of me. A practiced fist smashed into my face. I collapsed under the force of it. Darkness shrouded my vision. Buzzing invaded my ears.

He nudged me roughly in the ribs with his foot. "Get up. I didn't get to take my time with the others. I couldn't risk making any noise, so you're the benefactor of some pent-up hostility."

I pushed myself onto all fours. It felt like I had a burning hole in my face. I'd never been hit like that before. I touched my fingers to my cheek and winced. No blood. I was still ahead by that metric.

When I got to my feet, Ryan punched me in the stomach. I lurched forward as all the air left my lungs. He grabbed me by the hair at the back of my head and yanked me upright, then he slapped me.

The disrespect of that slap awoke an anger in me, displacing some of the fear. I punched at him, but he swiped it aside. It was nothing more than an inconvenience. "You'll have to do better than that, Alexis."

I didn't want his to be the last voice I heard. I didn't want him to be the last person to say my name. But no matter how mad I got, I was so over-matched as to be effectively helpless.

I took a play out of Jac's book and clawed his face. He let go of my hair, and I scurried away toward the shelter. Not to run away because I had nothing to run to. This was Butch and Sundance's last stand. I just needed some space, if only for a couple of seconds.

I spun around when I got to the shelter, thinking he must be chasing me. He wasn't. He stalked like a leopard going after an injured gazelle, picking its moment. He didn't immediately attack but circled me from a distance. Calculating the best angle.

I had only one trick up my sleeve. Courtesy of Tom.

I pivoted as he circumnavigated me, keeping what I thought looked like a fighting stance.

My plan — primitive though it was — was to sweep his leg out from under him, jump to my feet, and stomp on his face before he could recover. I wasn't an analytics person, but I wouldn't have placed favorable odds on my success.

Ryan dove forward.

I dropped to the ground, realizing on my way down he had only been feigning.

Still, surprise showed on his face.

I may have wasted my shot.

I hooked my leg around his ankles and jerked, while thrusting my top half forward to shove his hips or belly or whatever I could reach. The sand gave way under his feet, and he fell backward. I rolled and launched myself up, raising one leg in the air. *It worked! The idiot thing worked.*

But I nearly fell over while my brain tried to make sense of what it was seeing.

I planted my foot back on the ground.

Ryan hadn't fallen all the way to the sand. He was partly suspended in the air, though his heels, which were splayed out in front of him, dug into the sand. He didn't move, and his face was expressionless. His fingers touched the ground where his arms hung limply beside him.

What didn't make sense was that his torso was upright, and his butt levitated a few inches above the sand. I kicked at his foot. He didn't move.

Cautiously, and putting some space between Ryan and me, I moved around beside him and got my answer. When Ryan fell backward, he had impaled the back of his head on Tom's coconut spike.

My first thought was, *I told him someone would get hurt on that thing.* I couldn't have known it would save my life.

CHAPTER 54
KIND OF MESSED UP

AMONG THE MOST unpleasant things I have ever done was put my hand in the pockets of Ryan's too-tight pants to see if he was carrying anything useful. I gagged with revulsion at how warm he still was, though I suppose it may have been worse if he were cold. Maybe not. I don't have a lot of experiences with corpses.

Actually, that may not be true. This was the third one I'd handled inside of a week. That's probably more than most of the rest of the population, excluding first responders and morticians.

The knife he'd been using earlier was clipped to his right-front pocket. I snagged it and slid it into the waistband of my pants. It felt like theft, but he wouldn't need it anymore. Thinking that way seemed irreverent, but I needed that irreverence to act as a dam between me and the emotional river that was starting to crack. I had a lot to get done before I could allow a breach.

Before sticking my hand in his left pocket, I touched it from the outside to test whether there was anything in there. I felt something, so I dug my hand in. As I closed my fingers around the leather band and metal body, there was no doubt what I held.

I wrapped my watch around my wrist for the first time since the watch party. One of the last times we were all together. Though if what Ryan said was true, many of them were still together.

I hurried to the top of the dunes to put the plane in view. It rocked gently in the swells, most of it submerged. A sizable part of me doubted him. Another much smaller part of me wondered again if this was some elaborate hoax, and everyone was going to come out and be horrified that I'd killed Jac and Ryan. Except that Rhonda's grave marker caught my attention and disabused me of that notion. Everything that had happened was real and had actually happened.

But seeing is believing. Faith, however — at least according to a verse in the New Testament book of Hebrews that had always stuck with me — is the substance of things not seen. I couldn't take this on faith. Being by myself out here now, the gravity of which I was also trying to keep at bay, meant that my head was going to play a lot of games with me. Because I'd watched every season of *Alone*, I had some idea of what was coming. I needed certainty.

First, I had a couple of bodies to bury.

I grabbed Ryan by the ankles and lifted. I didn't think it through. When I did, nearly the entire weight of his body rested on the stake that I'd inadvertently driven through the back of his head. It drove in further. My hands felt the vibration when the point rammed into his skull.

If I'd had anything more than a bite of fish in my belly, I would have lost it. This was perhaps the only benefit of a mostly empty stomach.

I was committed now, and I couldn't think of another way to do this. I gave him a good yank, but it didn't do the trick. I yanked again and kept pulling until the stake gave way, and Ryan thudded to the ground.

The next part was even worse. Far worse. There was no way I could bury him with a spike sticking out of his head. The hole would have to be either too wide or too deep, and I didn't have the energy to do more than was absolutely necessary. It hadn't been that long ago that we'd buried Rhonda. My fingertips had only just healed, and this was going to be six times as much work — two bodies and no one to help. The sand was waterlogged now too. The fluffy top layer that had been relatively easy to dig through was gone.

I couldn't do it. In the most literal sense, I didn't have the capacity for it, besides the calorie burn. I was burning up far more energy than I was consuming, even without something like this. Digging two graves may mean I might as well dig a third. Actually, it was looking a lot like I would die out here anyway, but maybe I'd just be giving myself a head start.

I considered my options, talking through it out loud. It was only a matter of time before I started talking to myself anyway, and I may as well give in early. I walked to the dunes and sat down, watching the now-peaceful sea and rhythmic undulation of the waves.

"You could wrap them up in extra clothes and stash them in the cave. Nope. First, the stench would be unbearable for … for however long dead people stink. Second, you might need the cave again, and you don't want to share it with corpses. Third, you don't have a way to get them up there. Done. Out. Next idea.

"Funeral pyre. Maybe. It has some merit. It would take a lot of wood, though. How much? No idea. Well, that's a problem for two reasons. You only have so much wood before you have to widen your search radius really far, which means burning a lot more calories. More importantly, if you don't have enough wood or get the fire hot enough, you're stuck with two half-burned bodies.

"Good idea, but it has some problems. What else? Put

them on the raft and send them out to sea. No can do, sister. You may need that raft.

"Hang on. There's something here."

I thought back to our second day here after we made the raft, loaded it up with luggage and supplies, and ferried them back to the beach. I was closing in on an idea. My brain felt like an image on a camera that was all fuzzy and out of focus. I kept jostling the ring on the lens until … boom … there it was. Clear as day.

Turning, I looked over my shoulder at Ryan, who lay awkwardly in the sand. "I'll just do what you were doing. I'll put you and Jac on the raft — one at a time to minimize the chance of a mishap — and take you out to the plane. I'll buckle you in beside everyone else. Assuming they're actually in the plane, which I still need to confirm. Okay. That's the plan."

Timing was everything. I couldn't do this until low tide. I stood up so I could see the beach to my left. The waves had retreated from their highwater mark. I had until the afternoon to get everything ready.

I loved having a plan. It was almost exciting, in a way that I understood was kind of messed up, because everyone was dead and my plan had to do with stowing bodies.

I stood up and dusted the sand off of me, then returned to the fire to see if there was any more fish.

CHAPTER 55
WORSE FOR THE WEAR

IT WASN'T until I was walking in the sand between the dunes and the plane that I realized something which maybe should have been obvious sooner. On the day Ryan killed Denisha while she was making the S.O.S. signal, the footsteps I found probably weren't hers. They were more likely Ryan's on his trip taking her to the jet. The thought made my stomach cramp.

And when had he taken Daryl out there? It couldn't have been on the day that he had murdered him. The waves were a chaos that he couldn't have survived. I probably should have asked more questions before spiking him in the skull. Though, in my defense, I wasn't in total control of that situation.

I considered stripping down to my skivvies, not wanting to get my clothes wet again, but I didn't want to be nearly naked in front of my dead acquaintances. I know it's weird and nonsensical. My state of undress certainly didn't matter to them. It mattered to me, though, so the clothes stayed on.

I slipped out of my shoes, which had aged three years in the last three weeks, and flexed my toes in the sand. I steeled myself for what I knew was going to be truly atrocious. It was also, by all objective reasoning, unnecessary. Except that it was essential for my mental and emotional well-being.

Waves slapped at my feet and ankles as I walked toward the plane, reaching higher up my leg with each stride. I high-stepped until doing so became too ungainly, then dove forward, swimming out to the plane with its one intact wing pointing skyward.

As I swam along its length, I tried looking into the upward-pointing windows, but condensation and grime disallowed me from getting a look at what waited for me inside. By the time I reached the nose, my anxiety levels maxed out.

Despite the tide being out, most of the cockpit remained underwater. The passenger-side windshield peeked above the surface. I considered sliding onto the plane and dropping in that way, but I was concerned about laying myself open on the remnants of broken glass. I might dump Ryan in that way when the time came for it. I couldn't just leave him floating around in there, though. He could float out when the tide rose and beach himself, forcing me to deal with him a second time. By then, he would be bloated and decomposing. It would be a far worse experience, so I would take care to buckle him in, for my sake, not his.

I slid back to the side of the plane where the door should have been and realized that because of the plane's pitch, it was entirely submerged. I swam down several feet and found that much of the door was underneath the wreckage. When the jet rocked, it came close to occluding the doorway entirely for a few seconds until it rocked back to its default position. I surfaced to catch my breath and make a decision.

What was worse, tearing up some skin on broken glass with the possibility of it leading to an infection, or getting pinned under the plane and drowning? Ever since seeing an episode of *Rescue 911* where a woman drowned by getting her ring caught in a drain at the bottom of a pool, drowning by entrapment had been high on my list of ways not to die.

I threw in my lot with gangrene and hoped for the best, so I went back to the front of the plane and slid in without incident. Only then did I realize that pulling myself out that same way would be more problematic.

I visualized the inside of the plane. When I left the cockpit, I would be in the galley. I should be able to surface there, though there were cabinets and appliances that stuck out, which may be in the way. Beyond them was the main cabin and … we'd find out.

"Alright, let's do this." I wouldn't have made a good hype man.

A wave knocked on the plane, making the whole thing shiver.

I lowered myself into the water, eyes wide, giving myself only a moment to acclimate. Small fish swam around me. The visibility wasn't as good as I would have liked. Since the storm, the water was much murkier than its usual crystalline blue. I pushed through the cockpit into the galley, keeping my focus upward for a place to surface.

When something touched my hip, I looked down. A hand was reaching for me. I jerked away from it, kicking and inhaling water. I bolted upward, panicked.

The disturbance in the water pushed away the hair that shrouded Denisha's face.

I sputtered and coughed even before I broke the surface in the cabin. I sucked in air as soon as it struck my face. Death and putrefaction filled my lungs. I immediately became sick with the sharp, sickly stench.

When I finally opened my eyes, what was left of Henry's moldering face greeted me. I screamed and turned around, burying my face in the corner made by the intersection of the cabin and galley cabinetry. Pressing my nose against the wood, I got my breathing under control as I treaded water.

"Okay, okay. It's okay," I whispered, reassuring myself,

much the same as I had done with my nephews when they were fussy infants.

I didn't want to turn back around, and I didn't want to go back underwater and see Denisha. This was a terrible idea. A moving image projected itself into my mind of Gob Bluth sitting in a hospital bed, saying, "I've made a huge mistake."

Me too, dude. Me too.

Denisha's past words replaced the cast of *Arrested Development*. "Buck up, buttercup." I came here to do a thing. It was time to get it done and get out. I pulled my shirt up over my nose, a failed effort to displace some of the smell.

I turned and faced my decomposing boss. Across the aisle to his left, Norm's dark shape hovered beneath the surface. Behind him was the latest addition — my row partner, Daryl. Because he had an aisle seat, his head was entirely out of the water. But for his swollen, gray complexion, he could have been resting.

Tom sat behind Daryl. With the upward slope toward the rear of the plane, more of Tom's torso was out of the water. It betrayed signs of a struggle and one terrible wound to his throat.

With everyone accounted for, it was time to go. My eyes roved back to Henry's grotesque remains. He and Walt had been lucky, as it turned out. As I wondered if that's the suit he would have picked for his burial, my attention fell on something. A dark triangle was wedged between the seat cushions behind Henry's hip.

If I weren't bobbing while treading water and if the water level was any higher, I wouldn't have seen it. If the plane had still been flat instead of tilted on its side, courtesy of the hurricane, I wouldn't have seen it. If I'd been Ryan wrestling with a corpse and trying to fasten it in place, I wouldn't have seen it.

As it was, I barely caught a glimpse of Henry's satellite phone. I reached out, trying to divert my attention from the feel of his waxy flesh that it was impossible not to brush.

I cradled the phone in both hands and flipped it over to examine it from every angle. Aside from some seaweed I picked off, it didn't look any worse for the wear of three weeks under water.

265

CHAPTER 56

TREMENDOUS WASTE OF TIME

I SAT in front of my burgeoning fire for a long time, staring at the satellite phone. Henry was so proud of it when he got it a couple of years ago. His secretary brought the package in right after one of our all-hands meetings when it was just the two of us. "It's only for emergencies," he promised. The minutes plan was outrageous. He was giddy as a child at a candy shop, tearing the box open and giving me all the specs, as if I either knew or cared what they meant.

"You care now, don't you?"

Yup.

Only one spec mattered now. He had told me, "It's water resistant too."

I asked, "That's not the same thing as waterproof?"

It wasn't, and he gave an excruciating, informative lecture about the difference. Well, it would have been informative if I hadn't tuned it out after a few minutes. And frankly, it didn't really matter whether I understood the details. All that mattered was whether it had kept water out for three weeks when it was really only designed to do so for about thirty minutes.

What did I know about electronics and saltwater? It's a bad combination. Very bad.

What to do. What to do.

I stood up, caring for the phone as if it were a newborn. It was my only hope for ever getting off this island, so I was going to give it all the love and nurture it could stand, including a bath. I carried the phone to the stream and squatted beside it.

The phone was off for one of two reasons. Either the battery died because Henry was using it when we started going down and it never got turned off. Or the water had got in there while it was on and killed it. If the latter were the case, my plan for how I was going to spend the next few days would be a tremendous waste of time. Actually, that's inaccurate. *Waste of time* suggests I had something better to do with my time, which I absolutely didn't.

Of course, it's possible water hadn't penetrated the phone at all, and what I was about to do was an unnecessary risk. Possible, but unlikely. This was the safest course. If saltwater was inside the phone, it would leave salt deposits when it dried, and that could short something out. I had to eliminate that possibility.

I pushed the clip on the back of the phone and popped the battery off, then unplugged the ports for the charger cable and headphone jack. Taking a deep breath first, I dunked both the phone and its battery. I pulled the battery out first and laid it on my lap. I only wanted to rinse it. The phone, though, I wanted to fill it up with freshwater. I shook it underwater and wobbled it from side to side until all the air bubbles stopped emerging from the ports and it was good and truly drowned. The freshwater needed to replace the saltwater, not just join it, so I kept it under and continued shaking it much longer than was probably necessary.

In the immortal words of Eminem, I only had one shot, one opportunity to seize everything I ever wanted. If you compared how badly I wanted this to all the other things I ever wanted in my life, those desires were meager and insignificant.

With stage one of my four-prong plan complete, it was time to embark on the second stage: drying this thing out. On the way back to camp, I waggled the phone from side to side, trying to drain all the excess water.

Ryan was attracting flies. Regardless of anything else, I had to deal with him next. In the meantime, I took some satisfaction in knowing the last things that would ever be attracted to him were scavengers and carrion creatures.

I set the phone on the bamboo base of the shelter. Without a roof on the shelter yet, it would get plenty of sunlight. The walls and elevation would protect it from stray sand. I picked it up to give it a few more hard shakes, then set it back down. Worried that it would fall between the cracks, I went around the outside to see if we'd left anyone's bags behind. We had, but everything in it was still sopping wet. Returning to the front of the shelter, I slipped my shirt off, folded it neatly and set the phone on it. I could get another shirt once I made it back to the cave.

I was going to give it three days — at least three days — before I tried to turn it on. I had enough things to do in the meantime to keep me occupied so that I wouldn't sit by the phone willing it to dry faster.

Next up, dealing with Ryan's and Jac's bodies. Ryan was most pressing since I planned to sleep here tonight. I looked up at the sky, then remembered I had a watch. A little after 4:00. I had a few more hours of sunlight. I would deal with Ryan. Jac may have to wait until tomorrow.

I shuffled through the sand over to Ryan and looked down at him. The first task was to get rid of the new appendage sticking out of his head. It was going to be a ghastly task. Fortunately for me, I'd already emptied the contents of my stomach in the plane.

I went around to his head, wrapped both hands around the stake, and pulled. His head jerked back, but the stake didn't come free. I paused to gather myself for another effort, when I realized that because I wasn't burying him, the stake could stay put. Relief washed over me like a tsunami. Enough banshees were already running around in my head wailing as loudly as they could muster. I didn't need to add anything as gruesome as this to it.

I returned to Ryan and raised his arms over his head so that he looked like he was signaling a touchdown. Grabbing his shirttail, I pulled it up to his chest. "I'm sorry. Not sure for what really. It's your own fault you're dead. I guess I'm sorry it came to this."

It seemed inadequate, but I didn't have anything else to say. The last thing I did before loading him onto the raft and dragging him out to sea was finish pulling the shirt over his head as best I could so I didn't have to see his face.

CHAPTER 57
DRENCHED IN NOSTALGIA

WITH JAC safely tucked away beside Tom well before noon, I focused on phase three of my plan. As with all highly important plans, this one needed a name. After mulling over several dozen options the night before, I landed on the glaringly obvious: Operation Homeward Bound. It was drenched in nostalgia and wholly encompassed my mission.

The third stage relied heavily on the idea that the second (and ongoing) phase — drying out the phone with the idea that all the circuitry still worked — would be successful. This stage involved going through everyone's work bags, which we'd stored in the cave before the storm, to find a portable USB charger.

I had one in my bag, but it was dead because I never remembered to charge it until I needed it. In those moments, like this one, present-me became really disappointed in past-me's forgetfulness and lack of foresight. Not the specific foresight that I might be marooned on a deserted island, and the ability to charge a satellite phone may be my only opportunity to escape. But the more general foresight that in my past life a situation might arise where I need to charge an electronic device.

I ran from camp to the cave and scampered up the trail to the entrance. It wasn't wise to burn the extra calories, but I literally couldn't wait the extra few minutes to find out whether I was sunk.

Right before entering the cave, my nerves took a couple of hits. I hadn't been back to this spot since the thing with Jac. After that, the immediacy of the situation struck me. This was it. Everything hung on this next couple of minutes. My hands shook like I had a palsy.

I clapped them together hard enough to make them sting. It didn't make the shaking stop. I have no idea why I thought it would. My Daddy's voice leapt into my head, *Nothing for it but to do it, baby girl.*

"Truer words, Daddy."

I ducked my head and hustled into the cave, saddling myself like a mule with every work bag and briefcase stashed away in the tunnel. It only took a couple of minutes before I was back in the open air, sitting down with a pile of leather around me. I set mine aside, already knowing the state of affairs in there. The most useful thing I had to offer was a connector-adapter-thing with a bunch of cable endings, which only mattered if someone had a charger.

I grabbed Henry's briefcase first, thinking the satellite phone may have come with a charger. A three-number combination lock thwarted my efforts. Because it was a Halliburton Zero, I assumed it was going to require a bit more than banging at it with a rock for me to get that open. I set it aside, knowing I could come back to it.

Next up, Tom's canvas messenger bag. I had never considered before how much someone's bag says about them, but there were correlations to be made. No charger in Tom's bag, but I found a leather folio. When I slipped it out and opened it, the folio revealed itself to be a reMarkable tablet with a keyboard. I pressed the power button at the top. The screen flashed black, then white as it powered on, showing itself to have a full battery and no password protection. I smiled and patted it gently. I had something to do now that wasn't manual labor. The battery on these things lasted weeks. I had put one in a digital shopping cart a half-dozen times, but since I had a laptop and an iPad already, I could never justify spending that kind of money on a glorified notebook.

I put the tablet in my bag and moved along. "Eeny, meeny, miny, moe." I grabbed the next bag at random.

Inside was a black brick. I closed my hand around it with an obscene amount of hope attached. The brick didn't have a power button, just a screen and three ports, one marked *input* and the other two labeled *output*. Snatching the cluster of cables out of my bag, I plugged the USB cable into an output slot. The LCD screen illuminated with blue numbers — 97.

My sinuses flared with that weird sensation I get when I'm flooded with emotion. I pushed it back down. It wasn't time for that yet. Sure, I was one step closer. But the biggest question mark was hanging over my head. It would continue to dangle there like an unstable guillotine for the next three days. At least.

CHAPTER 58
NO SIGNS OF LIFE

DO you know what you do when all you have on your docket for seventy-two hours is waiting? You spend it typing the most incredible story. You write it while all the details are still fresh in your mind. You do this for a couple of reasons. One, you have nothing better to do. Literally. Nothing better. Two, you don't want to leave anything out or get it wrong.

I can't afford to get it wrong. Too many families deserve to know exactly what became of their beloveds. Assuming I ever get the chance to tell them.

So that's what I've spent the last three days doing. My fingers are as sore as any single part of me has ever been in my life. If I wasn't predisposed to developing carpal tunnel syndrome before, I've probably made up for it with the damage I've done on this tablet with a keyboard I now loathe. I never knew how much I would miss my mechanical keyboard.

I wrote everything. From the hour or so before the plane went down until I found the portable charger. Nothing notable happened between then and now. Finally, though, the moment is upon me to reassemble the phone. I've waited longer than I think I need to because I won't get any mulligans with this.

I pick up the satellite phone off the shirt pallet I created for it and hold it up to my ear, shaking it to listen for any liquid swishing around inside. As expected, there isn't any. But that's not the real danger. What I'm concerned about is condensation that could have accumulated inside. I think I've baked all the humidity out of it. The phone's been sitting in the blazing sun for a few days. I wouldn't have any moisture left in me if I'd done that.

After I clip the battery back in and plug in the ports, I hold the power button down.

Nothing happens.

Even though that was the expected result, a wave of nausea washes over me and lingers.

I take the black brick of a charger out of my pocket and plug in the cables to let it charge the phone. The LCD screen on the charger shows 97 again, while the phone shows no signs of life. Again, expected. But, geez. A girl could use some assurances.

How long do I need to wait? A full charge will take a few hours probably. But I don't need that long. A few minutes is enough.

I decide to go pee. Not that I really *need* to pee, but I do need to not stare at these two electronic devices while I wait.

The trip to the latrine and back doesn't take as long as I want. I go to the stream, check my reflection in the stillest water I can find and futz with my hair until it's not a disaster. I dunk my coconut canteen and fill it with water that I neither need nor want.

I set it beside the shelter. The charger's been pumping enough juice into the phone long enough that if it's going to power it, it'll do so now. I try to temper my hope with pessimism that, other than me still being alive, almost nothing has gone my way in the last almost-four weeks.

I nearly chicken out of turning the phone on. The stakes are too high. If it doesn't work, I'll die on this island, almost certainly. Not today or tomorrow, but months or even years from now. An existence that has no meaning or purpose and only continues because of inertia. I don't want to know if that's my fate. The only way to know otherwise is to act on a courage I've never felt.

On the other hand, who cares? Me pushing the button isn't affecting the outcome, only delaying my knowledge of it.

With my eyes closed, I hold down the power button for two seconds. I wait several more seconds before opening my eyes.

The screen is alive with information. Time and date. Menu options. A battery level showing it is charging. An indicator that the phone is acquiring reception. Seconds later, a tower appeared in the upper left corner with three bars out beside it. It's rather uninventive that they use a tower graphic when the technology is not reliant on towers.

My hands are so sweaty and shaking so badly that I have to set the phone down. I haven't planned for what to do next. It seemed so improbable that I would need to.

I wipe my hands on my shirt, kneel in the sand, and pick the phone up again. I dial the only number I can think of, the one that's been etched into my memory since I was in elementary school — my mom's cell phone.

I hit Send. There is an eternal delay before it rings on the other end. My heart beats faster with each ring. By the fourth ring, I have to sit down, afraid I'll pass out.

"Hey." It's the most syrupy sweet Southern voice you ever heard.

"Momma?" My voice is so constricted it hurts.

"You know what to do. Leave a message. I'll call you back."

I slump in disappointment but have to recover. I haven't planned what to say. I realize now that was a mistake.

As soon as the beep stops, I say, "Mo—" I can't even get it out and have to start again. "Momma, it's me, Alexis. Listen.

You've got to do exactly what I say. Do not call me back. I'm on an island somewhere in the Caribbean. Our plane crashed. I'm the … only one left. Give this number to the FBI or the Navy or somebody. I don't really know. What time is it now?" I look at my watch, and it occurs to me. There's going to be a lot to explain should that time come. "It's just after 3:00pm. Central time, I think. I'm pretty sure we never left Central time. I'll turn the phone on every day for an hour starting at 3:00. I only have a little bit of battery. Okay. I'm safe for now. I love you, Momma."

I wait several seconds after I stop talking to sever the only connection I have had with the outside world since we crashed. It is an extraordinary act of will power to hit the red button and end the call.

I don't know when she'll get the message, but there's no way she gets anything done in the next hour. *How long does a satellite phone battery last? A day? Maybe two? Probably not two.* I pick up the charger and unplug the phone, then re-plug in the USB cable to activate it. 68. So I have two more complete charge cycles with the phone. After that, it's over.

I power the phone down.

CHAPTER 59
A PICNIC IN PURGATORY

I THOUGHT WAITING on the phone to dry and then to charge was excruciating and taxing. I was wrong. Compared to this particular brand of waiting, that was a picnic in purgatory. This is hell. A hell in which I envision a thousand ways my mother never received or acted on my voicemail.

She changed her number after I went missing and was presumed dead. Because that's definitely what happened.

There's poor satellite reception, and the message is so garbled she can't make anything out and ignores it.

She thinks it's a prankster and ignores it.

Or she gets the message and calls the FBI or whoever it is you call — I really hope they can figure that part out — and they don't act on it.

I could go on. I am going on in my head. But I won't subject you to it, because it's a pretty miserable experience.

I have to occupy myself. In the three days that I waited for the phone to dry, I stocked up on firewood, replenished my supply of fruit, and put a roof back on the shelter.

After making my phone call yesterday, I brought the rest of the luggage back from the cave. I could only pull one suitcase at a time. The process took several hours at roughly twenty minutes a bag times nine bags. It was the ideal activity, occupying lots of time and exhausting me in the process.

Unfortunately, I don't have anything left I *have* to do. I've got to find something I *can* do.

Fishing. That's what I can do. Ryan managed to catch a fish. I can too.

My mother's voice crops up in my head. A memory — scratch that — an amalgamation of memories from my formative years. *"You know what your problem is?"*

I'm not going to enjoy this. "I'm sure you're going to tell me."

"You think anything the boys can do, you can do."

"Better," I say with crossed arms.

"Better what?"

"I think anything they can do, I can do better."

She takes two steps toward me and pokes me in the sternum. "Don't you sass me, missy."

"It's your own fault." I'm not backing down.

I didn't think it was possible for her cheeks to grow a brighter red. I was wrong. "Oh, is that right?"

"I have older brothers," I say dismissively. "They're always going to be bigger and stronger. Being smarter is a matter of survival."

"You ain't gonna find a man that'll put up with that mouth of yours."

Several cutting remarks reside on the edge of my tongue. She hasn't slapped me yet, and I don't want to push her to it this time. I take a half-step back, curtsy, and walk away.

I poke around in Rhonda's luggage for her sewing kit. When I find it tucked into a pouch, I take it to my fire pit. I wedge the butt end into a piece of hardwood and push it into the coals in the middle of the fire. A couple minutes later, it's glowing red. I press it against a rock until it bends, then repeat the cycle until the sewing needle transforms into a J-shaped hook.

I grab the kit and a stout bamboo stick, and head to the beach. I think about my odds of catching anything. Not great.

If I get into anything with teeth, I'll lose my hook. And since most ocean-dwelling fish have teeth — Is that even true? It seems true. Surely, you've got to have teeth to survive in the wild blue yonder. I'll happily be wrong on that score.

I traipse up the beach, with the plane showing its rear to me like the Scots in *Braveheart*, looking for bait. It doesn't take long for me to find a fish that must have been unfortunate enough to ride in the last big wave as the tide went out. I pick it up and take a whiff. It's definitely been dead for a bit. The smell tries to drag me back to the confines of the cabin, but I focus on my task.

Squatting in the sand, I use Ryan's knife to cut a smallish chunk out of the side of the fish and skewer it onto my hook. The only knot I remember is something resembling a clench knot, so I tie the hook to the line and the line to the pole after unspooling a bit.

With my feet in the surf, I twirl the bait over my head like young David preparing to hurl his stone at Goliath. Of course, if his release had gone as poorly as my first half-dozen, the giant would have squished him into a paste.

Eventually, I fling the bait in front of me, where I fiddle with the line, jerking it around a bit and hoping the aroma of rot will entice something to chomp down on it.

This goes on for a while, long after I sweat through everything I am wearing. In my past life in which I inhabited civilization, I didn't have the patience for fishing. But in that life, I had options for how to spend my time and how to stuff my face. Here, I am pretty limited on both.

A jerk!

Something tugs at my line. I start pulling it in, not being careful to avoid tangles like I was before. The fish on the other end doesn't like the resistance he's encountering and heads toward deeper water. "Too late, sucker!" A rush of triumph.

I clamp down on the thread. It bites into my skin. Only then do I remember that it's tied to bamboo on the other end.

I hold tension on the line with one hand while winding it around the makeshift rod with the other. After a couple of minutes, I can reel the fish in by spinning the bamboo. I inch it closer to shore until I get clever and start walking backwards. My very own cheat code. Once I'm about forty feet from the surf line, my fish flops onto the sand. I give the line a good yank to pull him further onto the beach, then run forward and smack it on the head with my rod. Twice.

It stops flopping.

In the process of removing the needle from its lip, I see my watch, its face glittering in the afternoon light. 2:50.

I drop everything except the fish and sprint to camp.

My work bag is under the renewed shelter. The phone is zipped inside one of the interior pouches. I power it up and stare at the screen, willing it to ring. It says it has reception. I check that every few seconds.

The next eighty minutes are the longest and most demoralizing of my life. Every doubt and fear I've ever had is realized and magnified, and there is nothing to hold back the crushing tsunami of despair.

CHAPTER 60
SUBDUED THUNDER

TIME PASSES. It must have. I don't know how much. I can't begin to guess. It's light again, and it wasn't before. I peed once. That's about all I remember of — I look at my watch — the last twenty-two hours.

Geez. I only peed once in an entire day. That's not good. I didn't eat or drink anything either. I'm pretty sure of that.

I force myself to sit up and swing my legs over the edge of the shelter. I've heard athletes who win championships in their sports talk about giving themselves one day to celebrate and revel in their accomplishment. After that, it's time to get back to work. At the opposite end of the spectrum, I gave myself a day to wallow in my misery. Now, it's time to get back to work.

Don't get me wrong — I'm still miserable, but I'm also not going to allow myself to die of dehydration because of it.

I grab a papaya from the larder and make my way to the fire pit, which is covered in a layer of ash. When I hold my hands close to the gray dust, it gives off little residual heat. It's going to take some love and attention to revive this thing. I use a stick to dig around in the coals and blow off the top layer of ash. An orange glow readily appears in the embers.

I work for a good thirty minutes at growing a healthy fire,

when the smell reminds me I'd been planning to cook something yesterday. "My fish!" I say aloud, catching myself by surprise. I run to where I left it the day before.

While I'd forgotten about it, the birds and crabs had not.

A loud chime permeates the air, disturbing the subdued thunder of the waves and chirping of the gulls. I don't recognize the sound until the third ring.

I spring to the shelter and hit the green button. "Hello? Hello?" My voice is soaked in desperation.

"Ma'am?"

"Yes. Hello. Who is this?"

"Ma'am, this is Seaman Nathan Higsby of the *USS Wichita*. Can you please identify yourself, ma'am?"

"Yeah. Of course. I'm Alexis Sullivan of some tiny speck of an island in the Caribbean?"

"Ma'am, could you provide me with you Social Security Number and date of birth?"

If this is an identity theft scam, it was well thought out. Normally, they prey on senile old people. Seeking out a desperate plane crash survivor is on another level. I don't really think that's what is happening here, but it occurs to me.

I give him the information. My hands and feet are sweating. I've never been so nervous in my life. What if they decide I'm not me? "Are y'all going to come get me?"

"Ma'am, we are triangulating your position as we speak. I need a little more information from you."

"You're very polite. Do you know that? Where are you from?"

"Yes, ma'am. Texas, ma'am."

"Listen, you have to quit calling me 'ma'am' or we're going to get sideways with each other."

"Yes, ma—10-4. Are you safe?"

A harsh bark of laughter escapes. I'm about as safe as it gets now. "Yes."

"How many are in your party?"

Whatever dark levity had visited immediately fled. I answer quietly, "Just me."

"I understand there were others on the aircraft?"

"Gone." I clear my constricted throat. "They didn't make it." It's true enough for now.

"I understand, ma'am. I'm sorry to hear that. Excuse me for just one moment." There's a scuffing sound that I imagine is a hand covering a receiver. The background noise on the other end becomes muted. Several seconds later, the noise picks up again. "Ms. Sullivan?"

"Yes?"

"We're going to direct a fast-mover to do a flyover to confirm your position. Are you able to make yourself visible?"

My heart bounds inside my chest. "Yes, I can do that. What happens after that?"

"We expect to coordinate a rescue operation. Can you keep your phone on?"

I pull it away from my face and look at the display. The battery is less than half full. I forgot to turn it off yesterday, but I've got at least two more charges left. "Yeah, I can do that."

"Very well, ma'am. Best of luck."

The line goes dead.

My brain shifts into overdrive. When I look at the state of my fire, I couldn't be happier with my earlier decision to get it back in order. But it needs to be bigger, much bigger, and dirtier. I gather palm fronds, fresh bamboo, and every other green thing I can find. The temptation is to throw it all on the fire, but I'm afraid I'll smother it. It needs a better base. I rummage through the woodpile for big chunks of wood that will burn for a long time. A month ago, I knew almost nothing about building a fire. Now, my life more or less depends on it.

Within twenty minutes, I transform my cozy bonfire into an inferno. It's time to add the greenery, which catches right away.

As I hurry to the beach, I try to do some rough math to figure out how long it will take a fighter jet to get here. But since I don't know how fast they fly or how far away it is, that task proves impossible.

Between the crashed plane, the coordinates they could establish through the phone signal, and the smoke billowing into the sky, I've made myself about as visible as I can. I decide on one more medium, but it's more of a sentimental endeavor.

I stroll down the beach to where the remains of Denisha's S.O.S. sign lay in shambles. I take care to rearrange the sticks and stones so that the first two letters are complete, then scrounge around among the sea oats and morning glories to find more rocks and driftwood to make the third letter.

A breeze blows in off the water, making the late summer heat less stifling. I sit in the sand, watching one jet rock in the waves while waiting on another.

I think with fondness and love and sadness and anger and regret about the people locked inside the confines of the cabin. And it occurs to me that I'll have to update my resume. There's no way the human resources director can survive the deaths of nearly the entire C-suite.

More pressing than that, though, I resolve not to take a beach vacation for at least a decade. For my first trip anywhere, I'm going to find the most inland place in America and go there.

I spot a dark speck on the horizon and wait on Maverick to rescue me.

AUTHOR'S NOTE

Writing *Watch Party* was an act of continuous revelation. When I embarked on the first chapter on January 1, 2023, I had a very basic premise in mind for how things would go. A small group of people would get in a crash – at that point I hadn't fully decided whether they would be in a boat or plane. Most of the group would survive, but then they would start disappearing one at a time.

I didn't even know who the predator was until well into the book. If you had asked me beforehand, I would have told you, I don't know how you write a book that way. Now, I get it. If you're following your characters' lead, things unfold in front of you. Often times, it's like a lantern, providing only enough light for you to see the next few steps. Every now and then though, those characters in your head hand you a spotlight that shines far down the path to illuminate where you're headed.

While *Watch Party* eventually wound up where I thought it would (mostly), the path took unexpected turns, all the way until the end. On June 21, I posted on social media than even in Chapter 54 (of 60), "the characters are still rebelling from doing what I orchestrated in my very detailed spreadsheet."

That's consistent with something I had posted eight days earlier: "the story is holding together with only the usual amount of times I get surprised by developments I didn't plot out."

The entire revelatory process of this novel reinforced for me the magic of the writing process. For this story, it began with a dream I had about a post-apocalyptic world in which a friend and I came across a pile of watches on a desolate, rocky beach. What good are watches when the world has burned? That dream evolved into the suspense novel you just read. The story could pretty easily have taken any number of other forms. I can't precisely say why this seemed like the best course.

The whole process frequently seems mystical to me, even though I'm the one taking often-ethereal concepts and making them concrete. This is embodied in something I wrote in March 2023, while still writing the first half of *Watch Party*: "The true magic of writing is that I started this morning's session with half of a first line in my head. 275 words later, I had the makings of the first quarter of a scene, which hadn't existed anywhere, even in my own imagination, moments earlier."

I still hold to that. Writing is its own form of magic. While the world around us becomes increasingly empirical, I am so happy to be a purveyor of stories that could not and would not exist were it not for me creating them.

For context, I had no idea what I would write in this Author's Note when I started typing a little while ago. I've been worrying for months over what to include. But 45 minutes later, here we are. Like I said … magic.

J. W. Judge
December 6, 2023

ABOUT THE AUTHOR

J. W. Judge lives in Birmingham, Alabama, also known as The Magic City. In his day job, he is a lawyer, practicing commercial defense litigation.

Watch Party is his fifth novel. His first three novels are all part of the dark fantasy series The Zauberi Chronicles: *Vulcan Rising* (Book 1), *Seeking Sanctuary* (Book 2), and *Forging Bonds* (Book 3). His fourth novel is a freestanding dark fairy tale, *Casual Business with Fairies*.

If you enjoyed *Watch Party*, sign up for Judge's newsletter for information about other stories he's working on. You can also follow him on social media for updates, developments, and news about other projects. If you'd like to reach out to him by email, please do so at jwj@jwjudge.com.

Please help others find and enjoy *Watch Party* by leaving a rating and review on Goodreads or your preferred retailer, or by sharing about it on your own social media.

WORKS BY J. W. JUDGE

Fiction

Watch Party

Casual Business with Fairies

Vulcan Rising (The Zauberi Chronicles, Book 1)

Seeking Sanctuary (The Zauberi Chronicles, Book 2)

Forging Bonds (The Zauberi Chronicles, Book 3)

The Murder Tree (A Short Story)

Non-Fiction

Write Your Novel One Day at a Time: How to Write a Novel While Having a Career, a Family, and a Life